He wasn't a man you could ignore...

In a sea of animated theatergoers, he was standing perfectly still. His eyes met hers, and from across the expanse of the lobby Julie couldn't see the color. But she registered an impression—icy, cold and calculating. She shivered from the chill, but continued her appraisal.

The lashes that framed those arresting eyes were thick, but did nothing to soften the bold planes of the face. The man had the alertness of a wolf who'd picked up the scent of a quarry.

Then a half smile flickered at the corner of his well-shaped lips, and in an instant the face went from harsh to engaging.

A wave of trepidation washed over her—a reaction to danger, she knew. But what kind of danger, precisely? Did it come from the political repercussions of the situation...or from the man himself?

Dear Reader,

Our "Decade of Danger & Desire" continues! To help celebrate and to thank you for your readership these past ten years, we've brought you a very special gift—Rebecca York's Peregrine Connection.

Since its original publication in 1986, the Peregrine Connection trilogy has been a favorite of romantic suspense readers—some of the most sought-after books, according to booksellers.

It's our pleasure to make them available to you once again. Whether you'll be reliving the danger and desire, or discovering it for the first time, enjoy!

Sincerely,

Debra Matteucci
Senior Editor & Editorial Coordinator
Harlequin Books
300 East 42nd Street
New York, NY 10017

Rebecca York
Flight of the Raven

This
Collector's Edition of

belongs in
the personal library of

Adela Rimson

Harlequin Books

TORONTO • NEW YORK • LONDON
AMSTERDAM • PARIS • SYDNEY • HAMBURG
STOCKHOLM • ATHENS • TOKYO • MILAN
MADRID • WARSAW • BUDAPEST • AUCKLAND

To our special research assistants, Norman and Howard

With special thanks to the staff of the United States Embassy in Madrid for their valuable assistance, and to John Riehl, for giving us the benefit of his expertise in Russian language and customs, and to Dr. Paul Burka for taking the time to answer our many medical questions

First published by Dell Publishing Co., Inc.

ISBN 0-373-22301-3

FLIGHT OF THE RAVEN

Copyright © 1986 by Ruth Glick and Eileen Buckholtz

CAST OF CHARACTERS

Julie McLean—When it came to spying, she was a rank amateur.

Aleksei Rozonov—Seducing Julie McLean was just part of his job.

Feliks Gorlov—The agricultural undersecretary cultivated form rather than substance.

Yuri Hramov—The KGB's secret weapon.

Georgi Krasin—The young political officer was in charge of monitoring—and sometimes abetting—terrorists' activities.

Dan Eisenberg—Was his death an untimely accident, or did it have darker implications?

Bradley Fitzpatrick—His unprepossessing exterior hid a sharp, analytical mind.

Amherst Gordon—He ran the Peregrine Connection with the skill of a veteran spymaster.

Constance McGuire—Data on all Peregrine agents was at her fingertips.

Cal Dixon—Officially an American embassy staffer, but he was rumored to have connections to the CIA.

General Bogolubov—He was obsessed with catching the Raven.

The Raven—A double agent on the run, with one last mission to complete.

Authors' Note

We were delighted when Harlequin Intrigue told us they would be republishing our Peregrine Connection trilogy. They are some of our favorite stories, and we had a wonderful time creating daring women and dangerous heroes and catapulting them into plots swirling with high-stakes intrigue and jeopardy.

With the fall of the Berlin Wall, the collapse of the Soviet Union and the restructuring of Eastern Europe, the world has changed at warp speed over the past eight years since the Peregrine novels were written. Yet, with spy scandals at the upper echelons of the CIA and even a terrorist attack at the World Trade Center, themes of preserving peace and the balance of world power are just as relevant today as they were in the eighties when the Peregrine Connection was written.

Ten summers ago we were held hostage by a darkly attractive, extremely dangerous KGB agent in Ruth's office. He's Aleksei Rozonov, the hero of *Flight of the Raven*, one of the most exciting adventures we've ever written. We did extensive research for this book, traveling to the American embassy in Madrid, visiting residences of the staff and deputy ambassador, exploring the Prado and combing the city for rendezvous spots.

While we were in Madrid, the embassy staffers urged us to visit a restaurant out near the air force base. Days after we left, the place was a target of a terrorist attack. Fortunately we missed it, but it gave us a dramatic opening for our spy story.

To get a handle on our Russian characters, Ruth read textbooks on Russian life and tuned in to Radio Moscow to listen to programs being beamed from behind the Iron Curtain. Eileen interviewed a Russian linguist and gathered data on Spanish terrorist groups.

The Soviet Union has dissolved since we wrote the tale of innocent-abroad Julie McLean playing a deadly cat-and-mouse game with KGB agent Aleksei Rozonov. Yet, if current headlines are any indication, spies are still around. And there are still fascinating stories to tell about what people will do for passion, loyalty and greed.

After reading *Flight of the Raven*—and all the Peregrine Connection books, we were pleased with how well the books stood the test of time. We hope you think so, too.

Rebecca York (Ruth Glick and Eileen Buckholtz)

Prologue

The roll of film in his pocket was a death sentence. And if he wasn't careful, it was going to be his.

It took all his discipline to feign interest in the flashy display windows lining the Plaza Mayor, but it was important to blend into the noisy evening crowd. He'd stopped under the shadows of the stone colonnades lining the square and doubled back often enough to assure himself that a KGB agent wasn't following. But the reprieve was only temporary for the double agent with the code name Raven. At any moment his cover could be ripped away with all the violence of a jealous husband who has discovered a naked lover in his wife's bed. The image brought a grim smile to his face. In this case he suspected that the injured party would shoot first and ask questions later.

A wiry youth in a black leather jacket jostled him from behind and mumbled a *"Pardon, señor."* The Raven's hand automatically shot to his pocket to make sure it hadn't been picked. Nerves.

Reaching a corner of the plaza, he started down the stone steps to the narrow street. The meeting place was around the corner. Instead of entering, he stopped at a *tapas* bar with a carryout window and ordered a plate of fried *setas*. Although tasty, the Spanish mushrooms didn't compare to the wild ones near his family's dacha outside of Moscow. The nostalgic memory from his childhood made his chest tighten painfully. How could you love your homeland yet be compelled to give away its most guarded secrets, he wondered for the thousandth time. Then his fingers curled around the roll of film. The thought of leaving the fate of the world to the tender mercies of the Kremlin strategists made him shudder.

From long practice at subterfuge, he gave no sign of recognition when his contact, Eisenberg, strolled past him and sauntered into the Taverna San Jeronimo. As though he had nothing more important to do, he washed down the mushrooms with a glass of sangria. But his thoughts were racing ahead. Soon the information in his pocket would be on its way to the one man who would know how to use it. After dropping a handful of pesetas onto the counter, he started across the street toward the San Jeronimo.

For a horrible, confusing moment the air around the tavern seemed to shimmer. Or maybe it was the deafening blast he heard first. In the next second, the wooden door of the tavern ripped from its hinges, and shards of glass and splintered wood flew through the air like tiny missiles. Several tore through the fabric of his suit, digging into his flesh and making him stagger, but he didn't stop to register the pain.

Next to him, an old woman clad in black doubled over and sank to the uneven pavement.

"Madre de Dios," someone else sobbed.

Suddenly the pavement was jammed with running feet heading away from the scene of the explosion.

But the Raven was riveted in his tracks. Holy mother! Eisenberg was in there and other innocent people too. From inside the tavern he heard the cry of someone in agony. He had to help get the people out of there.

It had been only seconds since the explosion. But his analytical mind was registering a whole series of damage assessments and speculations. The old stone building was already starting to collapse. He could picture the scene inside. Heavy wooden beams falling, plaster walls disintegrating, centuries-old floorboards giving way. Probably the bomb had been hidden in the front room. Could he get in at all? Could he get out alive?

Khaki-clad police with their ever-present machine guns materialized from the direction of the plaza, taking the decision out of his hands. His gut reaction was to stay, but there was too much at stake for him to be placed at the scene of what appeared to be a terrorist attack.

Drawing back in the shadows of a grimy doorway, he watched the Spanish civil guard begin coping with the chaos. From what he could see now, it looked as though they were going to be bringing out more bodies than survivors.

Turning reluctantly away, he shoved his hands in his pockets and felt the cold metal of the film spool. The implications of what had happened suddenly slapped him in the face. *Chyort!* He was in one hell of a fix now.

Chapter One

At the headquarters of the Peregrine Connection in Berryville, Virginia, Amherst Gordon blotted his lips with a white linen napkin. "Tell the chef the poached salmon was seasoned with just a bit too much tarragon."

Constance McGuire gave her gray-haired contemporary a sympathetic look above the rims of her half glasses. A visitor who stumbled into the country elegance of the Aviary would probably take the two of them for Virginia aristocracy. It was a pose that Gordon ordinarily relished. Yet she knew that on days like this, responsibility weighed heavily on his tweed-covered shoulders. He might be independently wealthy, but he wasn't Virginia gentry. He was a veteran spymaster known to a few highly placed members of the intelligence community as the Falcon. His daily business was coordinating the activities of a worldwide network of intelligence agents.

And when the Falcon started finding fault with the Aviary's exceptional cuisine, it was because he was really worried about one of his operatives.

Gordon stood up. Leaning heavily on his cane, he walked over to the doorway that led to the solarium. Lush with tropical plants and his cherished birds, it was his favorite part of the house. But today, gazing at his indoor paradise did nothing for his stress level. "I suppose the damn siesta's over in Madrid by now," he muttered. "And we'll find out what Eisenberg got from the Raven."

He'd had the feeling for weeks that both men were being maneuvered into a net, and he could sense it tightening around them. He'd already offered to pull them off. But the Raven had refused to abandon his dangerous perch. He'd insisted that the information just within his reach was too vital to abort the mission now.

The curt refusal had filled Gordon with a sort of fatherly pride. He'd found Justice Louis Brandeis's "spark of idealism" in the Raven and fanned it into a flame. But even he hadn't realized at first how extraordinary the man really was. By conventional standards he would be considered a traitor to his country. But to anyone who understood his motives, he was nothing less than a hero. The problem was to keep him from becoming a martyr as well.

Gordon's grim thoughts were interrupted by a chime that in an ordinary home could have been the doorbell. But this was no ordinary home.

"I think we'd better get to the office." Connie pushed back her own chair. The special bell always meant trouble. It was connected to the computer that monitored the State Department's most secure communications line. When a key word from their data base—like an agent's name or cover identity—showed up in text, the alarm would sound.

Connie never seemed to hurry, yet by the time Gordon reached the library she had already triggered the dual mechanisms that opened the section of wall leading to their shielded sanctuary. Age, he noted, had not impaired her economy or grace of motion.

Connie crossed immediately to the computer. For a man with a rebuilt kneecap, Gordon was at her side in surprisingly short order. Together they scanned the message on the screen. It detailed a suspected terrorist bombing of a restaurant in Madrid. One U.S. embassy employee had been among the victims.

Behind her, Constance could hear the spymaster utter a curse. "I was afraid of something like this. They got Eisenberg. I just hope they didn't get the Raven too."

"Maybe it was just bad luck."

"Not likely. The first thing I want you to do is get the whole damn political section of the embassy on the case. And drop a hint to Ambassador Thomas that U.S. defense strategy could be riding on his staff's detective work. I want immediate access to everything they find."

"The Raven could still be alive," Connie reminded him.

"If so, we've got to pull him out of there. When you've finished getting the embassy off their tails, transfer some funds from his Swiss bank account to Madrid."

"You know he's refused to accept any payment for what he's supplied to us."

"Dammit, this time he's going to have to burn his bridges. And that means he's going to need some cash."

JULIE MCLEAN had passed up an invitation from another embassy staffer to see a current Burt Reynolds movie dubbed into Spanish and had opted for a quiet evening at home.

She was just putting her dinner dishes into a sink full of sudsy water when the phone rang. Bradley Fitzpatrick, her immediate superior, was on the other end of the line.

"Julie, am I glad you're home!"

The clipped delivery told her it wasn't a social call. "What is it?"

"We need a fourth for bridge."

"Deal out the cards. I'll be there," she said. Neither one of them played bridge, which was why they had selected it as a telephone code. It meant she was needed at the embassy on the double.

After easing back into her pumps and pulling on the jacket of her navy suit, she paused to catch the shoulder-length mass of her dark hair in a wide barrette. Damn, she thought, she probably should have washed it when she'd gotten home this afternoon. From the strained tone of Fitz's voice, she suspected she might be on duty for the next twenty-four hours. Maybe it wouldn't be a bad idea to pack a change of underwear and a few toilet articles in a tote bag.

Eduardo, the *portero,* glanced up from his post in the lobby as the elevator door groaned open. "So you changed your mind about going out, after all." He looked pleased that she was taking his advice about enjoying herself more.

The stoop-shouldered man with the craggy visage was one of the reasons why Julie had moved into this particular building three years ago. Eduardo treated every one of his twenty-five tenants like family.

Julie smiled and nodded as though she were setting out on an evening of fun. "I may not be back tonight, so don't wait up."

"Have a good time, *señorita,*" he called.

As soon as she stepped out the door a grim expression captured her oval face. Her job in the political section of the embassy was monitoring terrorist activities. Fritz wouldn't have called her unless something pretty serious had happened—like last year when a restaurant near Torrejon Air Force Base had been bombed.

Her redbrick apartment building was only a fifteen-minute walk from the embassy, and she was tempted to make a beeline for the closest gate. Yet, despite her anxiety, she walked a block north before heading back toward the American enclave. Security had been adamant lately about employees not taking the same route to and from work every day. If somebody hostile had been listening to her conversation with Fitz, he could be waiting up the block.

The thought brought back all the reasons she had decided months ago that this would be her last post with the State Department. She'd been with the service for eight years, and at first she'd relished the chance to experience other cultures firsthand. But her last tour in Moscow had been like living in an isolation bubble where every word spoken was overheard. Madrid was a paradise by comparison. In fact it was a plum assignment. But over the last few years American embassies all over the world had turned from glamorous outposts into handy targets for leftist and rightist militants.

The compact umbrella she'd forgotten in the bottom of her tote bag made the metal detector at the consulate entrance buzz. With an apology she handed the canvas carryall over to the marine guard for a quick inspection. By the time she'd finally keyed in the combination for the black metal gate that barred the entrance to the third floor, Bradley Fitzpatrick was pacing up and down her office.

"What kept you?" he demanded.

"The security drill."

With his red hair, freckles, and stocky build, her boss hardly looked like a seasoned diplomat. But his unprepossessing exterior hid a sharp mind with enough political savvy to put him in the top echelons of the Foreign Service ranks. His rumpled brown suit and the tie loosened around his collar told Julie that he hadn't been home at all since morning.

"What happened?" she asked.

Now that they were in the protected environment of the embassy, he got right to the point. "Another terrorist bombing. One of the taverns near the Plaza Mayor."

"How do we figure in it?"

Fitz's voice was grim. "The civil guard is withholding the details pending positive identification. But one of the bodies pulled from the rubble was carrying Dan Eisenberg's wallet."

Julie sank down into the padded cushion of her desk chair. "Oh, my God," she whispered. The shock left her completely numb for a few seconds. Then tears started to well in her brown eyes. Ladies control themselves in front of others, a voice from her past reminded her sternly. With a fierce effort she held the drops back.

The man who'd broken the bad news studied her now chalk-white features from across the desk. Julie and Dan had been good friends ever since the lanky army captain had been assigned to the office down the hall six months ago. Fitz had even thought there might be a romance brewing, but Julie had deftly cooled down Eisenberg's ardor into a more manageable relationship. Maybe it was because her tour had been coming to an end, he reflected, and she hadn't seen any future in a romantic liaison.

Walking around the desk, he put a hand on her slender shoulder. Needing the comfort, Julie reached up and pressed her fingers over it. Her wide-set brown eyes avoided his, and her gently rounded lower lip was trembling. He knew she was struggling to rein in her emotions. He would help by giving her a job to focus on.

"Why Dan?" she asked, her voice quavering.

He shook his head. "It could just be a tragic coincidence. But we need to find out exactly what happened, who's responsible, whether the tavern was a random target, or whether there was some specific motive." His voice was businesslike now. "I've already been in touch with the police. But we're getting pressure from Washington to have a report ready in the morning."

"Give me a few minutes," she told him, reaching for a tissue. "Then I'll get on the phone to some of my contacts." She paused and looked up at Fitz, tears still glistening in her eyes. "And I can also go through Dan's things to see if there were any notes he left about what he was doing this evening."

He sighed. "That leaves me free to make the identification at the morgue and call his family in New York."

When Fitzpatrick reached the door, he turned back for a moment. Julie was sitting completely still, her face slightly averted. He was struck by how she looked in this moment of crisis. He'd always thought of her as sensitive and attractive but not beautiful. Tonight the unaccustomed pallor of her skin against the background of the dark curtains made her profile look like an antique cameo. Even now, her carriage and style spoke of wealth and culture, reminding him again of her privileged background. More than once he'd wondered how one of the wealthy Baltimore McLeans had gotten into this kind of business in the first place.

Not that she hadn't done an excellent job here, he reminded himself. But she wasn't detached enough. You had to know her well to see the symptoms of stress beneath her controlled exterior. Perhaps denying herself the conventional emotional outlets made things worse. He knew she'd already opted out of the service for a lower-key translator's job back in D.C. Too bad this mess had to cloud her last couple of months here.

None of the calls Julie placed netted much immediate hard information. Although Madrid was a city that kept late hours, most government offices were already closed. Even her contacts at UPI and Reuters were of little help. A rumor that the ETA, the Basque separatist activists, would claim credit for the bombing was still unconfirmed. Whoever wanted that report in Washington wasn't going to be happy with the dribble of facts she was able to collect.

Still feeling numb inside, she got up and crossed to the door. She wanted to put off going through Dan's office, but she knew that it was probably the most constructive thing to do now.

The only way she could cope with the smiling picture of him and his parents on the bookshelf was to lay it face-down before starting to go through desk drawers full of manila folders neatly labeled with project names. She recognized most of them, but the one at the very back, labeled Foolery, piqued her interest. It turned out to be full of risqué cartoons and jokes that had been passed around the office. They must have appealed to Dan's offbeat sense of humor, she thought, realizing with a painful stab that she was already thinking of him in the past tense.

Pulling out his appointment book, she flipped through the pages. His schedule, like her own, had been full of meetings with Spanish government officials, briefings for visiting U.S. dignitaries, and the long afternoon lunches where the Spanish habitually concluded a surprising number of business negotiations. Most of the entries were complete with names and phone numbers. But on a few scattered dates there was simply a capital *R* lightly penciled in the lower left-hand corner. Julie thumbed back through the previous six months and found they came in pairs—about twice every three weeks, but never on exactly the same days. One, she noticed, was for today—Wednesday, May 15. Another was for this Friday. The *R*'s might designate the days he practiced on the rifle range out at Torrejon. Or maybe they indicated when his laundry was supposed to be returned from the Rodriguez cleaners. She had no way of knowing.

Closing the book, she went on to the other contents of the center desk drawer. Tucked in the back was a carved wooden box full of ticket stubs to the bullfights and other attractions Dan had enjoyed. She'd attended some of them with him, and again her emotions welled up at the thought of the friend she'd lost. She'd known that he'd wanted to be more than friends, but he settled for what she was willing to give to their relationship.

At the bottom of the pile was one ticket that was not torn in half. It was for the revival of a class Spanish play, *La Dama del Alba*. With Dan's Spanish she couldn't imagine him catching the subtlety of such a downbeat tragedy. Had someone given him the ticket? She glanced at the date. It was for this Friday. The day clicked in her mind. It matched one of the cryptic *R*'s in the appointment book. Flipping through the pages, she matched a dozen *R*'s to torn ticket stubs. They were all for obscure events in out-of-the-way places where you wouldn't expect to see an American.

Her brow wrinkled. She'd thought she'd known Dan pretty well. But now she was wondering if he'd had a Spanish girlfriend on the side.

The door opened, and Fitzpatrick stuck his head inside. His abrupt reappearance made Julie jump.

"Sorry, I didn't mean to startle you."

"That's okay. I could use a break," she admitted, reaching around to massage the ache in her shoulder blades with her finger tips.

"Then how about coming back to my office for a cup of tea and some Oreo cookies I've stashed away for an emergency?"

Julie slipped the ticket she'd found into the pocket of her skirt.

"Find anything unusual?" Fitz asked.

Had she? She didn't want to stir up anything if there was some perfectly innocent explanation for the tickets. "Not yet," she answered, "but there are some phone numbers I'll check out in the morning."

"I hate to tell you, but it's *already* two in the morning," Fitz replied, "and neither one of us can go home till we get some kind of report on the wire back to Washington."

How UNFORTUNATE that General Bogolubov had picked this week to inspect his field sites in Spain, Aleksei Iliyanovich Rozonov thought as he read over the night report and made notes for the general's nine a.m. briefing. All hell had broken loose yesterday evening, and in the midst of it the general had arrived. Yet only the hand Aleksei unconsciously ran through his black hair betrayed his anxiety. The strong lines of his angular face might have been carved from stone.

The reports said a terrorist attack had destroyed a tavern near the venerable Plaza Mayor. Five people had been killed in the blast. One of them was an American army officer attached to the embassy. Another was a Russian KGB agent carrying a French passport that identified him as a wine merchant.

Aleksei shifted his almost six-foot frame in the desk chair that, even cranked to its full extension, never gave him quite enough leg room. The ironic humor of the San Jeronimo situation didn't escape him. Somebody was going to have the very devil of a time explaining that "innocent victim" to the Spanish authorities if they figured out the Kremlin connection. As the cultural attaché, he was glad that it wouldn't be in his official province.

Of course, he was on the senior KGB staff at the embassy, which did mean certain duties connected with the incident. The problem was, he was having trouble getting any hard information, and it wasn't from lack of trying. He would have given a case of export-quality vodka to know what Kiril Ivanov was doing at the San Jeronimo last night.

Aleksei glanced at his watch and stood up. Bogolubov was obsessed with promptness, among other things. Taking his dark blue European-cut jacket from the coat tree in the corner, he shrugged into it and straightened his tie, noting with relief that even with his eyes half-closed he'd somehow managed to pick an ensemble that actually matched. The duty officer had rung his apartment at five in the morning. Aleksei had been at his desk not much more than a half hour later. But Bogolubov wasn't going to be concerned with his lack of sleep, only his ability to do his job under pressure.

He and the general's son, Leonid, had been in the same class at MGIMO, the foreign ministry's diplomatic training school. Despite his father's high connections, Leonid hadn't done well, and the disappointed father had apparently blamed that failure on those who had excelled in the class. Although the hostility was discreetly hidden, Aleksei suspected that the general was waiting for him to make a mistake so he could pounce.

Carlotta, one of the Spanish secretaries employed in the cultural section, looked up with expressive dark eyes as he opened the office door. "I've fixed some coffee, strong and black the way you like it," she said.

Despite the stress of the morning, he flashed her a quick smile that transformed his carefully disciplined countenance for just a moment. Carlotta took care of him well at the office, and she'd offered none too subtly to take care of him during off-hours as well. He could have used the human comfort, but it would have brought complications he couldn't afford.

Accepting the coffee, he took a few quick swallows and left the half-full cup on her desk. "I don't know how long I'll be up there with the general. But I'm expecting some important calls. Transfer them to Ivan and record the conversations. I'll listen to the information later."

"Of course, Señor Rozonov."

The strong Spanish brew helped sharpen his wits for what he knew was going to be a verbal fencing match. From long experience at self-preservation, officers in the Soviet higher echelons were skilled at speaking without saying exactly what they meant. Bogolubov was a master at obfuscation.

Aleksei met Georgi Krasin in the elevator. The young political officer with the mop of sandy hair and somber intellectual face had also been summoned to the early-morning inquisition. But that wasn't surprising, since he was in charge of monitoring—and sometimes abetting—terrorist activities.

Feliks Gorlov's presence at the meeting was another matter. Gorlov had been busy with trade negotiations for months trying to buy wheat from anyone who had a spare hundred kilos. So what was he doing here? The nattily dressed agricultural under secretary with the razor-cut brown hair was lounging back in his seat, giving the impression that he and the commanding officer on the other side of the desk had been exchanging confidences for some time. Aleksei shrugged. His own impression of the man was that he cultivated form rather than substance.

Tabling his opinion, he shifted his attention to the person who had called the group together.

In deference to the foreign setting, the general was also in mufti. Unlike Gorlov, he was dressed in a boxy, wide-lapel wool suit that would have stood out on the Paseo de la Castellana like a Spanish olive in a jar of Black Sea Caviar. As he took time to shuffle through the folder on his desk,

Bogolubov ignored the new arrivals. Finally he cleared his throat.

"Well, what have you got on that damn bombing?" he demanded.

Georgi, obviously eager to please, began to summarize what he'd been able to glean from a half-dozen sources. It didn't impress the general very much.

"The Kremlin will want an angle we can use to make the Americans look bad. See if you can invent a link to that protest against NATO last month," he prompted.

Georgi scribbled madly on the pad he'd brought along.

"And what about you?" Bogolubov asked, turning to Aleksei.

He began with a concise appraisal of the damage sustained and the latest list of the victims. "Before we make a political issue of this, Comrade General, I recommend we find out what Kiril Ivanov was doing there," he concluded.

The general flashed him a triumphant look. "He was shadowing Eisenberg—on my orders."

Aleksei, like Georgi, didn't have to fake astonishment. "You mean the American who was also killed?" he asked.

"Yes. We've been uneasy about his activities for months now, but I'd just gotten approval from those dunderheads at the ministry to put him under surveillance."

The general was gauging reactions around the room. "You think he was working for the CIA?" Aleksei asked.

The portly man on the other side of the desk snorted. "If he'd been working for the CIA, we would have had a file an inch thick on him. No, this is something else, something I intend to get a handle on."

As the others stood up to leave, the general motioned to Aleksei. "Just a minute, Aleksei Iliyanovich, I need something else from you."

"Of course, Comrade General. I just wish you'd brought me in on this sooner."

Bogolubov closed the door behind the other two men. As the general leaned back in his chair again, Aleksei thought he looked very much like a fat toad that had just snapped up a couple of juicy flies. Others had seen the resemblance, too, because he was often called "the toad" behind his back.

The general shrugged. "The ministry preferred to restrict the information. But now that Eisenberg's mission in Madrid has literally been blown to bits, there's no point in keeping you in the dark. Kiril Ivanov searched the American's quarters and found some of his secret papers hidden in a corn flakes box, of all places. From them we've been able to deduce that he was working with someone right here at the embassy who uses the code name Raven. Your job is to find out who it is."

"Where do you want me to start?"

The toad stood up so that he could slide his hand into his too-tight left trouser pocket and pull out a slightly crumpled white envelope, which he handed to the younger officer.

Aleksei's brow wrinkled as he slid a blue theater ticket from the envelope. "I don't understand. What does a performance of *La Dama del Alba* have to do with any of this?"

"Ivanov saw Eisenberg pay for two tickets to the performance and pick up one. The other is still at the box office but may be claimed by performance time. This is a seat near the matched pair. I want you to go and see who shows up."

Chapter Two

Julie folded the message from Cal Dixon and slipped it in her desk drawer. Nominally, he was the mid-level consular officer in charge of dispensing U.S. government benefits to Americans living in Spain and checking the credentials of Spanish nationals wanting U.S. visas, but it was whispered around the embassy that he was connected to local CIA operations. It was considered bad form to mention the suspected association to his face.

He looked, Julie reflected, like a slightly older but still well-conditioned version of a high school quarterback. His suits and shirts were expensive yet not flashy. More than once she'd seen him in the area's plushest restaurants obviously cultivating Spanish contacts. She'd never quite been able to put her finger on what she didn't like about the man.

Ostensibly, Cal wanted background information about the political affiliations of several visa applicants. But she had to wonder, given the crisis mode of the past twelve hours, why that routine piece of business couldn't be taken care of on the phone instead of in a personal meeting.

Julie sighed wearily and picked up a notebook, wishing she were out of the Foreign Service and back in her cozy Washington town house. But despite her present state of mind, she was a woman who honored her obligations—and completing this tour was one of them.

A few minutes later she pulled open the door to the waiting room of the consular section of the embassy. It was one of the few areas to which Spanish nationals had access, subject to security clearance at the door. Although the room had been recently redone, the plastic furniture and government-green walls had all the ambience of an unemployment office. It was probably to encourage the petitioners to fill out their forms as rapidly as possible and be on their way, she speculated.

A secretary buzzed Julie through to the "employees only" area, where she made her way past desks of junior-grade clerical workers checking visa applications and benefit forms.

"It's unlocked," Cal called out in response to her knock on the door to his private office.

As she entered the room, he logged off the computer terminal and swung his chair back toward the desk. "Thanks for sparing me some time this morning," he said. "I hear you had a busy night."

"Bad news travels fast."

"Unfortunately that's true. Listen, Julie, I'm going to come right to the point. The note I sent was just to get you down here. I really want to talk about Captain Eisenberg."

"Oh?"

"The two of you were friends, weren't you?"

"Dan was a very likeable guy. He was friends with a lot of people."

"But the two of you were 'close friends.'"

Julie sat up straighter. "My past relationship with Dan Eisenberg is no business of yours. But my God, what does it matter anyway? The man's dead."

"I was hoping you might be in a position to tell me if he was up to anything—shall we say—that might not have been in the best interests of the U.S. government."

She struggled to control her anger. "I had absolutely no reason to question his loyalty, and *you* have no reason to question me like this." Her fingers pressed painfully into the spiral binding of the notebook as she started to stand up.

"I think you'd better stay. I'm not making any accusations. but I am conducting an authorized investigation."

"For whom?"

He hesitated, a look of indecision crossing his guileless features. "What I'm going to tell you is strictly confidential. The investigation is for the Director of Central Intelligence."

Julie felt her stomach knot. It had crossed her mind last night when she'd been going through his desk that she hadn't known Dan Eisenberg as well as she'd thought. She couldn't picture him as a traitor, but that's what Cal was hinting. Her own doubts fueled the vehemence of her response. "You can sort through the contents of Dan's day-old garbage, but I doubt it will turn up anything criminal in his background."

"Hey, don't take offense. I'm only doing my job, the same as you are. And since you've been working the embassy side of this, we ought to at least touch base and share information," he said.

She nodded tightly. "If I find anything that I think will be of interest to you, I'll pass it on. But my own opinion is that poor Dan was at the wrong place at the wrong time."

Cal steepled his hands and looked thoughtful. "To show you my spirit of cooperation, I'll start by sharing some privileged information with you."

When she didn't ask what it was, he continued. "There were a number of unsavory characters in that tavern last night. One of my underworld informants say that a local drug kingpin escaped with minor injuries and has gone into hiding. And if that isn't interesting enough, there was also a KGB agent enjoying the local color. He was a clandestine operative named Kiril Ivanov. I'd like to ask him some questions about what he was really doing there, but unfortunately he bought the farm along with the captain."

Julie received the new information in stunned silence. Cal's sources must be a lot better than hers. The consular officer pressed his advantage. Getting up, he went to a combination safe in the corner and pulled out two fat folders, which he dropped in her lap. "The first file has pictures and fact sheets on all the known KGB agents in the area. Naturally, a lot of them have cover jobs at the Russian embassy. The second one has a number of miscellaneous troublemakers that have come to our attention. I'd like you to look through the pictures and tell me if you've seen any of these people with Dan. And note the names in case they come up in any of the information you find out about the incident. I expect you to report any of that back to me."

"Is that all?" She stood up, the folders clutched in her hand.

Cal ran blunt fingers through his close-cropped light brown hair. "You can't take that material out of this room. Sit down at the table in the corner and go over it. I'll lock it up again when you're finished."

Julie nodded. She should have realized that Cal's connection with the CIA was probably as classified as the material he had in the folders. Without another word she took the files over to the table he'd indicated and set to work.

THE REST OF THE DAY was not much better. Because Cal's unpleasant assignment had taken up the morning, there wasn't time to spare for even a late lunch away from her desk.

"I'm going down to pick up something to eat before the snack bar closes. Do you want me to get you a sandwich?" Paula Collins, one of the junior political aides, asked sympathetically, popping her blond curly head in the doorway of Julie's office. Like the rest of the staff, she knew who was drawing extra duty because of the bombing.

Julie looked up gratefully from the newspaper she was scanning for details on the incident. "That would be wonderful. Do you know what's edible down there today?"

Paula laughed. The basement cafeteria was one of the embassy's secret weapons. It was often bandied about that all they'd have to do to disable the Russians would be to invite them in for a fast-food snack. "Probably nothing's edible, but I hear today's special is pizzaburgers."

Julie grimaced. "Oh, what's the difference! Everything they fix tastes the same anyway."

"Isn't it the truth," Paula agreed. She hesitated for a moment. "You know, Julie, everybody was really shocked to hear about Dan. But since the two of you were..." She let the sentence trail off, not knowing quite what the relationship had been. "If there's anything I can do, just let me know."

"Maybe you could start a collection envelope, and we could send it to the hospital for handicapped kids across town where he was donating some time."

"Gee, I didn't know he was doing that."

"He didn't talk about it, but I think it's because his older brother died of cerebral palsy. It really hit Dan hard, and he wanted to make a difference." Julie felt her vision begin to mist again. Dan had been such a good person. It wasn't fair that this had happened to him.

"I'll take care of it," Paula assured her. "But let me get you something to eat now."

Julie nodded, reined in her emotions, and turned back to the papers that had been delivered that morning. Spain's terrorist activity was relatively minor league, compared to that in the Middle East or Northern Ireland, for example. But there were sporadic outbreaks and always the chance that the U.S. presence could be the target. Scanning the local media for articles on the ETA, FRAP, and other agitators was part of her routine. Today, stories about the bombing covered the front page and spilled into the other sections. There was a lot of speculation on who was responsible, but despite earlier rumors, no one had claimed credit for the destruction.

The bombing had pushed to page five a story about a cornice from a library under renovation falling on the king's limousine. Luckily, Juan Carlos had been inside the library making a speech. Other than that it had almost crushed the monarch's car, Julie reflected, the accident wasn't all that rare. Supervision of public construction under the previous regime had been all too lax, and almost every other month a part of a building came crashing to the pavement.

After thanking Paula for the hot sandwich and Coke, Julie turned quickly back to her newspaper. She didn't really want to encourage any more sympathetic conversation about Dan, no matter how well-meaning. The subject was still too painful.

Later in the afternoon she canvased her contacts again and wasn't surprised to find that there were details the newspapers didn't yet have.. The type of bomb had been determined. It had been a plastic explosive detonated by a clockwork egg timer. Tentative identifications had also been made on the other four victims. If the authorities had discovered a KGB link to one of them, they were still treating the intelligence as confidential. Because Julie had no official reason to know either, she couldn't ask.

Hour by hour, she added bits and pieces of information to the file she was compiling, all the time trying to put the puzzle together.

Fitz came in at five-thirty and found her staring vacantly at the folder. Giving her an understanding look, he closed the file and locked it back in the safe.

"Enough for today," he proclaimed.

Julie scanned the new lines etched into his freckled brow. "You look about as wrung out as I feel. I'll quit for the day if you will."

"Deal. I'll even drive you home."

It was an offer she couldn't refuse.

As Fitz pulled his blue compact car up in front of her apartment, he put a hand on her arm. "I know this has really been an ordeal for you."

She nodded.

"I wish I could say it was over, but I'm still getting pressure from Washington. There's some extra research we're going to have to do."

"What?"

"We'll talk about it in the morning—in the office. You just get some rest tonight."

She sighed. Fitz was the kind of guy who leveled with you, even if it kept you on pins and needles all night wondering what he was going to drop on you tomorrow.

Julie was glad she'd opted for a building with an elevator as she leaned her head wearily against the brown-painted metal walls. Her eyes ached from perusing columns of tiny black type, her back ached from sitting in one position for too long, and her heart ached whenever she thought about Dan's untimely death. After opening the front door to her apartment, she set her purse down on the carved-oak sideboard that she'd picked up at El Rastro, Madrid's famous flea market.

A very private person, Julie had taken special joy in making her apartment into a haven where she could reenergize her spirit after a hectic day at the embassy. Every piece of furniture and accessory, from the Icelandic fur throw rug to the embroidered pillows on her Shepherd's bench sofa, was there because it brought her pleasure. She stopped for a moment in front of the shelves that held her porcelain menagerie. She'd collected the delicate little animals from around the world. Often their appealing expressions amused her. Tonight there was nothing that could make her smile.

Sinking into a leather easy chair, she rubbed the throbbing tension spot between her brows. She'd been too busy to think about her surprise morning interview with Cal Dixon. Now the reaction was setting in.

After almost three hours with Cal's rogues' gallery, she'd been relieved to tell him that she hadn't seen any of the men and women. Many of the candid shots depicted Soviet chauffeurs and clerical staffers. Others could have been vacation photos snapped at nearby castles and cathedrals—except that the multilingual tour guides, not the tourists, were the focus of the camera's lens. She hadn't thought about it before, but of course it would be easy for congenial "guides" to pick up tidbits from businessmen and military personnel enjoying the local sights.

The confirmation that Soviet spies moved in the same circles that she did was even more disconcerting. Naturally, being cautious about what one said and did in front of foreign nationals had been drummed into her head so thoroughly that it was almost as automatic as brushing her teeth before going to bed. Still, she was surprised by photos of people with whom she'd interacted. Feliks Gorlov, the Russian agricultural under secretary, for example, had seemed quite personable at the French Bastille Day fete last year. Yelena Danchev, who held a position similar to her own, had started a pleasant conversation with her at last month's diplomatic speaker's forum.

Then there was Aleksei Rozonov, the cultural attaché. Her hand had paused on the photo. This morning in Cal's office she had been trying to get through the material quickly, but there was something about the picture of the man that had warranted a second look. The candid shot of Rozonov had obviously been taken at a garden party. Though he was standing with a tall glass in hand, she saw that his shoulders were squared and his darkly handsome features alert. But his good looks were pushed to the background by a tangible aura of danger about his person. Julie had shivered and quickly turned the page.

In an effort to put Rozonov and his cohorts out of her mind, Julie strode purposefully into the bedroom and began sorting through the clothes she intended to drop off at the cleaners tomorrow. It was a relief to focus on a simple domestic chore rather than the morass of confusing details Cal had tossed in her lap.

One of the items that needed attention was the navy suit she'd worn for eighteen hours the day before. As she checked the pockets, her fingers closed around the ticket from Dan's desk she'd stuffed there the night before. She'd forgotten all about it. When she drew out the blue rectangle, she felt an odd, disorienting sensation, as though she were looking through a kaleidoscope and some unseen hand had twisted the tube, giving the little pieces of glass a completely different pattern. She'd thought she knew Dan, but all her previous assumptions were being called into question.

Julie wanted to believe the ticket was the most innocent thing in the world, yet she couldn't help remembering Cal's veiled accusations. He suspected that Dan was involved in some sort of debatable activity—maybe even espionage. Did he know something more about her friend, something he wasn't sharing with her?

The ticket, she knew, should be turned over to him. But then, if it were really something innocent, why get Cal involved? Why not just go to the play herself? When nothing out of the ordinary happened, she could toss away the ticket stub with a clear conscience.

She looked at the date. The performance was for seven o'clock tomorrow. As a Spanish major in college, she'd been interested in Alejandro Casona, and she had promised herself to see some of his work performed while she was in Spain. Somehow, with the pressures of her job, she hadn't gotten around to it. This might be her last opportunity to see his dramas before her tour was up.

WITH A THEATRICAL flourish, Amherst Gordon tossed the report from Madrid into the office burn bag. "This doesn't have any more details than *The Washington Post*," he complained.

His assistant fished out the computer printouts, and smoothed the crumpled sheets. "I'll bet those poor staffers were up all night putting it together. And I think if we read it carefully we'll get some insights."

The Falcon changed the subject. "There are just too many variables, and I don't like it one damn bit."

"Well, it could be worse. At least we know the Raven wasn't killed in the blast," Connie pointed out.

"But I'll bet that Soviet 'wine merchant,' Ivanov, wasn't there to sample the sangria."

"I'd like to know who he was taking orders from," Connie mused.

"The Raven might know. I'd give away the Liechtenstein diplomatic codes to have a ten-minute chat with him about it."

Connie laughed at the inside joke. "Of course, that's impossible. Right now, he doesn't even have a contact for passing information."

The Falcon balled his veined hand into a fist. "There are some even murkier details you haven't heard yet. Dan's theater ticket for the fallback meeting has vanished." The fist came down and hit the mahogany surface of the desk.

Connie looked up sharply. "Wasn't it in the box in his desk?"

"No. I've seen facsimilies of the pictures taken in his office—and the printed inventory of his effects. It's missing. The mate's still at the box office. I had an operative check on that last night. But the Russians have apparently expressed an interest too."

The Falcon's assistant uttered one of her rarely used expletives. "You don't think they have someone *in* our embassy, do you?"

"It's always a possibility."

"Who inventoried Dan's effects?"

The old spymaster pulled a crisp new folder out of his desk drawer. "A third-tour political officer named Julie

McLean. She's the same one who turned in this damn report full of empty speculation and holes."

"Is she any relation to Senator William McLean?"

"Her uncle. It's all in here." He slapped the rigid file against his desk top. "On the surface she comes up clean. But I suggest you do some more digging into her background. She could have been recruited while she was stationed in Moscow during her last tour, for all we know." He paused and rubbed a finger across his usually smooth-shaven cheek. The rasp of skin against gray stubble testified that he, like the embassy staff in Madrid, had been on overtime alert. "But Julie McLean isn't our most urgent problem," he reminded his assistant. "Dan was our only communications link to the Raven, and we've got to set up something else. The trouble is, almost any approach we make could put him in more danger."

"What about the dead drop at the Prado?" Connie asked. She was thinking about the loose molding in a stairwell of Madrid's world-renowned art museum where the Raven had once picked up and left enciphered communications.

"It's a possibility. But we'd have to let him know it's not a trap."

"You're already thinking of something, aren't you?" Connie asked, noting the familiar glean in her employer's green eyes.

"Yes. You do remember it was the Raven who told us the Russians were reading our communications on one of the European satellite links?"

She nodded.

"Since he routinely monitors those communications as part of his job, why don't we send some carefully worded messages to the U.S. military of Torrejon. The Russians should be interested in that. If we embedded a code word the Raven has used, he ought to pick up on what we're doing."

Connie looked at him knowingly. Like a chess master planning a devious assault, he was deep into the strategy of this particular game. Only he wasn't playing with carved figures on a red and black board. He was manipulating men's lives.

BECAUSE JULIE HAD PUT in so much extra time over the bombing incident, she was entitled to get off early the next afternoon. But the project Fitz had hinted at involved going through three filing cabinets full of newspaper clippings looking for a link between known terrorist organizations and what had happened at the San Jeronimo. The search yielded a few tentative suspects who might be backed by European leftist groups, but the connections were well hidden, if they existed at all.

By the time she finished, she didn't think she had the energy to drag herself to the theater. But as she walked past Dan's closed office door on the way to the elevator, her resolve strengthened. She had felt helpless to do anything about the tragedy of his death. Well, this was one final loose end she could tie up.

She had time for only a quick shower before the 7:00 p.m. performance, but the needle spray hitting her bare skin had a reviving effect. Soon she was sweeping her hair up with silver combs and slipping into a soft green silk sheath.

To compensate for the weariness in her brown eyes and the pallor of her complexion, she took a bit of extra care with her mascara and green eye shadow and dabbed some blush onto her cheeks. A few minutes later, as she surveyed the effect, she decided that she would pass for someone out for nothing more than an evening's entertainment.

As her cab pulled up in front of the small theater on a side street off the Gran Via, she noted that it was sandwiched between a leather boutique and an antique shop. The location didn't seem very promising, but the auditorium was a charming surprise. With its gold pilasters, crystal chandeliers and faded red brocade walls, it had once been elegant. Now, although it looked a bit like a dowager who had come on hard times, it was obviously enjoying a new popularity with Madrilenos interested in Spanish culture. She noted that the ground floor was already three-quarters full.

There were about a hundred people in the balcony. She glanced at the row the usher had indicated and saw two empty seats close to the center aisle. One was hers. Had Dan planned to meet someone here? If so, he or she had better hurry. Mentally shrugging, Julie began to descend the steps.

WHEN ALEKSEI ROZONOV arrived a few minutes later, he paused to scan the lower auditorium looking for familiar faces and noting the location of the exits. You never knew, he reflected soberly, when you might have to leave before the curtain calls.

When a bell sounded, signaling that the first act would begin soon, he turned and headed for the stairs, thinking that it would have been a lot more profitable to spend the evening going over embassy cables. Despite the general's paranoia, he didn't expect anyone to be occupying either seat he'd been sent to monitor. Under ordinary circumstances, that would mean he could go home after the first act. He would bet, however, that Bogolubov had someone working double time translating the play into Russian so the old toad could spring a quiz on the last act tomorrow morning.

The wry thought was in his mind as he quietly descended the steps toward the front of the balcony. The ticket the general had given him was for a seat a row back and five over from the ones in question. He didn't glance in that direction until he'd sat down and thumbed through his program for a minute. But even before he looked, he had a strange, sick feeling that there was somebody there. The intuition proved correct. When he lifted his eyes, he found himself staring at the back of a long, thick fall of rich coffee-colored hair secured at the crown by a set of silver combs.

Chapter Three

In the few seconds before the lights dimmed, the woman turned toward the empty seat next to her and set down a dark coat. Aleksei allowed himself no more than a casual look in her direction, but his powers of observation were acute. In that instant, it was as though his clear blue eyes had snapped her picture. As the room darkened he brought her face up in his mind like a color slide projected on a screen.

With her thick curly hair and olive skin she might well be Spanish. But the wide-set eyes and high brows spoke of a more hybrid heritage. In any case he doubted that Eisenberg would have risked involving a Spanish national in the all too deadly intrigue that had cost him his life.

Who was she, he wondered—Eisenberg's mistress? The man would have been fortunate to have someone so striking warming his bed. For a moment his mind followed that line of thought. She wasn't classically beautiful. Yet the contours of her face and her aristocratic posture added up to a very attractive woman.

He glanced in her direction again. In the dim light he could see little more than her outline. But that, coupled with his quick first impression, was enough to convince him that she wasn't a kept woman. He could still see the confident set of her shoulders and almost sense the quiet air of refinement she projected so naturally. Of course, he reminded himself, he'd only seen her for a few seconds. Was he really able to draw an accurate character profile from just one look? Or was he weaving a fantasy about the mystery woman who had claimed one of a pair of seats he had been sure no one would occupy this evening?

The curtain had risen on the interior of a farmhouse, and a bent old man had started to speak. Aleksei shifted his attention to the play. There was nothing more he could do until intermission besides sharpen his Spanish.

When the lights came on again at the end of the second act and the applause had died down, the woman rose and set her program on the chair. She also left the coat as she stood and began making her way toward the back of the balcony. That meant she must be going downstairs for some refreshments. As she climbed the stairs, her gaze, which was lightly skimming the audience, passed Aleksei by and then jerked back like a snapped rubber band. For just an instant a look of shocked recognition flickered in her eyes. Then she quickly hurried toward the exit.

Julie's heart was pounding, and it wasn't just from the rapid climb to the back of the balcony. She knew where she'd seen the tall dark man sitting behind her. In Cal's rogue's gallery of KGB agents. She even remembered his name—Aleksei Rozonov. Officially he was the cultural attaché, which meant he could conceivably be here as part of his cover job. Or maybe he was into classic Spanish drama. It could even be a coincidence that his seat just happened to give him an excellent view of the one she'd been occupying. But the carefully constructed explanations somehow failed to give her any comfort.

Without conscious thought, Julie followed the rest of the well-dressed crowd down to the lobby. Around her, men and women were discussing the first and second acts. She wished *she* had nothing more pressing to think about than Maria Lopez's interpretation of the *madre*. As she waited in a short line at the bar, she considered simply leaving her coat upstairs and walking out of the theater. Vanishing now might be a way of steering clear of whatever mess Dan had gotten himself involved in. On the other hand, she'd already plopped herself right in the middle by sitting down in that seat.

She wondered what she had stumbled into. Was this KGB agent expecting some information from Dan? Or was he here to monitor a meeting between whoever showed up in her seat and the one next to it? It now seemed less likely that the seat beside her was empty by chance. Dan must have intended to meet someone here, and his death had canceled the rendezvous. The possibilities made her thoughts swirl. She was playing out of her league trying to resolve the mystery of the ticket by herself.

After paying for her white wine, she began to make a circuit of the room, focusing on the framed posters of plays previously produced at the theater. Most were Spanish classics. But she noticed that some were translations of American and English works.

As she sipped the mellow wine and studied the bright placards, her mind began to slip back into a mode that had helped her handle fears as a child. Then she'd been afraid of a large black dog whose huge fenced yard she had to pass on the way home from school. The animal had once leaped the chain-link barrier and attacked a teenager who'd been teasing him, so the fear was not without foundation. She'd gotten past that yard every day by telling herself that if the dog didn't jump the fence before she counted to a hundred, she was home safe.

Now she resorted to the same technique. If she made it all the way around the room and Aleksei Rozonov didn't come downstairs, his being here had nothing to do with Dan or the theater ticket.

Five minutes later she let out a deep breath. She'd been under a lot of stress during the past forty-eight hours, and her imagination was working overtime. As soon as she finished her wine she'd go back upstairs.

She was about to set the almost empty glass on a tray when a prickly feeling at the back of her neck made her want to whirl around. Instead she turned slowly. Ten feet away, through the crowd of strangers, she saw the Russian. His lean hand wrapped around a highball glass, he wasn't talking to anyone or pretending to admire the wall decorations. As in the candid photograph she'd seen in Cal's office, his light eyes were alert. He appeared to be studying her with the unabashed frankness of a man taken with a particular woman. She couldn't mistake the sexual element of the appraisal, and she knew the Spaniards around them would understand that. But there were more disturbing undercurrents that reached out toward her from his sharp eyes.

Her legs felt shaky. To compensate, her fingers tightened on the tapered base of the wineglass. She wanted to look away, but avoiding his gaze wouldn't change the situation: she and this man were already linked together in a way she didn't understand. For one reckless moment she thought about marching across the room and demanding to know exactly what was going on. She dismissed the impulse almost as quickly as it occurred. As the thought crossed her mind, her chin lifted defiantly. Rozonov's eyebrows raised ever so slightly in answer.

He wasn't a man you could ignore, she acknowledged. He was dressed impeccably in a dark pinstripe suit set off by a white shirt and a burgundy tie. That alone wouldn't have distinguished him from the other male theatergoers. But Spanish men tended to be short, and the Russian was almost a head taller than most of the men in the lobby. In a sea of animated conversations, punctuated with expressive hand gestures, he was standing perfectly still. His eyes met hers, and from this distance she couldn't see the color. But she did register an impression—icy, cold and calculating. She shivered from the chill, but continued her appraisal.

The lashes that framed those arresting eyes were thick and black, matching the dark brows and the straight midnight black hair. They did nothing to soften the bold planes of the face, she thought, noting the deep creases that cut from the corners of the well-shaped lips upward toward the straight nose. The man had the alertness of a wolf who'd picked up the scent of a quarry.

A wave of trepidation washed over her. She told herself it was a reaction to danger. But what kind of danger, precisely? Did it come from the political repercussions of the situation or from the man himself and her response to him? The laughing, talking people in the room might as well be stage props. With one penetrating look, Rozonov had let her know that she alone was his prey.

As she watched, he put down the half-full glass he was holding and began to weave his way through the crowd toward her. Her survival instinct told her to turn and run. Yet some primitive reaction to the man kept her rooted to the spot. He stopped a few feet from her, a half smile flickering at the corners of his lips. Even with that small compromise, the change in his face was remarkable. In an instant it went from harsh to almost engaging. Unaccountably, she found herself sensing gentler qualities below the threatening surface. His eyes were no longer ice. They had melted into the silvery blue of a lake shimmering in the sun.

"Are you enjoying the performance?" he asked in a voice as rich and smooth as a dark sable pelt.

"It's quite good," she replied, and then realized in horror that he'd asked in English and she'd automatically answered in the same language. So much for pretending to be just another *señorita* enjoying an early show.

"Yes, but I have the feeling Casona is setting us up for a tragedy."

Julie met his gaze, hoping that he couldn't read the fear in her own eyes. Did his casual comment hold a hidden threat or warning? Up close the man's dark fascination was even more compelling. But she was determined to hide the impact he was having on her. "As I remember, the daughter isn't really dead. But she comes back and drowns herself when she finds out she's been replaced in her family's affections," she informed him.

"Well, I won't be waiting in suspense for the fourth act," he replied dryly. The Russian accent and speech pattern were more pronounced now.

"Oh, I didn't mean to..."

"It is not important."

It certainly wouldn't be if he hadn't come here to watch the play in the first place. Chimes sounded, signaling the end of intermission. With relief, Julie turned toward the stairs. But the Russian put a detaining hand on her arm. "Surely you're not going to leave without telling me where we've seen each other before. Could it have been at the British Embassy garden party last month?"

Julie had collected her wits by now. "I don't believe so," she murmured as the crowd thinned around them. "I think we'd better go back to our seats."

"If you insist," he said with a slight bow. "But perhaps we'll be meeting again."

All the way back up to the balcony she could feel the Russian's eyes drilling into her back. She had ample time to reflect that his parting words weren't exactly reassuring.

As the curtain rose, Aleksei settled back and focused his eyes on the stage. However, his mind was far from the pastoral setting of the farmhouse depicted below him. He still didn't know the identity of the woman to whom he'd just been talking, and he didn't know what she was doing in that seat. But she was almost certainly an American. An associate of Eisenberg? An innocent bystander? Or someone deeply embedded in the intrigue that swirled around the seat she occupied?

Talking to her had only confirmed his first impressions. She was a damn attractive woman. And despite the reason that he was here, his interest was more personal than he would have liked. Slowly he replayed the whole encounter from the moment she'd registered dismay at seeing him behind her in the balcony. Was it the mere fact of his nationality? Or did she know something more that made her wary? He strongly suspected the latter. But how much did she know? And where had she gotten her information? From the CIA? From the late Dan Eisenberg? There was no way of knowing—yet.

Downstairs, he'd admired the way she'd held her ground. *Bozhe!* He'd simply admired her. It was amazing how many details had registered, he mused, as he remembered the lines of her green dress and the way the silky fabric had emphasized the curves of her slender figure. The color had been a perfect foil for her olive skin.

When he crossed the room to speak to her, more intimate details had come into focus. Her expressive eyes were coffee brown and flecked with warm gold. And that luxurious hair was a barely tamed cascade of natural curls. Standing close to her, he'd been able to detect the warm fragrance of her skin. The observation gave him pause. This was the second time tonight he'd been thinking about her in blatantly sexual terms, even though there'd been nothing overtly sensual in either her manner or her words. In fact, she'd been unable to completely hide her fear of him. Yet fear hadn't been her only response. A man knew when a woman was reacting to him on a sexual level.

He had a sudden desire to get up and walk out of the theater, to go back to his office and write up a false report of the evening—a report that made no mention of the woman. He was almost certain she was not a trained espionage operative. That meant either some resourceful agent was using her as bait, or she had stumbled into a situation where she didn't belong at all.

Of course there was another possibility. She might be a very good actress, as good as the young woman now reciting her lines so convincingly down there on the stage. Suppose the mystery woman's ingenuousness was just a pose? Suppose she had come here to deliberately trap him into some false step? He'd always laughed off the security lectures about beautiful spies working their wiles on unsuspecting diplomats. But in this case maybe the warnings weren't so funny. He could imagine a confidential report in a file folder somewhere speculating on how long he'd been without female companionship. There might be someone who was hoping that he'd be susceptible to just the right approach.

All right, Aleksei Iliyanovich, he reminded himself, *that is one more thing you are going to have to guard against.*

There was one final reason why he had to report the evening's encounter. He didn't trust Bogolubov, and the feeling was certainly mutual. Chances were the comrade general had dispatched someone to shadow him. No, the best policy was to get up and make the phone call the duty officer back at the embassy had just been told to expect.

IT WAS IMPOSSIBLE for Julie to concentrate on the last two acts of the play. The men and women emoting on the brightly lit stage below her were mere shadows. She was much more aware of the man she couldn't see, Aleksei Rozonov. Now that she knew he was sitting just a row behind her, it took a considerable amount of discipline to keep from turning and glancing back anxiously in his direction. She simply couldn't suppress the feeling that his assessing blue gaze was still burning into the back of her head. The knowledge made shivers crawl up her spine and play with the wisps of hair at her nape.

She had been a fool not to turn the theater ticket over to Cal Dixon. First thing Monday morning she was going to have to tell him what had happened this evening, and then she was going to have to explain why she hadn't confided in him. The prospect wasn't pleasant.

When the actors had finally taken their curtain calls, Julie gathered up her coat and turned to leave. Unable to keep her eyes from flicking to Rozonov's seat, she was surprised to see that it was empty. When had he left? She looked for him in the lobby and in the crowd lingering on the wide sidewalk in front of the theater. But he was gone. For the moment she was safe, and she breathed a sigh of relief.

She was heading for one of the taxis pulled up at the curb when she caught sight of one of Madrid's more incongruous sights. Down on the next block was a McDonald's. The well-known golden arches were a reminder that she'd skipped dinner in order to make the early performance. Unexpectedly they also brought forth a wave of longing for something familiar in this foreign city. She had always scorned Americans who traveled halfway around the world to eat Yankee junk food. Now, after her disturbing encounter with the Russian, she craved the comfort of a Big Mac with fries and a Coke. Turning from the line of cabs, she started off down the street toward the brightly lit windows.

She wasn't the only one heading toward the American restaurant. Surrounded by a crowd of men and women, she didn't notice a shadow detach itself from the shelter of a store entrance and follow several paces behind her.

A number of conversations around her still focused on the play and the death at the end. Julie didn't want to think about death or anything else unpleasant tonight, so she quickened her steps. The steps of the man who was following also quickened, but she was oblivious. A short gray-haired *viejo* held the door open for her, and she nodded her thanks before stopping to look around.

The foot-high menu over the counter was a delightful mixture of Spanish and English. When the food arrived, she looked around for a table. Most of the seats were occupied, since Madrilenos usually didn't even think of having dinner until after nine.

Seeing that a spot near the door had just been vacated, she made a beeline for it. At the next table a young couple with Boston accents were discussing their afternoon's shopping expedition to the plush mall at Madrid Dos. The sense of familiarity about this place and its occupants was just the kind of reassurance she needed after her earlier encounter with Rozonov. She felt insulated and safe—almost as though she were back home already.

As she bit into a french fry, she closed her eyes and sighed. It was almost as good as she'd anticipated. Before she realized it, she'd eaten half the bag. She was just reaching for the Coke when the woman at the next table stood up and grabbed her arm. Julie looked up in alarm.

"What?"

"That man." The woman gestured excitedly. "It happened so fast. He just cut your purse off the back of your chair."

Automatically Julie turned and felt the strap. It was no longer taut from the weight of the bag, but dangling loosely. In the next moment she looked with a feeling of sick dismay toward the door of the restaurant. It had just slammed closed.

The husband of the blond woman was already out of his seat. He reached the door, pulled it open, and vanished. People at other tables had become aware of the incident. *"El hombre huerto su monedro,"* she heard a large woman explaining excitedly in the corner. The news buzzed from table to table, now in Spanish, now in English. Everyone was looking curiously in her direction. Other women who had casually hung shoulder bags on the backs of their chairs transferred them to their laps or jammed them between their feet on the floor.

The husband was back in a few moments, shaking his head apologetically. "I ran down to the end of the block in both directions, but I think the fellow disappeared before I got to the sidewalk."

"You poor thing," the wife murmured solicitously to Julie. "Is there anything we can do?"

She shook her head and sank back into her seat.

The manager, a distressed look on his rounded face, bustled up and began apologizing profusely in rapid Castilian.

Julie stared at him, still disoriented. She could feel the french fries she'd eaten congealing in her stomach. She knew from the half-dozen distressed travelers who showed up at the embassy daily that this sort of thing was common.

Silently she cursed her stupidity and tried to remember exactly what she had transferred to the black kid evening bag before going out.

"Did anyone see the incident?" the manager asked the crowd.

The American woman began to give a description of the thief. It could have fitted a dozen Spaniards in the room.

Julie wasn't really listening. What a fitting end to an upsetting evening. And then a new and more frightening thought struck her. Did her encounter with the Russian at the theater have anything to do with this? She fervently hoped not and tried to reassure herself that the theft was an unfortunate coincidence.

She thought back over how she must have appeared as she entered the restaurant. She'd probably looked like an easy mark. Certainly she'd been lulled into a false sense of security by the nostalgia of the setting, and she was paying the price. But right now, unless she wanted to borrow cab fare from this American couple, she was going to have to call Paula or Fitz. "Can I use your telephone?" she asked the hovering manager in Spanish.

"Sí. Sí, señorita."

Chapter Four

"Good morning, sir," the uniformed guard at the checkpoint greeted him.

The Raven's only acknowledgment was a curt nod. In the Soviet chain of command, dour demeanor was the rule when dealing with underlings. And if there had been any tendency to relax, everything had tightened up like a shoe factory struggling to meet a suddenly doubled quota when Bogolubov had appeared on the scene.

After signing the log, the Raven waited until the guard clicked the lock on the heavy door. Once he had stepped inside, it closed behind him with the sound of steel meeting steel. It had often crossed his mind that if someone happened to drop a nuclear bomb on Madrid, this would be the safest place in the city. But with the guard outside dead, there wouldn't be any way to get out again.

The room was filled with half a dozen noisy Teletype machines spewing out pages of Cyrillic text. Five of them monitored sensitive but ordinary diplomatic communications. But one machine was for top-secret material. It was a newer Western-made model that had been on the U.S. export prohibited list. But that hadn't prevented its acquisition via an agreeable Middle Eastern exporting firm and its subsequent modification in a Moscow electronics lab. The U.S.-made hardware was more reliable than anything manufactured at home, the Raven reflected. But when it did break down, spare parts were a bitch.

However, that wasn't his problem. He was more interested in the data than the terminal. It was on this line that he had picked up a lot of the information he'd passed on to the Falcon. Until nine months ago his personal code of honor had restricted the exchange to material that wouldn't damage his country's own national security. That meant he'd stayed away from almost anything with military ramifications. But then he'd gotten a hint of something that could change the whole balance of world power.

At first he had thought it was simply part of the extensive Soviet propaganda effort, the most effective tool of which was disinformation. Moscow had always prided itself on the creative use of half-truths and fabrications that were close enough to facts to sound plausible. The technique was used on every front. When Arkady Shevchenko had defected, he'd been smeared as an alcoholic and a womanizer to discredit his disclosures. After the accidental release of cyanide in Bhopal, India, TASS had rushed in to inform the world that the U.S. was testing deadly poison gas on a guinea pig community. And Moscow had even tried to scare black and oriental athletes away from the Los Angeles Olympics with a hate flier purportedly prepared by the Ku Klux Klan. At its most successful, this war of words had toppled whole governments. Even when the lies didn't stand up to scrutiny, they cost the West millions of dollars to counteract the libel.

The Raven stepped over a snake pit of heavy extension cords and cables, heading for the Western-made machine against the wall. Though the noise level always gave him a headache, at least it wasn't like the comms center in KGB headquarters, where the operators lost fifty percent of their hearing within five years. But the clatter here, he reminded himself, was a mixed blessing. It meant that there was no one assigned to the room who might be looking over his shoulder.

Quickly he began scanning the output of the last twenty-four hours for the information he hoped to pass to the Falcon. He was looking for references to material classified under the project name Topaz. The access was so tight, he doubted that even a dozen men knew the significance of the word.

He'd always harbored a grudging respect for the power of a successful disinformation assault. But under Topaz the trickery promised to escalate from shaping opinion to manipulating the spending of U.S. defense dollars. The first Topaz reference on this communication link nine months ago had aroused his curiosity. The weeks had crawled by as he'd doggedly chipped slivers of information from the monolithic bureaucracy. Even though he still didn't have the whole story, what he'd learned made his blood run as icy as the Volga River in the dead of winter.

The scheme had been to trick the U.S. Defense Department into wasting billions of dollars by making the Western forces believe they had captured the nerve gas antidote Quadrozine. The Western commanders had snapped up the first part of the bait when they'd started making decisions based on "stolen" Soviet documents. The next phase of the operation had involved letting rebel forces in Afghanistan capture a Russian tank with syringes of the supposed antidote stashed inside. The Pentagon chiefs had been elated with the discovery and were now reconstructing their entire defense system around it. Now Moscow was getting ready to put the next step—whatever it was—into operation.

He was so damn close to finding out the critical details. Yet, at the same time, he felt as though a noose were being lowered around his neck and slowly tightened. Sometimes in the middle of the night he could feel the rough hemp choking off his windpipe. The hunters were closing in, and his survival instinct urged him to abandon the search and defect. But the very reasons why he had begun this double life kept him coming back to the deafening clatter of the communications room every morning. If he could hold on till he got one more break, he'd really earn the welcome he knew the Falcon had waiting for him.

Of course, he did have something. On a trumped-up trip back to Moscow, he'd photographed an initial planning memorandum that should stir up a bit of doubt in the Pentagon. That film was now sitting innocently with the other photographic equipment in his apartment. It would have been in the Falcon's hands by now except for the tragedy at the San Jeronimo. The fact that they'd identified his contact made his situation even more desperate. The only stroke of luck was that he hadn't actually been seen with the dead man.

So how was he going to get that film to the Falcon now? And what if it came to a choice between getting the proof out or saving himself?

He had reached the bottom of the pile of classified messages and was about to signal the guard to let him out when a piece of informal traffic addressed to General Dwayne Brewster at Torrejon Air Force Base caught his eye. It was from one of the general's colleagues at the Pentagon and advised him of a surprise upcoming visit by the inspector general's staff. There was nothing of particular importance in the communiqué except that it used the caution "Don't put this one in your file."

That was one of the phrases he and the Falcon had used for identity verification back when his every action hadn't been subject to examination under a microscope.

He looked down at the white fanfold paper in his hand. The choice of words could be coincidental. Yet somehow he didn't think so. This was coming in on the line that he had warned the Falcon his government was reading. Using the Soviet's tap to send a message back to him was a form of poetic justice that would appeal to the director of the Peregrine Connection.

After taking a precautionary glance at the door, he turned his back to it and pulled out a standard-issue KGB pen that contained a miniature camera. First he pulled the pocket clip forward to activate the hidden mechanism. Then he held the instrument over the communiqué and clicked the point return button twice before returning the pen to the breast pocket of his suit.

The Raven picked up the stack of routine output he retrieved daily from the room and glanced around once more, assuring himself that everything was in order. Then he ran the buzzer alerting the guard that he was ready to return to his desk job.

THERE WAS SO MUCH KGB work to take care of that Aleksei often came to the office on Saturdays to deal with the normal duties of his cover job as cultural attaché. But he wasn't the only one. A fair number of staffers had to put in weekend time. He was just going over the schedule of a Ukrainian folk dance troupe which would be arriving in Barcelona next month, when the phone rang. He wasn't surprised that it was a summons from Bogolubov. When Aleksei entered the upstairs office, the general was sitting forward glaring at Feliks Gorlov and Georgi Krasin. "Well, Aleksei Iliyanovich, you seem to be the only one capable of following orders," he observed.

Aleksei took his seat without comment. A compliment from the general was like a two-edged blade. You never knew when you were going to get the other side of it.

"You schoolboys," he addressed the other two professionals in the room. "If you don't do a better job on your homework, your next diplomatic assignments are going to be in Nicaragua and El Salvador."

Georgi covered his cringe by pretending to straighten his steel-frame glasses. Gorlov merely inspected his carefully manicured nails.

"But we'll discuss your shortcomings later. Right now I want to show you what Rozonov bagged last night at the theater where I sent him to make some observations."

"Not on the Spanish drama, I assume," Gorlov murmured under his breath.

The general either didn't hear the remark or chose to ignore it. Sliding his chair back to reach in a drawer, he pulled out a black leather pocketbook and slapped it down on the polished surface of his desk as though it were exhibit A at an espionage trial. Even Aleksei looked surprised, although he recognized the black evening bag as the one the woman at the theater had been carrying. Apparently his phone call had inspired more than a simple surveillance. For a moment he felt a pang of regret. Then he reminded himself that he hadn't gotten her into this. She'd done it herself as soon as she'd taken that seat.

Bogolubov emptied out the contents of the purse onto the desk top with careless nonchalance. Reaching into the small pile of personal effects, he fished out a wallet and flipped it open, revealing a personal identification card. From across the room it was impossible to read the information, although Aleksei could see it was neatly printed.

"I believe we've flushed out Eisenberg's replacement. At least she showed up for a clandestine rendezvous that he'd set up before his accident."

Three sets of eyes were riveted on the comrade general. He paused and pulled a crisp manila folder out of the same drawer that had held the evening bag. "She's a mid-level political specialist at the U.S. embassy named Julie McLean." The general stumbled over the consonant that began her first name since there was no *J* sound in the Russian alphabet. "Her last tour of duty was in Moscow," he added. "And who knows what kind of damage she did there."

Aleksei saw Georgi swallow convulsively as though the general's supposition was causing him personal discomfort. Didn't he see that the older man was just playing for dramatic effect? Americans in Moscow were watched more closely than bacteria under a microscope. He doubted there was much chance any of them could pull off an espionage coup. Still, he couldn't help finding the information about Julie McLean's last post interesting. The name fit her, Aleksei thought, remembering the way she'd looked standing with a glass of wine in her hand across that crowded theater lobby. Despite the circumstances, being able to put a name to her face brought him a surge of satisfaction.

"The tour in Moscow means we've got a file on her," Bogolubov was saying. "I've had a facsimile of selected pages sent from headquarters. The microfiche will arrive by diplomatic pouch."

He passed the sheets around and let the three men look them over. Aleksei quickly scanned the biographic material. Julie McLean was twenty-nine and single. A graduate of the Foreign Service school at Georgetown University. He raised an eyebrow at the notation on her uncle, Senator McLean, a hard-liner when it came to Soviet-American relations. Would he have encouraged his niece to become a spy?

His eyes moved down the page. She'd attended public school in the elementary grades and then switched to a private girl's academy. She'd been raised in Baltimore, a city he'd once visited when his father had been with the Soviet delegation to the U.N. He and his parents had taken the train down to watch a friendship tour by the Bolshoi.

Gorlov was holding up a poor-quality facsimile of what looked like a newspaper photograph. "I think I met the woman," he mused.

Bogolubov gave him a direct look. "And?"

"It was at one of the embassy nation-day parties—the German, I think. No, the French."

"I don't give a pig's teat which party it was. What did you think of her?"

Gorlov was unfazed. "Polite but guarded. Not my type, really. You know how Western women are—not enough curves."

The general grinned and nodded before turning to Aleksei. "And your opinion?"

A dozen details and perceptions leaped to mind as he remembered the green dress that had molded her slender but very appealing figure, the intelligence mirrored in her dark eyes, and the fear she'd struggled to suppress when she'd sensed his interest. "If she's a spy, she's new to the game."

"Why?"

"She made too many mistakes."

"Like what?"

"Using Eisenberg's ticket in the first place. That was too big a risk. Or answering me in English when I spoke to her. But all that's in my report."

Bogolubov leaned forward so that his double chin was resting against his fingertips. His expression was thoughtful. "Perhaps she wanted to convey a certain impression."

"To throw us off our guard," Feliks Gorlov added, picking up the theme.

"Or maybe she was floundering because Eisenberg hadn't given her the name of his contact," Georgi interjected.

"Um." The syllable, which might have signified agreement came from the general as he scooped up the contents of the black leather bag and returned it to his desk drawer. "The question is, can we use any of this information to our advantage?" he asked.

"You mean turn her?" Gorlov said.

"Too crude an approach. Besides, I suspect we only have one thing she might want."

"Money?" Georgi Krasin asked.

The general snapped angrily. "You're starting to believe all those Western news magazines. They're not all motivated by greed."

Aleksei filled in the blank. "She needs to make contact with Eisenberg's turncoat."

"The man who's using the code name Raven," Bogolubov added.

"But we can't use him for bait. We don't know who he is," Gorlov pointed out.

"Not yet." The general paused and looked around the room. "But I'm thinking of offering her a convincing substitute. And since she's not Feliks's type, and Georgi hasn't had enough experience for the job, I think we'll try Aleksei Iliyanovich."

"You want me to pretend to be the Raven?" he clarified.

"Possibly. Or maybe just a comrade interested in selling some information—or even defecting. Either way, McLean ought to jump at the opportunity, and you can use your charm to find out what she knows."

"Yes, Aleksei Iliyanovich would be a good choice," Gorlov agreed, studying his colleague thoughtfully. "Women respond to him, and he's got an excellent command of the English language."

"Didn't you spend several years in the U.S.?" Georgi asked, unable to disguise the tone of envy in his voice. Hardline propaganda to the contrary, a posting in Washington or New York was coveted by Soviet diplomats.

"Off and on, almost six."

"So you've got a pretty good handle on how they think," Gorlov said.

"Even in my father's time we didn't exactly mix freely with the natives."

"More than the rest of us."

"You don't look pleased," Bogolubov observed, addressing Aleksei. "What's the matter? If you play it right you may get—what do the Americans call it?—a roll in the hay out of the assignment." His use of the crude Western expression drew appreciative laughter from the other two men in the room.

After they had left, Aleksei remained seated.

Bogolubov raised his heavy-lidded eyes. "Yes?"

"This is a rather unusual assignment, Comrade General."

"You're not up to pretending to be the defector?"

Aleksei gave his superior a measured look. "That's not the issue. I gather you're taking sole responsibility for this operation."

"Of course."

"Then that increases the risk to me personally. What if someone who doesn't know about the operation misinterprets what I'm doing? What if they think I really *am* the Raven? My career could be destroyed, or I could end up as dead as Kiril Ivanov."

The general stroked his chin. "You accepted certain risks, Major Rozonov, when you joined our ranks."

"Granted. But I'd be happier about this project if you would document your orders and put them in my file."

Bogolubov shrugged. "As you wish."

"Thank you, Comrade General." Aleksei's tone of voice was deferential but both men knew who had won that round.

BRADLEY FITZPATRICK zipped up the black evening bag that had been dumped downtown in a Madrid mailbox and returned to the U.S. embassy by the Spanish civil guard Sunday morning.

According to the inventory Julie had given him, nothing inside was missing except the ten thousand pesetas she'd tucked into her wallet. However, the lining of the bag had been carefully slit in several places, as though the thief had been searching for something hidden inside. And when Fitzpatrick began to look more closely, he noted that her identification card was bent, as though it had been hurriedly stuffed back into its plastic holder. He'd seen his share of personal belongings returned to American citizens via the mail once the cash and values were removed, but the condition of this purse and wallet didn't match the scenario of a simple robbery.

His mind flashed back to the note of panic in Julie's voice when she'd called him from the Gran Via Friday night. Then he'd put it down to the stress of having been victimized.

Lord, he thought. Last Thursday Cal Dixon had called him in and made some pretty nasty allegations about Dan Eisenberg before firing off a barrage of questions about Julie's relationship with the captain. Fitzpatrick had prac-

tically laid his career on the line defending her. Now he had
to wonder exactly what the hell was going on.

Sighing, he picked up the phone. He had no choice but to
call Cal.

Forty-five minutes later, Eduardo buzzed Julie's apartment to tell her two colleagues from the office were downstairs. The Sunday paper was spread across the kitchen
table, and she hadn't yet bothered to get dressed.

"Send them up in five minutes," she instructed the
portero. By the time the knock came at the door, she was
tucking a plaid shirt into the waistband of her jeans.

"Fitz, Cal?" Julie peered into the hallway, looking from
one unreadable face to the other. A wave of apprehension
suddenly made her feel cold in the cotton shirt she wore.
"What's happening?"

"We've come to take you for a walk, Julie," Fitz replied,
his voice vaguely apologetic.

"A walk?" What in the world was going on?

"In Retiro Park," Cal added.

The well-groomed area with its wide paths, gardens, and
lake was one of her favorite parts of the city. But from the
tone of Cal's voice and the somber expression on the two
men's faces, she suspected she wasn't going to enjoy this
particular Sunday outing.

Chapter Five

"Just let me get my purse."

Cal and Fitz exchanged cryptic looks.

"Maybe you'd like to put your wallet in it," the CIA man murmured.

She whirled to face him. "Was the evening bag returned?"

"Yes."

Fitz offered her the brown paper bag that had been tucked under his arm.

When Julie reached inside, the purse was missing. Only its contents were there.

"Where . . . ?"

Cal answered the question before she'd framed it. "We've sent it out to be cleaned."

Oh, no, she thought. *The cleaners* was the code word for the forensic lab at Torrejon. She'd almost convinced herself that she'd been the victim of a simple robbery. Now she knew Cal Dixon didn't think so. The realization made it suddenly hard to catch her breath. There were a dozen excuses she wanted to make and questions she burned to ask. But not until it was safe to talk.

Cal, who was dressed in a navy jogging suit, nodded to Eduardo as the threesome crossed the lobby. In their casual attire, they looked as though they might have been going out for a Sunday stroll. But from Julie's perspective, with a large man at either shoulder, she felt as though she were heading for her own execution.

Though she had planned to talk with Cal first thing Monday morning, it was obvious the CIA man wanted some answers now.

She stole a quick glance at Fitz. From the tight look on his familiar freckled face she could tell Cal had already convinced him she had made a serious breach of security.

Only the inevitable Sunday choir music on the radio broke the silence as they rode down Paseo de la Castellana and turned off on Calle Alcala.

As they got out of the car and approached the park's decorative iron fence, Julie could see dozens of Madrilenos enjoying the warm morning sunshine before the day grew too hot for more than sitting at one of the shaded café tables with a cold beer.

Many of the strollers were still wearing their Sunday best. Others had changed into jeans and casual shirts. She and her escorts didn't look out of place.

It wasn't until they had passed through the wide gates, and Cal had set a moderate pace, that he came to the point.

"Your bag was stolen and searched by professionals, Julie. Why?"

She glanced left toward Fitz. He kept his eyes straight ahead, his lips clamped together.

"I don't know." Though she tried to remain calm, her voice was quavery and barely above a whisper.

"Come on. You must have some clue."

She sighed. "I was going to tell you about this tomorrow anyway."

"Sure."

"Keep it civil, Dixon," Fitz broke in. She felt his shoulder press against hers for just a moment.

The small gesture made her turn to him. "Fitz, do you remember when I went through Dan's office drawers?"

"Yes. You said you didn't find anything important."

"That's right. But there was a theater ticket that matched an odd notation on Dan's calendar."

She wished Fitz would say something. Across the wide lawn, the strains of a guitar reached the threesome. "I put the ticket into my pocket and forgot all about it—until after Cal grilled me in his office. I suppose I should have given it to him the next morning. But I wanted to prove to myself that it was something innocent."

"But it wasn't, was it?" the consular officer interjected.

"No."

"In fact, I'll bet you found other notations on Dan's calendar that look 'odd.'"

"Yes." Damn the man!

"Who was Dan meeting Friday?" Cal pressed.

"There was an empty seat next to his, but no one claimed it."

"Then what had you so frightened that you didn't tell Fitz about it when he came to pick you up after the robbery?"

"Someone I recognized was sitting in back of the two seats."

"Who?"

"One of the KGB agents in your mug book."

Cal swore under his breath, but the imprecation held a strange note of triumph. "I knew it."

"Who was it?" Fitz questioned.

"Aleksei Rozonov."

"The cultural attaché?"

"Yeah, he's one of their top boys," Cal said. "This is going to be very tricky," he added to himself.

Julie felt as though a weight had been lifted off her shoulders. Why hadn't she come to Cal in the first place? He was a lot better equipped to deal with this sort of thing than she. "I've hardly been able to sleep since Friday night," she admitted.

"Tell me what happened and don't leave anything out," Cal directed.

She hesitated for a moment. So much of the encounter had been in nuances she didn't want to examine too closely. Yet her sense of being in danger had been very real. "I could feel him watching me at the intermission. Then, just before the third act started, he came up and asked me how I was enjoying the play, but it wasn't a casual conversation. I felt he was looking for something."

"That was it?" Fitz prompted. He sounded relieved, as though he'd expected her to admit going off into a corner with the man and exchanging secret documents.

Cal continued the interrogation. "What did you think of Rozonov?"

"Intelligent. Polished. Dangerous." *Darkly handsome. Devastatingly sexy. Too confident.* Her response to the Russian had been powerful and disturbing. That put her in an even more precarious position than merely using Dan's theater ticket. But she wasn't about to share the insight with Cal.

They had reached a little circle called the Plaza de Nicaragua. In the center was a fountain decorated with dolphins and cherubs. A sudden shift in the wind sent the spray in their direction. Cal put his arm up to shade his face but Julie welcomed the cool mist of water. When she turned to face the fountain, he grasped her forearm and steered them back in the direction of the lake. Fitz wheeled with them as though they were in military formation.

"We've got to find out what Eisenberg was up to and why the Russian is interested," Cal said.

"Maybe Dan was doing some sort of government undercover work," Fitz suggested.

"If that were true, I'd know about it," Cal snapped. "Get it into your head that the man was involved in something unsavory. And I'm going to find out what it was." He was silent as they skirted the crowd at the edge of the lake, where street vendors were selling trinkets and candy. When they'd gained one of the less traveled jogging paths, he turned to Julie.

"Aleksei Rozonov thinks you know something."

"But I don't."

"That's beside the point."

"Cal, I don't want to get involved in whatever this is."

Fitz sighed. "I'm afraid you got involved when you used that ticket."

She'd been worrying about that since Friday night. Now it was out in the open. "Can't someone else handle it from here on out?"

"I'd like nothing better than to put a professional on the case. But it would tip our hand to switch dancers in mid-waltz, so to speak," Cal pointed out.

"And it's vital that we find out what's going on," Fitz added.

Julie took a deep breath. "Then, what am I going to have to do?"

"Get to know Rozonov a little better."

An image of a sacrificial goat tethered to a stake leaped into her mind. Her heart started to pound. From the moment the Russian's icy blue eyes had locked with hers, she had known the man was a threat. She had sensed danger and intrigue swirling around him like demons in a mist. But her apprehension had been on a personal level as well. Even though their encounter had been brief, she had felt a dark attraction pulling her toward the man. It had made her want to run the other way. Now—my God!—Cal Dixon was practically throwing her at him.

IT HAD BEEN a long time since he had prowled the marble galleries of the Prado, the former palace that housed Spain's national art collection. Now, as so often in the past, the Raven's footsteps brought him to the paintings of Hieronymus Bosch, the fifteenth-century Dutch master whose works had been collected by Philip II.

Bosch had been obsessed with retribution for sin—like some of the great Russian novelists. But his artistic expression was so startlingly different. His huge canvases were often divided into several parts, some depicting in intricate detail throngs of men and women enjoying the pleasures of the flesh. Other equally elaborate sections illustrated their eternal tortures in hell. Bosch liked to make the punishment fit the crime. The Raven's eyes were drawn particularly to the men falling under the blade of a long, phallic looking knife and the woman whose naked ivory skin was being fondled by the spidery claws of a green monster.

He could easily picture Bosch exchanging creative ideas with the twentieth-century torture masters who ran the Gulag Archipelago, the chain of prison camps where so many Soviet citizens had disappeared. The thought made a sudden chill dance down his spine. If his own sins against the state were discovered, he'd rot in the Russian version of hell. That was a risk he'd chosen to take, but still, Bosch's graphic nightmares disturbed him.

Turning away, he headed toward the Rubens collection, knowing that less moralistic subjects would lift his spirits. The amply endowed females the painter had favored reminded him of many of his countrywomen. But a Russian painter would have covered them in furs and heavy garments rather than mere wisps of lace.

To even the most alert observer, his progress through the crowded galleries would seen random. He might be just another tourist taking in Madrid's most celebrated cultural attraction. But he was really making his way toward a little-used stairway at the west end of the building. Just above the ground floor, a piece of marble molding was loose. Behind it, was the dead drop where he and Peregrine agents had left material for each other before the net around him had begun to tighten. On his way down it was impossible to stop because there were a number of people on the stairs. So he passed by the drop and went to look at some of the Flemish baroque paintings. Fifteen minutes later the stairwell was clear, except for a man holding the hand of a small girl. After waiting until they were out of sight, the Raven reached down quickly, slid the piece of marble aside, shoved an envelope into the opening, and replaced the marble. Then he strolled back to the main floor and out of the museum. In keeping with his tourist pose, he turned in the direction of the smaller building several blocks away that housed Picasso's famous *Guernica*.

The information he'd left was merely a test of the communications link with the Falcon—a photocopy of the embassy's confidential telephone directory, information that would be of minor use to the West. Since the material could have been supplied by anyone on the staff, it wouldn't point an incriminating finger at him. Now he'd just have to wait and see what sort of return message appeared in the clandestine mailbox.

The strategy was sound. But waiting was like sitting on top of a live grenade that could go off at any minute.

JULIE TOOK two 100-peseta notes from her evening bag and handed them to the cabdriver. After withdrawing her party invitation, she stepped out onto the sidewalk and allowed the folds of her long burgundy dress to settle gracefully into place. Then she made her way toward the high wall that shielded Byne House from view.

She'd attended only a few previous soirees at the mansion. The occasions had simply been an extension of her business dealings with officials in the Spanish government. This evening was still business, but of quite a different type. It was to be her first contrived meeting with the Russian spy. The assignment had her nerves stretched taut. To calm them, she forced herself to think about the opulent setting rather than the dangerous man she'd been sent here to meet.

Byne House was actually a small palace and one of the most carefully preserved legacies of Madrid's elegant past. Ironically, it had been the home of an expatriate New York millionaire, Arthur Byne, whose widow had willed it to the United States. Now it was the official residence of the embassy's second-in-command, Henry Sloane, and his wife Margaret.

Much of the American's diplomatic entertaining took place in its gracious public rooms and gardens. Tonight Byne House was the scene of a reception for the highly acclaimed Philadelphia Opera, which was mounting its first European tour. Though the opera singers had been well reviewed by the Madrid press, Raphael Conti, the flamboyant artistic director, had stolen the show. When Paula and the other staffers in Julie's section had learned she was attending the reception for him and the rest of the cast and orchestra, they'd been jealous. Word had it that her uncle's political connections had procured her the invitation. She'd been grateful for the misconception.

Because Aleksei Rozonov had known Conti in New York, there had been no questions asked when the Russian cultural attaché had been added to the invitation list. Cal Dixon had called Julie to his office to apprise her of the game plan.

"Rozonov must be anxious to renew his friendship with Conti. They went to high school together in New York, and by all accounts, they were quite a pair. I see from the Russian's file"—which had expanded by at least an inch since the last time Julie had seen it—"that they once took the Conti limousine for a joy ride into Canada. If Rozonov's father hadn't pulled some strings, that stunt would have gotten Aleksei Iliyanovich sent back to school in Moscow."

It was hard for Julie to picture the man with the penetrating ice blue eyes participating in such a prank. But the KGB agent, like everyone else, must have been young once. Quickly she blocked out the mitigating thought. Rozonov was the enemy, and the only safe course was to keep reminding herself of that fact.

Julie knocked on the heavy wooden door and waited while a tuxedoed butler carefully inspected her engraved invitation. She knew the precaution wasn't simply to keep out gate-crashers. For the safety of the high-level diplomats gathered here, security had to be stringent, even if it was disguised in gracious party regalia.

The gate opened into the garden and Julie stood for a moment surveying the glittering scene. Men and women dressed in evening clothes were gathered in small groups, chatting casually. Waiters circulated among them with silver trays of champagne and canapés. The courtyard was illuminated by lanterns strung between the trees.

Margaret Sloane, dressed in a stunning ivory gown, was welcoming guests as they arrived.

"I'm so glad you could join us this evening," she said. "You know your way around, don't you, my dear?"

Julie nodded. Her background had well prepared her to mix and mingle with the high-society crowd. She'd learned early from her mother that in social situations you did what was correct, not necessarily what was natural.

She brought a courteous yet slightly reserved smile to her face as she complimented her hostess on the setting before moving into the garden.

A waiter stopped to offer her a glass of champagne, but she declined and asked where she could find the bar. A glass of club soda with a twist of lemon was more appropriate to the evening's game plan.

As she made her way along the circular path that skirted the small fountain, she passed Ambassador Thomas, enjoying an animated conversation with one of the featured sopranos, Geraldine Lowery. The tall, distinguished-looking man glanced up at his young staffer, seemed momentarily surprised, and then nodded a greeting. She returned the salutation with an automatic smile. Although she'd been afraid to ask, she suspected that Cal was running this operation without the knowledge of the embassy's senior staff. Now that suspicion was even stronger.

The bar was set up near the French doors that connected a casually decorated garden room to the courtyard. After getting her soda, Julie drifted inside.

Where was Rozonov? she wondered. Had he arrived yet, or had he decided to skip the party after all? She'd spent the past few days psyching herself up to confront him this evening. Although she still dreaded the meeting, she wanted to get it over with.

In the wide hallway one of the senior political officers gave her an appreciative smile. "You look absolutely terrific, Julie. You ought to dress this way for the office. It would certainly liven things up."

Julie accepted the compliment graciously. In truth, she had dressed carefully for the occasion, finding it easier to think about her hair and makeup than about her assignment for the evening. Her dark tresses were swept up in a French twist with just a few dark curls artfully arranged at her cheeks. The upswept hairstyle was a perfect foil for her long burgundy evening dress. From the front it was almost demure. But the provocative back plunged almost to her waistline.

Upstairs, she could hear one of the musicians engaged in an impromptu performance. As she climbed the wide marble steps, a piano rendition of the overture to *The Barber of Seville* drifted downward. Ordinarily its energetic baroque rhythm would have put her in a carefree mood. But not this evening. Even the seventeenth-century splendor of the house with its carved stone fireplaces and elaborately painted ceilings failed to capture her interest for long.

Many of the singers and orchestra members had gathered in the music room. Julie skirted the entrance and made her way to the main reception hall. The moment she entered she felt a chill down the bare expanse of her back. Rozonov was there. She knew it.

Her eyes scanned the crowd and found him standing near one of the stone columns that decorated the room. He was turned away from her, talking to Conti. Even in a black tuxedo, the male uniform for the occasion, he was instantly recognizable. Had she really memorized the erect carriage of his broad shoulders and the way his dark hair tapered at the back of his neck?

All the anxiety that had enveloped her in the theater suddenly came swirling back, threatening to suffocate her. Just as it had before, her survival instinct urged her to turn and run. But it was too late for that.

She walked toward the fireplace, where she could get a better view of the two men. They were both tall, dark, and good-looking, though Conti's skin had a deeper, more Mediterranean cast. But their personal styles were quite different. The Russian was dressed to blend into the crowd. The conductor, with his scarlet cummerbund and matching bow tie, obviously wanted to be noticed. After all, he was the star.

Conti must have been approaching the punch line of an outrageous story. He gestured expansively with his hands, punched his friend's shoulder playfully. Both men appeared to be enjoying the joke. Julie's ears caught the deep resonance of Rozonov's laugh. The shared merriment softened his austere face for just a moment. Then he looked up and caught her appraisal. Taking a deep breath, she fixed a polite smile on her face and ordered her legs to take her across the room.

She'd prepared a complimentary opening line addressed to Maestro Conti, but she didn't get a chance to use it.

"Ms. McLean, what a pleasure to see you here this evening. Let me introduce you to my friend Rafe Conti."

Julie shot the Russian a startled look. He had used her name as though they were old friends. Recovering, she turned to the conductor. "Maestro, I've been a fan of yours since my uncle took me to hear you conduct the *Eroica Symphony* at the Kennedy Center."

"I'm always delighted to meet such a charming admirer," he drawled in a cultivated voice that held just the hint of an Italian accent. Instead of shaking her proffered hand, he lifted it to his lips. "You've just made me wish our tour wasn't moving on to Barcelona tomorrow."

"If the newspaper accounts of your week's stay here are true, my friend, you've probably already broken your quota of hearts in Madrid," Aleksei cut in.

"Well, you Russians may be confined by quotas, but thank God for good old capitalistic enterprise." While he chuckled at his own witticism, Julie's brown eyes met Aleksei's blue ones. For just an instant they seemed to be conspirators in a private observation. When she realized what was happening, she quickly lowered her lashes.

"But the press exaggerates," the flamboyant conductor continued, addressing himself to his old friend. "Anyway, I get the feeling you've already staked out a claim on Ms. McLean."

An automatic denial leaped to Julie's lips. But before she could voice it, Aleksei corrected the impression. "The lady and I have only recently met, although I won't deny that I'm very interested in getting to know her better."

The fact that he was making her assignment easier did nothing to steady her pulse. And when a group of admirers came to claim Conti's attention, leaving her standing with the Russian, her mouth was suddenly dry.

"I'm surprised to find you here," he remarked, leaning slightly toward her and lowering his voice.

"I didn't expect to see you either." She knew instantly from his expression that he knew she was lying. The cat-and-mouse game had begun.

Chapter Six

"Well, perhaps it's what you Americans call fate," Aleksei continued. "You may recall that I predicted we'd meet again."

"Yes." Almost every word he'd spoken had engraved itself on her mind.

"You've visited Byne House before?"

Julie nodded. He was so close, so overwhelmingly attractive. She had tried to prepare herself to fight the sexual pull she'd known she'd feel. Her defenses were inadequate.

"It's fascinating. You must show me around." *So no one can listen to our conversation,* she thought.

"I'd be glad to." She was about to lead the way when she turned back to him, her brown eyes lifting questioningly to his face. "Would you rather converse in Spanish? Or maybe Russian?" Cal had told her to be accommodating.

The offer to continue in his native tongue was all too tempting. His English had once been excellent. But he knew from experience that subtleties of expression and word choice were easily forgotten. That meant he was going to have to keep a step ahead of the conversation, anticipating her responses and weighing the precision of his own. "My English is far better than my Spanish, and I'm afraid Russian would be a bit conspicuous here. But where did you learn my language?"

"My last tour was in Moscow."

"Oh."

Somehow the single syllable told her he'd already possessed that piece of information. The insight was a reminder to stay alert. They weren't just a man and a woman enjoying each other's company at a party, although on one level she couldn't help wishing that were true.

"Do you know the history of the house?" she asked.

"Only that it was owned by an American millionaire. And that it's supposed to have a resident ghost."

"How did you know that?"

"Oh, we have our sources." His voice was low and confiding. "It's hard to hide anything from us—even something as insubstantial as a ghost."

Did he mean the KGB or just the Soviet bloc in general? And then she laughed, realizing the absurdity of trying to find hidden meaning in a joke.

As they had been speaking, they had made their way across the main reception room. Several couples were standing near the door, and Aleksei put his hand on Julie's back to guide her out into the hall. He felt her little shiver of awareness as his fingers brushed her bare skin. Even this light touch of flesh on flesh brought back all the sexual feelings he'd fought against that first evening at the theater. He didn't know whether to be irritated or elated that she'd picked such an alluring dress. He did know that he had to fight the desire to stroke his thumb across the warm, velvety surface of her exposed back.

"Arthur Byne, the man who restored the house, was an architect. He was killed in a car accident at Christmas time, and his wife is supposed to have grieved for him for eight years before she died, too. She's the one who's said to be haunting the premises. But from all reports she's friendly— or at least not unfriendly," she informed him in a breathy rush of words. She wasn't even quite sure what she'd just said. The warmth of his strong fingers against her bare skin made it hard to think coherently.

To her relief he removed the disturbing hand once they'd passed through the doorway.

"A benevolent ghost. You Americans have all the luck." He looked down at the dark tendrils of hair curling around her face and the equally dark lashes that all but brushed her cheek as she looked down. Why did this woman have to be so damn attractive to him? Why did her every unconscious gesture have to let him know that the feelings were not one-sided?

They paused at the entrance to the music room, where members of the chorus had begun to sing along with the piano player. Sometime during the evening he'd switched from Mozart to Broadway tunes.

"I enjoyed your show music when I lived in New York," he remarked. "But if I join in the singing, it's going to worsen Soviet-American relations."

She laughed. "You must be exaggerating."

"Don't put me to the test."

Julie had been searching for other topics of conversation. He had just given her the perfect entrée. "You lived in New York?"

"Yes. My father was a member of the Soviet U.N. delegation for a number of years. Getting to know your countrymen has proved very helpful in my work."

"It would." *And which line of work was that—diplomacy or spying?* She gave him an appraising look. "But I'm curious about something. I thought Soviets living abroad, especially in the U.S., were pretty limited in their contacts." *Except for their assignments as intelligence agents.*

"That's certainly true now. But in my father's day we had a bit more freedom. I went to a private school in Manhattan."

"That's where you met Maestro Conti?"

"Yes." *So you've been reading my file too.*

Her curiosity about this man was stretching beyond the scope of the assignment. "What was it like growing up as a foreigner in New York?"

A shadow crossed his face. "New York is an exciting city. But it's hard not to be homesick so far from your own country."

"I know." The melancholy note in his voice struck a responsive chord within herself. She knew too well the loneliness of living surrounded by foreigners. For her that had been a recent discovery. She could imagine it would be worse for a young boy with parents who had their own concerns and problems to cope with. But why, she suddenly asked herself, was she starting to identify with the enemy?

The music faded as they moved into the dining room. Julie paused and gestured toward the paintings on the wall. "I've been told the house boasts a good 'second-rate' collection."

Her companion smiled. "So you're interested in art as well as the theater."

Although she really didn't need reminding, the casual remark made her vividly aware again that she and Rozonov were playing a game of cat and mouse, only she wasn't sure who was stalking whom. Her chin lifted slightly and she forced her eyes to meet his unwavering gaze. "I have a variety of interests, as I know you must, too."

His dark eyebrows arched slightly. "Perhaps we even have some in common. I look forward to our discovering them together."

Cal had cautioned her not to risk pumping the Russian for information at the party but to hint that she was interested in a more private meeting. Clearly, it wasn't going to be all that difficult to manage. The realization made her feel a bit like a butterfly fluttering dangerously close to a flame.

"That sounds intriguing," she murmured.

"Does your interest in Spanish culture extend to the local cuisine?"

"Yes."

"Then perhaps you might allow me to show you one of my favorite restaurants some time soon. It's off the beaten track and very quiet. You Americans don't appear to have discovered it yet. It would be a good place to get to know each other better."

She could feel her heart rate accelerating. Although she was inexperienced in setting up clandestine meetings, she knew he was making this too easy. That meant he had his own reasons for establishing contact. For a moment she studied his features. A casual observer might have thought they were relaxed, but she already knew enough about him not to make that mistake. Even at ease, he projected a sense of leashed power that she found both frightening and exciting.

"I'd like that," she managed. "Perhaps you could call me next week at home."

He pulled a small black leather notebook and pen from his inside breast pocket and waited for her to give him the number.

She complied. But even as she spoke the numerals, she felt a sense of trepidation. When he snapped the book closed and put it back into his jacket, she felt almost as though he was pocketing her as well.

By PREARRANGEMENT the call from Moscow on the secure line was timed for the middle of the siesta, when most of the embassy staff was at lunch. But General Slava Bogolubov had prudently stayed by the phone. For the past few weeks he had been resenting the fact that Department H was looking over his shoulder. This afternoon he was actually anticipating the call. There was a major development to report and he was going to make the most of it.

When the phone rang, he picked up the receiver and identified himself. "Bogolubov here."

"Good of you to make yourself available."

The general rolled his eyes. As if he had a choice. "Just doing my duty as a servant of the state." The platitude was calculated to annoy the caller, but it couldn't be faulted for its orthodox dogma.

"Yes. Well, that's as it may be. But I don't have to remind you that we're at a critical stage in this operation. I suppose you still haven't made any progress exterminating that mole burrowed in the embassy?"

"It's hardly my fault that my main operative was blown up shadowing the American agent."

"But it was bad timing, Comrade."

Bogolubov repressed the retort that was begging to tumble from his lips. "I agree. According to our police sources, it looks as if the incident was drug-related."

"Last week you reported that it was a terrorist attack."

"The police have unearthed some new information. A local drug dealer was the target, and the hit man wanted to throw the authorities off the track."

"Of course all this has nothing to do with *our* problem."

"On the contrary, Comrade. It's helped me narrow my investigation down to three prime suspects. And I'm putting the pressure on. At this point, our mole must feel as though all his escape holes are being locked."

"I was hoping for something more concrete than a psychological analysis of the suspect's state of mind."

"Then perhaps you'd be interested to hear the latest development." The general paused and stroked the waddle of his double chin.

"Yes?"

"One of my agents uncovered a dead drop at the Prado." He let that information sink in for a minute.

Actually, recovery of the photocopied phone directory had been a stroke of pure luck. It had been discovered by one of the museum's maintenance workers, who was just literate enough to recognize Cyrillic characters when he saw them. Making the brilliant deduction that the hidden material might be something of value to the Russians, he'd phoned the embassy to arrange a sale. But Bogolubov saw no reason not to claim the credit. "The papers inside could only have been left by someone with access to classified material."

"Do you think it was the spy Eisenberg referred to as the Raven?" There was a note of excitement in the other man's voice that couldn't be completely hidden.

"Let's hope so. At any rate, I have a plan for trapping him."

"What?"

The general briefly outlined his strategy.

"That sounds reasonable. But remember that the man you're trying to snare has been eluding our clutches for years."

"This time he's met his match."

"I hope your self-confidence is warranted. We've discovered some evidence that he may be after Project Topaz. So if you don't bring him to ground soon, you'd better at least eliminate that new American female agent." The man in Moscow paused for a moment. "Remember, if Operation Topaz is jeopardized in any way, your head is going to be on the chopping block."

The general ran a pudgy finger underneath the coarse material of his shirt collar and then unfastened the button that was suddenly pressing against his windpipe. Even he didn't know the full details of the supersecret project called Topaz. But he knew millions of rubles and the next five-year defense plan were riding on its success. His voice, however, conveyed nothing but confidence. "When I succeed, I'll expect that promotion I've been waiting for."

"*If* you succeed, you'll be able to name your reward."

GEORGI KRASIN cast another nervous glance at the doorway of the blue and beige dining room. His stomach fluttered every time he wondered why Feliks Gorlov, a man who didn't socialize much with lower-rank embassy staffers, had extended this luncheon invitation.

Since Gorlov had a morning appointment at the Ministry of Agriculture, they had arranged to meet at the small but comfortable restaurant in the Hotel Suecia. But the older man was more than fifteen minutes late. To pass the time, Krasin had used the restaurant's linen napkin to clean his glasses and then had ordered a pitcher of sangria. The waiter had brought it, along with a plate of octopus vinaigrette and the inevitable basket of hard white rolls. One of the things he liked least about Spain was the food. But he was sure the food here was a damn sight better than in Nicaragua.

He looked up to see the always impeccably dressed Gorlov threading his way through the tables of Spanish businessmen enjoying the customary extended lunch.

"Sorry I'm late," he said as he slid into the blue banquette across from his junior colleague. "But Moscow is pushing me to firm up that agricultural exchange program. When Gomez finally got down to business just before I was due here, I could hardly walk out on the man."

Krasin nodded and poured his colleague a glass of sangria, noting that while he might sound a bit distressed, there wasn't a lock out of place in his stylishly cut hair. He'd wondered more than once how his fellow agent managed to live so well on his salary, even taking into consideration the perks that went with their particular line of work. Did Gorlov have something else going on the side? He kept that particular question to himself. "So what else is new in your department?" he asked instead.

Gorlov shrugged and gave a brief summary of the week's ups and downs before opening his menu. The next several minutes were taken up with a discussion of what *chanfaina,* the restaurant's special of the day, might be, and what precisely was in the seafood salad. There was no hope that the waiter could provide an explanation in Russian, so they were on their own.

After ordering, the two men continued to exchange inconsequential pleasantries. Spreading a thick layer of butter on the dry bread, Krasin reminded himself that lunch at a fine Spanish restaurant was never less than a two-hour affair. There'd be time enough to find out what Gorlov really wanted to talk about.

After the seafood bisque had arrived, his companion finally cleared his throat. "How's your assignment for Bogolubov coming?"

Sensing more than casual interest behind the question, Krasin looked up cautiously. "Slow, but I'm making progress."

"Glad to hear it."

"And you?"

"About the same."

"What aspect of the case are you working on, anyway?" Krasin tried. Gorlov and the general had seemed rather chummy, and he had wondered what was going on.

The other man picked up his butter knife and tested its edge against his thumb. There was a favor he needed, and he was confident that he could get it if he went about things in the right way. "I've been assigned to gather background information on our embassy personnel."

"Oh?" Krasin's face remained impassive, but he could feel a muscle twitching in his neck. No matter how careful you were, there was always some smirch on your record that could be dragged out in case Moscow needed a scapegoat.

"I just happened to be reviewing your file yesterday. You have had your share of minor infractions, haven't you?"

"But you didn't find I was a security risk."

"No."

Georgi let out the breath he'd been holding. "Then what are you getting at?"

"There are a few details I chose not to call to Bogolubov's attention."

No one did favors for free in this business. "I assume there's something you want in return."

"You're a fast learner. You'll probably go far in the service."

Silence hung over the table as the waiter came to refill their glasses of mineral water. There was a chance that he might just understand Russian. When he had departed,

Gorlov returned to his soup for a moment. "Not bad," he commented. "But the squid's a little rubbery."

Georgi waited. He hadn't known some of the seafood in the soup was squid, and he wished Feliks had kept that bit of information to himself.

"You know, the general and I have been working very closely on this case," Feliks confided.

"I had that impression."

"I understand there's some pressure from Moscow to clear this whole thing up. And, I've been thinking, it will be a credit to both our records if we come through with what the general needs."

"I'd been thinking the same thing," Georgi agreed. But insuring that his reports on the explosion at the San Jeronimo met expectations had made him feel like an infantry man stumbling through a mine field without a metal detector.

"Why don't we collaborate on this," Feliks suggested. "If you show your raw data to me first, I can make sure it's in the form Bogolubov wants and also alert you to any areas that need fleshing out."

Georgi pushed his steel-rimmed glasses onto the bridge of his nose. There was no way Feliks was making this offer out of the goodness of his heart. It sounded as though he wanted access to the police reports of the investigation. But why? To find out, he'd have to play along.

"It's flattering to have a senior officer taking a personal interest in my career," he observed dryly.

"Then we can work together."

"Yes." For now, anyway, Georgi thought slyly.

ALEKSEI ROZONOV hoisted his lean body out of the easy chair where he'd been watching the evening news. The material that was aired in Europe, as well as in the United States, never ceased to amaze him. The Soviet censors selected news for its propaganda value. The West seemed to choose it for sensationalism.

After switching off the set, he crossed to the bookcase that served as a makeshift bar and poured himself a double shot of vodka. He didn't like to drink alone, yet there was no one he really cared to drink with either.

He started to carry the glass back to his chair, then changed his mind and brought the bottle along. Vodka, he thought disconsolately, was a ready anesthetic for the Russian soul. He'd never understood the Western taste for whiskey, because it left you with an aching head. Overindulging in vodka only led to numbness which made it easy to drink too much. He'd seen too many of his disappointed contemporaries turn into alcoholics and had vowed it would never happen to him. But there'd been a time after Anna and the baby had died that he'd come close.

He downed the burning liquid in the glass and poured himself another. Then his eyes focused on Anna's photograph in its silver frame on the mantelpiece. They had only been married for three years. Not very long, really. There were weeks now, sometimes months even, when he didn't look at her picture anymore. He knew that if he closed his eyes and tried to bring her once-familiar features into his mind, he wouldn't be able to recall them. The admission was painful.

She had been blond, he remembered, with green eyes that darkened to emerald when she was caught up by some strong emotion. It was strange to think how much he had changed since she had died. But she would never change, never age, never again enjoy the pleasure of snuggling under a heavy quilt and making love on a snowy Moscow evening.

They'd done their share of that. The memory no longer had the power to warm him. After almost a dozen years, the anguish was gone too.

He didn't realize that he'd been sitting in the dark until the siren of a fire truck or ambulance speeding by on the street below brought him back to the present. He shook his head to sweep away the specters of the past and then glanced at his watch; it was almost ten. He'd planned to call Julie McLean tonight. Maybe it was too late. Or maybe not. After all, this was Madrid, where the siesta stole a chunk from the middle of the business day and where eight in the evening was still considered late afternoon.

"Dzulie." He said the word aloud as it would transliterate into his own language. Then he practiced for a moment until he was satisfied that he'd been able to almost capture the true pronunciation.

The thought of talking to her lifted his spirits. For years he'd felt like a mountain climber pulling himself up a weathered crag one handhold at a time. When he'd met Julie, it was as though he'd suddenly reached a peak where he could take in for the first time the glory of a secret valley spread out below. He recognized the feeling for what it was and swore vehemently under his breath. Why, he asked himself once again, did he have to desire this particular woman?

He still didn't know whether she was acting for some intelligence agency or simply being used by someone who wanted to get to him. He'd bet on the latter, but it didn't matter. She was a threat to his survival. Yet, as he remembered the way she'd looked in that burgundy gown, her rich brown hair swept up to reveal the graceful line of her neck, the warmth in her large dark eyes as she gazed at him, it was impossible to think of her that way.

He swore again. *You're a fool, Aleksei Iliyanovich,* he told himself. *What do you imagine they want you to think about her? They want you to see her as soft and feminine, vulnerable and desirable.* But even as his mind registered the sardonic observation, his hand reached for the phone.

She answered on the fifth ring, just as he was about to put the receiver down. "Julie, am I disturbing you?" he asked.

She knew who it was at once, and not just from the slightly exotic pronunciation of her name. Every time the phone had rung during the past few days, she had picked up the receiver expecting to hear the rich timbre of Aleksei

Rozonov's voice. She had been hoping for the call and dreading it by turns. Now she found the mere fact that he was on the other end of the line disturbing.

"Yes. I mean no," she said, trying to keep her reaction in check so that she could carry out the assignment Cal had given her.

He laughed. "I hope I didn't get you out of bed."

"Oh, no. I was washing my hair." *My God, why did I tell him that?*

"Shall I call back later so you can dry it?"

"No." The denial came to her lips too quickly. "I've wrapped it in a towel."

He caught the uneasiness in her voice. Had she really been washing her hair or was that just an excuse to throw him off guard? Whether it was or not, the tactic was working. He found himself wondering whether she'd been in the shower or just leaning over the sink in the type of lacy lingerie he'd seen in Western magazines. Or was she naked, her olive skin glistening with water? When the wayward thought flitted through his mind that it was too bad the KGB hadn't installed a hidden camera in her apartment, he brought himself up short. Back to business. "I was calling to ask you to lunch this Friday, if you're free," he said.

With the phone between her shoulder and her ear, she shrugged into the light robe she'd brought from the bathroom. Of course Rozonov couldn't see her. But the intimacy of talking to him with nothing on, coupled with the menace he presented, still had its effect. "Yes, Friday would be fine." She hoped he couldn't hear the tremble in her voice.

"I can make reservations at the restaurant I told you about for one o'clock."

Her fingers played nervously with the belt of her robe while she waited for him to name the place.

"It's near the Puerta de Alcala."

"You mean in the Plaza del Independencia? I know where that is."

"Good. Then I'll meet you at the central archway and we can walk over to the restaurant together."

That was a rather unusual way of doing things, she thought, and then she realized that he didn't want her to know where they would be going. So the KGB would be aware of their destination, but not Cal.

"Will that be satisfactory?" he questioned. "Or would you prefer some other arrangement?"

She heard the silence lengthening between them, knowing that the longer she waited to answer, the more chance there was of arousing his suspicion. Feeling as though she were diving into uncharted waters, she answered. "Your arrangement will be fine."

"Then I'm looking forward to having you all to myself for the afternoon." The silky note in his voice made her feel as though she'd just agreed to a romantic rendezvous instead of an appointment to exchange secrets. She wondered which would be more dangerous.

She took a steadying breath. "I am too." To her horror she realized that, despite the risk, the words she had spoken were true.

"Good night, then. And pleasant dreams, Julie."

Chapter Seven

The young boy with the sealed envelope stuffed into the pocket of his navy shorts hurried along one of the wide pedestrian parkways lining the Paseo de Castellana. He was coming from the direction of the Prado. Drawing abreast of an outdoor café where afternoon strollers were seated at green-and-white tables, he stopped and looked around. As he expected, the tall, well-dressed foreigner who had given him a thousand-peseta note and sent him on the unusual errand was nowhere to be seen.

The man had had a summer cold, he recalled, and had held a handkerchief to his nose, effectively obscuring his features. His voice had been hoarse. But it was the eyes he remembered most. They had been intense and steely. And they had impressed upon the boy the importance of carrying out instructions. Those had been very precise. The boy was to walk down the Prado stairway closest to the Calle Felipe IV exit. If he found anything behind the loose marble baseboard near the first floor exit, he was to deliver it to the man selling ice cream and mineral water.

The boy waited patiently behind several patrons buying cold drinks. When he reached the front of the line, he fished in his pocket for the crumpled envelope and laid it on the counter. The white-jacketed attendant whisked it out of sight and handed the boy a second thousand-peseta note and an ice-cream bar. For a moment they looked at each other.

Then the attendant shrugged, and the boy turned away and began to unwrap his confection. It was an unexpected bonus.

Half an hour later, a teenage girl dressed in jeans and sandals showed up and asked the ice-cream man if he could tell her what time the cathedral in Toledo closed for the afternoon. He gave her the correct answer and the envelope. Had it been unsealed, he might have satisfied his curiosity about the contents. But if he looked inside, he had no way of returning the package to its original condition. Since he suspected he was acting as a go-between in some underworld payoff, he refrained from meddling. Taking good money to hold a small envelope for part of the afternoon was one thing. Incurring the displeasure of whoever had purchased his services was quite another.

The girl, who took the envelope from the café, delivered it to a leather repair shop off the Gran Via, where it was picked up by the Raven, along with the pair of shoes he'd left to be resoled. Before heading home, he stopped at the specialty food department of El Corte Inglés and bought a bag of the freshly ground Columbian coffee he'd grown fond of.

There was a certain risk, he acknowledged, as he waited for the elevator to descend from the fourth floor of his apartment building, in relying on such a circuitous delivery route. But he had weighed that risk against the more obvious danger of returning to the Prado.

Not until he had double-locked the door to his apartment did he remove the crumpled envelope from his breast pocket. Inside was a folded sheet of paper with a message typed in English. It specified an emergency evening meeting for the next Thursday at Café Sabatini in the old quarter of town. Though the message looked as though it could have come from Eisenberg's replacement, he knew it wasn't from one of the Falcon's agents. The headers and trailers that bracketed the message were similar to what he had expected but the validation sequence was missing. Peregrine agents didn't make mistakes like that, which meant the message was forged.

Chyort! How in the devil had Bogolubov found out about the dead drop? Either it was horrible luck or the comrade general was a lot craftier than he'd thought. Either way, the noose around his neck was drawing tighter. The urgent request for a meeting was a trap.

THE ATMOSPHERE of tension in the Aviary was so heavy that Gordon's beloved parrots were squawking like the chorus in a Greek tragedy. Constance McGuire closed the door to the concealed office, effectively cutting off the screeching. Gordon's mood had deteriorated as the day had worn on. He'd gone from sending back the crab salad to the kitchen because the plate wasn't chilled to dumping a box of government pens in the trash because they were the wrong shade of blue.

"Was there a break in the police investigation of the terrorist attack?" Connie asked as he put down his growing San Jeronimo folder.

"Damn right. It wasn't terrorists at all."

"Really?" Connie couldn't keep the astonishment out of her voice as she swiveled to face him. She was thoroughly familiar with the terrorist modus operandi. This had matched up on almost all counts.

"Someone went to a lot of trouble to make it look that way," Gordon informed her.

"Who?"

"The police have discovered it was drug-related. The bomb was intended to assassinate Juan Inurria, a local underworld kingpin who was trying to extend the boundaries of his territory and apparently stepped on someone else's toes. Incidentally, he wasn't killed. But he's in hiding—supposedly on the Costa del Sol."

Connie thought for a moment. "I hate to even ask, but are you sure there's no possibility that either one of our men could have been involved?"

From the way Gordon tensed, she knew she'd hit a nerve. Maybe this very question was what had been bothering him all morning.

"Not the Raven, certainly," he said quickly. "Since he hasn't touched our money, I can't imagine his going after dirty cash."

"And Dan?"

A weary look crossed the veteran spymaster's craggy features. "Connie, I pride myself on being a good judge of character, but there's some angle to this that I just can't figure out yet. I don't want to think Dan had branched out from intelligence work to underworld activities. But right now I just can't be sure."

Connie had seldom seen her employer so distressed, but she knew the only comfort she could give him was to be as businesslike as possible. "So what sources of information are you tapping?" she asked.

"Well, there's the report Cal Dixon made to the Director of Central Intelligence in Langley last night. He seems to have good connections with the Madrid police department, and that's to our benefit, since we're on the hidden drop list for all his communications."

"Then why do I detect a note of reservation in your voice?"

"I've never met Dixon, but I have a gut feeling about him that makes me uneasy. The man's ambitious, maybe too ambitious. And he has the potential for screwing up this whole delicate operation."

"Couldn't we just tell him what's going on?"

"Negative. If the Kremlin gets even the smallest hint that *anyone* in the U.S. intelligence community knows about Topaz, our source of information is going to be cut off as effectively as a guillotined head."

Connie shuddered at the graphic image, picturing the Raven's neck under the guillotine blade.

The Falcon broke into her thoughts. "You'll want to look at Dixon's report yourself," he said. "Whatever else you can say about the man, he's surfaced a number of interesting possibilities.''

Connie picked up a pencil and notepad.

"It's not there in so many words, but I think Dixon suspects that the Russians are somehow tied to the drug angle.''

"I'll get our other sources working on that,'' his assistant promised.

"Thanks. And pull Dixon's personnel file. I want to know everything about the man, including how he thinks. It's just a hunch, but I'm beginning to suspect that Dixon is holding something back from the DCI.''

"Why would he do that?''

"I think he wants to pull off some sort of grand coup.''

Connie tapped her pencil on the desk. That kind of grandstanding had gotten more than one agent killed. She hoped that in this case the Falcon's hunch was wrong. "Are there any other leads you want me to follow up?'' she asked.

"Maybe you can find out why that hole at the Prado is empty every time we send somebody to check it out, and see what you can discover about a KGB agent named Yuri Hramov.''

His assistant's hand froze in the act of jotting down the Falcon's request. "Hramov! How does that beast figure in this?''

"So you know of him?''

Connie shuddered. "Only by reputation. Doesn't the KGB use him when they want to make a victim into an object lesson?''

Gordon nodded. "Yes. He's also an expert in faking accidents, and he was spotted at the airport in Madrid. I have a feeling that Bogolubov brought him in to replace Ivanov.''

Well, Connie thought, so there was ample reason for the Falcon's black mood. There were already so many disturbing twists and turns in this damn case that she felt like a boatman lost in a swamp. And if she and Gordon couldn't find their way out, the whole U.S. defense effort might sink with them.

CAL DIXON had his expression back under control, but when Julie had come in to report Rozonov's call, she'd seen the surge of excitement in his hazel eyes.

"You should have reported to me as soon as he hung up last night."

"It was pretty late." Julie didn't tell Cal, but she needed time to think and distance herself from the phone call before talking to him.

"Tell me about it," he demanded.

Dutifully she began to recount the conversation, carefully omitting the personal byplay between herself and the Russian. She'd spent much of the sleepless night planning what she was going to say this morning. That is, when she wasn't analyzing her conversation with Aleksei for the sexual awareness that had simmered beneath the words.

Cal rubbed his hands together. "Pretty clever of the bastard not to name the restaurant. But I have a few tricks up my sleeve that will fix his wagon. If we can't bug the place ahead of time, we'll wire you for sound and get every syllable that comes out of his mouth on tape."

"No!" The word was out of Julie's mouth before she had time to think. Damn! But Cal's enthusiasm for spy hunting made her edgy. She'd intended to play it cool during this interview, and here she was losing her composure when they'd barely gotten started.

"Listen, Julie, I can understand your concern, but I've had years of experience in this kind of operation." His smooth voice let her know that his only concern about her was whether she'd mess up his plans.

"And I've had years of experience with Julie McLean."

"What's that supposed to mean?"

"I don't even feel comfortable talking to a telephone-answering machine. I know I'd give it away if I were wired."

Cal leaned back in his chair and drummed his fingers on the desk. "That's going to make it a lot harder to protect you. What if he pulls you into a waiting KGB car and goes off to who knows where? There are ways to force anyone—especially defenseless women—to talk."

She knew the intimidating words were exaggerated. If Rozonov wanted to stuff her into a car, he could do it when she walked out the door of her apartment house. Nevertheless, the threat had the desired effect. She felt goose bumps rise up on the skin of her arms. "Cal, I don't know *anything*. What's he going to get out of me?"

"Julie, that's what they all say, whether they know anything or not. Even if you swear on Lenin's grave, do you really think he'd believe you right away? And when he finally finds out it's true, that would be even worse. If he thinks you're expendable, he might just eliminate you."

Julie took a deep breath and straightened her shoulders. "Quit scaring me. I agreed to help you, but you're going to have to let me do it my way."

Cal studied her set features, noting the look of determination in her dark eyes. On that little stroll in Retiro Park he'd made her think she had no choice about cooperating. Now if he gave her the illusion of some control over the situation, she might be a little easier to handle. "Okay, we'll do it your way," he said.

"Then I want to get one more thing straight before we continue this discussion."

"Yes?"

"You know that my tour is up in six weeks. I'm not extending it even a day to continue in the spy business."

Getting out of the "spy business," as Julie called it, was not something easily done. But explaining that wasn't going to help him achieve his present purpose. "All right."

She seemed to visibly relax.

"So let's get down to work." Cal opened a thick folder that had been sitting in the middle of his desk and began to thumb through it. "We need to spend the day prepping you on what to say and how to behave."

The thought flitted through her mind that she'd almost rather be spending the day in Rozonov's company than in Cal's. That she was identifying more with the Russian than with her own countryman was unsettling. She knew she had to get a grip on herself. The better she got to know Cal, the less she liked him, but that was irrelevant. The advice he was going to give her might keep her from ending up like Dan.

For the next two hours she was a very attentive pupil as Cal gave her a crash course in the basics of undercover intelligence work.

THE RUSSIAN HAD PICKED a well-traveled part of the city. Julie watched the midday traffic speed by as she waited for the light on Serrano to change. The Puerta de Alcala was located in a small *parque* where two major streets intersected. Carefully tended flower beds surrounded the limestone and granite triumphal arch that seemed to shimmer in the early afternoon heat.

There was no place to park on the busy avenues that flanked the arch. Anybody who wanted to observe a rendezvous here would have to station himself in a nearby building and bring along a telescope.

Julie shaded her eyes and looked up at the Ionic columns supporting the cornice at the top of the monument. Guarding it were several groups of warrior angels. Angels with swords and shields had always struck her as a contradiction in terms. But they seemed to appeal to something in the Spanish character.

Though the angels were visible, the man she had come to meet was nowhere in sight. Had second thoughts made him decide to cancel the appointment? Or was he late?

The light changed and Julie crossed the avenue to the arch. The day was clear and bright, with none of the smog that sometimes hung over Madrid. It was too beautiful an

afternoon for espionage. That was an activity better
shrouded in mist and fog.

The thought made her heart start to hammer against her
ribs. For most of the morning she'd kept a lid on her emotions by doggedly working on the material for the NATO
meeting that had been receiving so little of her attention
lately. In actuality, much of her regular workload had gotten short shrift during the past couple of weeks because both
Cal and the ongoing investigation of the San Jeronimo attack had been taking up so much of her time. Fitz had been
understanding about not pressing her to meet the usual
deadlines. But she didn't feel comfortable about having him
shift her assignments to other already overburdened staffers. What's more, Cal had blandly advised that she keep
things at the office as normal as possible. So she'd even
agreed to a leisurely lunch with Paula early in the week, although keeping her mind on friendly chatter had taken
considerable effort.

As she stepped up onto the curb, she wondered how she'd
been able to concentrate at all on something so removed
from this afternoon's appointment. Pausing by a bed of
yellow and orange marigolds, she forced herself to take
several deep breaths before threading her way through the
flower beds toward the monument.

The man Julie had come here to meet had been standing
in the shade of the central archway for half an hour, letting
himself absorb the feel of the park. He had selected the location because it was so easy to see anyone approaching on
foot. Of course, that didn't preclude the possibility of a car
circling the arch, but the traffic here was heavy and the red
lights long. A car that tried to stay abreast of two pedestrians heading down one of the nearby streets would have
trouble keeping pace.

His attention switched from the surroundings to Julie. A
casual observer might simply think how attractive she
looked in her royal blue dress, light stockings, and white
shoes. But he had learned to see past the props people chose

o support the various roles they played. He watched her
scan the monument's facade and noted the deep intake of
breath as she paused beside a flower bed. He knew from her
artificially rigid posture that the extra oxygen hadn't done
much to steady her nerves. She was off balance. All to the
good. He'd never fished with a rod and reel, but he'd been
fascinated by Hemingway's descriptions. He'd come to
think of cultivating intelligence sources as a similar process. After they'd taken the bait, you played out the line to
let them think they had some control. Then you gently
reeled them in so that they didn't have a clue about what was
happening until they found themselves out of familiar waters and in your wicker basket.

She was almost in the shadow of the arch before she saw
the Russian standing with his back to the gray stone. The
suit he wore was practically the same color. His white shirt
and navy tie did nothing to alter the subdued effect. Suddenly she felt very conspicuous in her royal blue dress. She'd
picked it because she knew the color was flattering, and that
had made her feel confident. Now she wished she could fade
into the monument walls as effectively as Rozonov.

He waited until she was only a few feet away before he
spoke. "I'm so glad you didn't change your mind," he said,
his resonant voice conveying the impression that the words
were more than just a conventional greeting. His blue eyes
seemed to deepen as they made a frank inspection that began with her white pumps and ended with her face. "You
look lovely this afternoon," he added.

"Thank you." His closeness was affecting her again as it
always did, and she found she couldn't quite meet his gaze.

"Perhaps we'd better head for the restaurant."

She nodded. "You still haven't told me where we're going."

"It's just down Serrano." He gestured in the direction
from which she'd come. "If we hurry, we can make the
light."

Before she knew it, he had taken her arm and was escorting her rapidly back through the flower gardens to the curb and then in front of the lanes of stopped cars. They reached the opposite pavement just as the light changed. Instinctively Julie knew that he had been watching the flow of traffic and had timed their departure to make it more difficult for anyone on foot to follow.

She sensed a certain reluctance to break the contact as he let go of her arm, and they started down the wide avenue. The shops in the area were some of Julie's favorites, although she usually waited for a sale, an *oportunidad,* as the Spanish said, before she bought. Despite the circumstances, or maybe because of them, she found herself inspecting the contents of the store windows they passed.

"Do you like to window-shop?" he asked.

"Yes."

"Here in Madrid you can assume that you'll find the same thing inside. In Moscow, you know, the displays are often better than the actual merchandise." He paused. "It's the price we pay for keeping up with the arms race."

"I noticed that when I was there." She stole a glance at her companion, wondering why he'd chosen to make that particular observation. Was he trying to hint at some dissatisfaction with his life-style? With his government? Or was he giving her an opening to express her own dissatisfactions?

"The goods here may be attractive, but the prices are pretty high."

He paused in front of a shop that sold imported English china and turned slightly, glancing unobtrusively back the way they had come. She knew he was checking to see if they were being followed and that the precaution must be an ingrained habit. That told her volumes about the life he must lead.

"With your salary, surely you can afford to buy whatever you like."

She laughed. "Almost anybody could use more money."

"True. But few are honest enough to admit it."

Or dishonest enough. She didn't voice the thought. The turn the conversation was taking made her uncomfortable, and she found herself wanting to change the subject. "Look at that matched pair of borzois. They've always struck me as such aristocratic animals." She pointed toward a set of fine porcelain figurines in the window.

"Ah, yes, the Russian wolfhounds. They were originally developed to run down wolves for the idle rich who had the time to hunt." He began to walk again.

Julie's eyebrows lifted at the insinuating statement, but he didn't elaborate.

They had reached a crossing. Aleksei gestured toward the right. "This way."

As they turned the corner, Julie was struck once again by the sharp contrast between Madrid's wide, straight main thoroughfares and the narrow, twisting side streets. At the next crossing they turned down a narrow lane.

The restaurant, which was called Casa Mendoza, was in the middle of the next block. From the outside it was modest enough, but the interior was warm and homey. There were large painted plates displayed on the wall and dark oak tables and chairs. Only a few other lunchtime patrons were seated at the tables, Julie noted as she and Aleksei waited beside a carved antique server.

The man who came bustling out from behind a set of swinging doors was short, lean, and probably around thirty-five, Julie judged, noting all the details for Cal. Mendoza, if that was his name, seemed to know Aleksei quite well. The two men stood for a few moments talking in low but rapid Spanish, both glancing in Julie's direction several times. Then the proprietor turned and bowed to her. "This way, *señorita*."

"What was it you told me about your Spanish?" Julie whispered to Aleksei as they followed the man toward the back of the establishment.

"I said it's not as good as my English. That's true enough."

But it must be quite sufficient, she thought.

Julie waited until they had been seated in an alcove that overlooked a small courtyard where bright flowers bloomed in decorative planters and lush green and white vines trailed downward from the balconies above.

"And what exactly did you tell him in your very serviceable Castilian?" she inquired, gesturing toward the proprietor's retreating back.

"I told him that I wanted a table where you and I could be very private together."

"He probably thinks we're having an affair."

"What better excuse for a man to have an intimate lunch with a beautiful woman? Perhaps we're being cautious because you have a jealous husband." The look in his eyes was devilish. Was he actually teasing her.

"Aleksei..." Julie started to protest and then realized that this was the first time she'd spoken his name aloud. Was he aware of the breaking of that barrier?

"Ah, Julie, so you understand the wisdom of the little deception." Again the blue of his eyes seemed to deepen. Or was she reading her own emotions into his gaze?

She tried to remember Cal's instructions. They didn't cover this particular scenario. Before she could think of an appropriate rejoinder, she heard footsteps on the tile floor. As Mendoza rounded the corner carrying two menus, the Russian reached across the table and pressed his hand over hers. Julie's eyes were drawn first to the strong, well-shaped fingers covering her own; then to the unusual silver ring he wore. Its serpentine design featured a dark sapphire center. A KGB class insignia or a family crest? Julie wondered. Yet even as the thought flitted through her mind, she was aware of other sensations.

His skin was warm and dry, the pressure of his hand powerful and gentle all at the same time. His touch brought a warmth to her and that was frankly unsettling. Suppose they really had come here for the reasons he had given?

Risking a glance at him from under lowered lashes, she was struck by the intensity of his expression. She had expected to see triumph. She found something closer to vulnerability, but it vanished so quickly that she wondered if she'd imagined it.

"Ah, Mendoza, what do you recommend today?" the Russian inquired.

"For an appetizer, we have the asparagus and pastry. And the hake is very fresh. You could have it grilled or poached with a creamed wine sauce."

"That sounds good. I'll have the hake grilled. *Bien hecho, por favor.*"

She and Rozonov exchanged knowing glances. So the Spanish habit of passing the food lightly over the grill before serving it didn't sit well with the Russians either. To ensure that it was half cooked, you had to ask for *bien hecho*, "well done."

The proprietor turned to Julie. "Would you like to see a menu?"

"No, I'll have the same as the *señor. Bien hecho tambien.*"

Aleksei ordered a bottle of Portuguese white wine to go with the fish. When Mendoza had left, she was once again conscious of the hand that covered hers. The nails were blunt-cut, and a fairly recently healed scar ran from his little finger toward his thumb. Her own pulse was none too steady. Could he feel her reaction? Casually she slipped her hand out from under his and asked, "How did you get that scar?"

"I got in the way of some flying glass in Berlin."

What did that mean? she wondered. "That sounds hazardous."

He shrugged. "It goes with the job."

"I hadn't imagined your duties put you in jeopardy."

"Didn't you?"

The way he asked the question made her chest tighten. Unconsciously her fingers began to pleat the linen napkin on her lap. "You're right. Working at any diplomatic assignment these days has its risks."

"You could even go out for a drink in a tavern and get caught in a terrorist attack."

She forced herself to give him a direct look. "Are you referring to the San Jeronimo?"

"Yes." He paused. "Your friend wasn't just out for a casual drink—he was playing a very dangerous game."

Julie felt her stomach knot painfully, but she tried to hide her reaction. "I know."

Before her companion could answer, a waiter appeared with their asparagus appetizers and wine. She wondered how she was going to choke the food down, but the Russian didn't seem to be feeling the effects of the tense conversation. His blue eyes, which had been coldly appraising her reactions only seconds before, softened.

"I promise you'll love the food here, *querida*," he said, his voice low and intimate.

His sudden change of demeanor threw her off balance. He was such a convincing actor that when he called her sweetheart, she could almost believe he meant it. But then, she reminded herself, he was a professional and she was a rank amateur.

After ceremoniously opening the wine and putting the food on the table, the waiter departed. "We were speaking of your friend," Rozonov resumed without missing a beat.

Julie marshaled her courage. "I'm prepared to take his place."

He looked up sharply and she knew that now she'd caught him by surprise. A point for my side, she thought, enjoying the small triumph. But the satisfied feeling faded almost at once: she still didn't know what game they were playing.

Chapter Eight

Rozonov recovered quickly. "That should prove interesting," he murmured, leaning back and regarding her above the rim of his long-stemmed wineglass. She watched as he reached out, almost in slow motion, and lifted the glass to his lips. His eyes didn't leave her face, even as he sipped the pale liquid. "It's very good. You should try some."

Julie reached for her own glass and sampled the dry but pleasant vintage. She was determined to play with as much aplomb as he. "To our mutual interest, then," she offered.

A ghost of a smile flickered at the corners of his well-shaped lips. "Indeed."

She expected him to continue, but instead he turned his attention to the food. The silence stretched as he savored the fresh asparagus in its flaky crust.

When he finally spoke, it was not to give her the cue she needed to steer a safe course through this precarious interchange. "The vegetables here in Spain are quite extraordinary, don't you agree?" he asked.

"Definitely." Her years of social training were standing her in good stead. She must preserve appearances at all costs. This afternoon she was succeeding at hiding the stress. She was even able to cut the buttery crust that surrounded the asparagus, and carry the fork to her mouth. But despite her unruffled appearance, she was unable to relish the food.

For all she knew, the well-prepared first course might have been steamed grass.

By the time the hake arrived, Julie had thought up and rejected a dozen subtle ways of asking Rozonov what this luncheon was really about. Finally, when the waiter had left again, she settled on the direct approach.

"Why don't we get back to our discussion."

The Russian poured himself some more wine and filled her glass up again too. "I don't think we can go into any detail here." He paused and looked around significantly at the hallway and the open courtyard where an off-duty waiter was lounging at an empty table. "So why don't you indulge me in one of my passions."

Julie carefully laid down her fork. "And what exactly is that?"

"I'm a devotee of your American contemporary fiction. But there are so few people with whom I can discuss the subject. What do you like to read?"

The question took her completely by surprise. "Why— uh—mysteries and thrillers." She stopped and shook her head, realizing the irony of what she'd just said. It was one thing to be a vicarious participant in international intrigue. It was quite another to be caught up in the real thing.

"Ah, American thrillers. I've read a number myself. The trouble is, we Russians are too often cast as the villains."

"I see your problem."

His face threatened to break into a grin. "If you promise to keep my secret, I'll admit that I pick up a Ludlum or a MacInnes whenever I get the chance."

He was giving her the opportunity to switch to a safe topic and she accepted. For the rest of the meal they exchanged opinions on books they'd read. He hadn't been exaggerating about his enthusiasm for the topic. Was it her imagination, she wondered, or was he a frustrated writer? But she had little opportunity to pursue the thought.

After Rozonov had paid the check, he pushed back his chair. "You know, I think we must make arrangements to meet again."

"Yes," she agreed quickly, fighting down the apprehension that had been dissipated somewhat while they'd chatted about bestsellers.

"Somewhere outside where we can stroll and talk."

"There's always El Rastro on Sunday morning," Julie suggested.

"Sunday is fine. But the flea market is too crowded. What about Casa de Campos?" He named the sprawling park that had once been the carefully tended property of Spanish royalty but was now partially reclaimed by nature.

Another conversation in a park, she thought. Maybe this one would go better than the last time with Cal and Fitz. It seemed a bad omen, but she couldn't think of a good alternative. "All right."

"Shall we say Sunday morning at ten, across from the boat dock?"

"I'll be there."

The business settled, he stood and she followed suit. He waited for a moment looking at her. Then, instead of moving toward the door as she had expected, he took a step closer to her. "You know, we really ought to reinforce the impression that our business here was very personal."

"I think you've succeeded at that already."

"One can never be too thorough." As he spoke, he reached out and put his hands on her shoulders. She had been anticipating and dreading some kind of personal contact since the moment in the theater lobby when the Russian's silver blue eyes had locked with hers. Now reason urged her to break the bond. But her body was powerless to obey her mind. Her senses were too full of the man who pulled her gently toward him. The warmth of his touch penetrated the cotton of her dress. The clean male scent of his body, unobscured by spicy cologne or after-shave lotion, seemed to envelop her. His face filled her field of vision as he lowered his lips toward hers.

Just before her lashes fluttered closed she saw that his eyes had deepened to the cobalt of a storm-dark sea. Then his lips were on hers, warm and firm and exciting with the taste of the wine they'd shared at lunch. His mouth moved back and forth, and then settled with a steady indrawn pressure that sealed their lips together with mutual heat. She felt totally captivated, almost dizzy, as though the wine had finally gone to her head. But she knew the sudden intoxication wasn't from alcohol. To steady herself, she found his shoulders with her own hands. They were broad and rock-solid, a fortress to save her from the whirlwind.

She forgot the restaurant, the wine, the purpose of their meeting. There was only this man and the way his mouth felt locked to hers as though drawing her essence into himself. His body seemed to turn her own to fire as he pulled her more tightly against his unyielding length.

For Aleksei, the kiss had been an impulse, but he wasn't a man who yielded to impulses. Or perhaps it had been a challenge—to her, to himself. Now he was a hunter caught in his own snare, a deep-sea diver tangled in his own oxygen line.

He had told himself that her mouth would not taste this sweet and that her lips would not feel so incredibly tender and yielding beneath his own. The assurances had been a lie. He thought he'd be able to use the sexual tension that had been sparking between them to his advantage. Now he realized the arrogance of that assumption. The reality of folding her close was more than simply the physical pleasure of holding a woman in his arms. Just before her dark lashes had lowered, he'd seen the golden highlights in her eyes glimmer with desire. They had sparked an ache inside him. Now he was mesmerized by the way his fingers tangled in the raw silk of her hair, the way her delicate hands gripped his shoulders, and the pressure of her soft breasts against his chest.

Regret mingled with relief as he became aware of footsteps in the hall. Slowly, with the reluctance of a man concerned with protecting his lover's reputation, he lifted his head and put a few inches of space between their bodies. But the movements were just slow enough so that when Mendoza rounded the corner with a tray of chocolates and change, his two patrons were still in a somewhat compromising position.

When Julie heard the restaurant owner clear his throat, her eyes snapped open. Suddenly she was catapulted from a world of sensation back to the inescapable truth that she and this man could never be more than deadly foes. The kind of mistake that she'd just made might be fatal. No matter how much she was attracted to Aleksei Rozonov, she must never forget that they were adversaries in the most basic sense.

CAL DIXON PUT DOWN the phone and pressed his weight against the adjustable back of his desk chair, realizing how tense his muscles felt. That call wasn't the one he'd been expecting. But the information he'd just picked up was certainly welcome.

So his suspicion was confirmed. There *was* a Russian link to the San Jeronimo bombing. He'd already learned earlier in the week that the incident wasn't what it had appeared to be. But had Eisenberg's presence simply been bad luck, or was he into drug trafficking as well as spying? He was going to find out.

There was a lot riding on this case, he reminded himself, standing up and stretching before walking to the window. A blue-and-red cab pulled up in front of the embassy gate, and he waited to see who got out. It wasn't Julie McLean.

Sighing, he looked back toward the pile of visa applications on his desk. They were going to have to wait. He had more important things to do.

The national security implications of this case were enough to justify any action he might have to take. But above and beyond that, this was the first operation of consequence that he'd had full responsibility for. He'd come up through the ranks doing his share of grunt work. Madrid had seemed like just another post where you cultivated the local contacts and hoped for tidbits of information on terrorist activities and technology export violations. Until he'd started digging into the San Jeronimo explosion, he'd almost given up hope that he was going to get a chance to match wits with the Russians. Now it looked as though he might be sitting on something almost as big as the Walker spy case.

The thought set his adrenaline pumping. He began to pace back and forth between the desk and the window, pausing every time he reached for the latter so that he could survey the street. Under his breath he cursed his luck at having to work with someone as green as Julie McLean.

She should have turned that theater ticket over to him in the first place. Instead she'd stupidly gone off on her own and made the contact with Rozonov. Now he was stuck with her, and he didn't like it.

Julie's unwillingness to wear a transmitter, coupled with Rozonov's refusal to reveal the meeting place, had put her in a precarious position. The only choice had been to send two mobile units to the monument. But the Russian had chosen his location well. The heavy traffic and that quick evasive maneuver crossing the street just before the light changed had lost both the car and the van. Cal had been stewing over that ever since the report had come in.

He glanced at his watch. It was after four. What was the woman doing, bedding down for a siesta with the KGB? He'd take information any way he could get it, but he couldn't picture proper little Julie McLean carrying off that kind of assignment, or anything else that required deep deception. For the security of the mission, he'd be smart to tell her the bare minimum of what she needed to know. He could just imagine her confessing everything to the Russian cultural attaché at the least provocation.

He'd arranged for her to report back to Fitzpatrick's office for a number of reasons. She tended to get defensive the moment she walked through the door to the consular office. But more than that, he suspected that people were beginning to wonder why she was coming down here every day for a long meeting.

Another cab pulled up. This time the passenger was a woman with long brown hair wearing a bright blue dress. Julie was finally back. Cal was across his office and out the door before she had climbed the short flight of steps to the main entrance.

JULIE CHECKED with her secretary to find out if anything urgent needed her attention. Unfortunately, there were no messages that couldn't wait. She had no excuse not to head for Fitz's office. When she knocked on the door she'd been in the building less than ten minutes.

"What kept you?" Cal Dixon asked as she sank into the armchair across from her boss's desk.

"I just got back." She looked over at Fitz, who was sitting with his elbows on his desk and his hands clasped. Even though it was in his domain, it was obvious that he was going to let the CIA man run the meeting.

"I mean why the three-hour lunch?" Cal persisted.

"Have you ever tried to hurry through lunch in Madrid?"

"Rozonov's not a Spaniard."

She nodded tightly. "You're right. He wanted to have an extended discussion about American bestsellers."

"That can't be all."

"You didn't expect him to come right out and recruit me as a spy, did you?"

"Don't be ridiculous! Why don't we take it from the top. Where did you have lunch?" Cal reached down and picked up a small tape recorder that she hadn't noticed sitting beside his chair.

Julie's chest tightened. "Is that necessary?"

"I'm assuming you have no objections to my taping this session," he said. "I want to be able to go over the details later." He turned on the machine. "Where did you have lunch?"

"A place called Casa Mendoza."

"And what was the Russian's cover story to the management?"

"He implied we were there for some sort of lover's tryst."

"How did that make you feel?"

Julie shrugged. "It didn't bother me."

Cal studied her tense expression. God, what he'd give for a polygraph machine right now—and a free hand to use it effectively. He wanted the facts. But this woman's emotional response to the meeting might be just as important. What had been her real reaction to the Russian's ploy? he wondered. Was she embarrassed? Insulted? Intrigued? She wasn't saying, and he wanted to know why.

For the next fifteen minutes he fired questions at Julie, trying to get her to respond without censoring her comments. He'd been trained in reading facial expressions, and he watched them carefully for clues to her state of mind. He sensed that she wasn't telling him everything. Was it from loyalty to Eisenberg or other motivations altogether?

"So you think there was something going on between Rozonov and the captain? Or at least that the Russian was aware of some 'game' Eisenberg was playing?"

"I didn't say that."

"But you think so."

"Maybe Dan was trying to recruit him."

Cal snorted. "A seasoned KGB agent? You can do better than that."

For the first time, Fitz inserted himself into the conversation. "This isn't an interrogation."

Don't I wish, Cal kept himself from snapping back. He turned to Julie again. "Did he set up another meeting?"

"Yes. At Casa de Campos."

"That probably means a rowboat in the middle of the lake. So much for overhearing the conversation."

"Maybe we've run out of things to talk about," Julie tried.

"Don't count on it. You seem to have gotten him interested when you volunteered to take over for Dan. Now you can hint that you're willing to trade some classified information for money."

"Cal, I can't—"

"Yes you can."

"What information?" Fitz interjected.

The consular officer thought for a minute. "Files on NATO troop strength, strategic weapons, other things that Julie would have access to through her job."

Fitz's eyes widened. "Are you crazy?"

"I can sanitize the information so it will still look authentic but be worth less than a pound of Spanish olives on the open market. Besides, she doesn't have to deliver right away."

"But if he finds out she's playing with him . . ."

"We'll just have to hope he doesn't find out."

IT WAS DARK. Julie lay in bed, a sheet pulled up to her chin. Madrid's sultry heat had penetrated her apartment, but she couldn't bring herself to throw off the light covering. Somehow it made her feel safer, as though a thin piece of fabric could ward off the hobgoblins of the night.

Since she'd left Fitz's office, exhausted from the day's verbal sparring, she'd been thinking about "The Pit and the Pendulum," Poe's story of terror and inquisition. Like the hapless narrator, she was caught between two unattractive alternatives. And like him, she was sick unto death of it.

Cal, fair-haired CIA operative. He ought to be protecting her. But if he was her friend, who needed enemies?

Rozonov, the KGB's best. He should be her enemy. But this afternoon when he'd kissed her it was as though the world had been turned upside down. She remembered the feeling of clinging to him as though he were the only an-chored rock in an earthquake.

What gave the man such power over her? Perhaps it was the attraction of the forbidden. Did danger turn her on? Or was it something more basic, like explosive chemistry be-tween two people whose lives never should have touched? Even thinking about the way his lips had caressed hers and the way the lean length of his body had molded itself against her own made her start to perspire under the sheet. Sitting up, she turned on the bedside lamp. As usual when she couldn't sleep, she picked up a book. But though she was in the middle of an adventure novel, it was impossible to keep her eyes focused on the letters, which seemed to blur on the page.

When Cal had asked her about this afternoon, she'd done her best to hide her true feelings. Her emotions had always been very private, and baring them in front of co-workers had gone against all her training. Now, in the solitude of the night, she wanted to come up with some rational explana-tion for why she had reacted so strongly to the Russian's gambit.

She wasn't a trembling virgin, going all squishy the first time a man touched her. Over the years she'd drifted into a number of relationships. They'd been companionable, and she'd enjoyed the physical aspects of them. But sex just hadn't been the awesome experience *Cosmopolitan* had taught her to expect.

So what was building between herself and Aleksei Rozo-nov? It couldn't be that she'd suddenly found Mr. Right.

She started to frame an imaginary letter. "Dear Cosmo, I'm deeply involved with a wickedly attractive KGB agent. Can we reconcile our differences and forge a meaningful relationship even though I'm afraid he'll murder me in my sleep? Signed, Anxious in Madrid."

She laughed at the absurdity of her situation. The laugh-ter triggered a shiver that traveled the length of her spine. Though she couldn't help acknowledging her attraction, she was afraid of the man, and she had every right to be. He was an expert in a profession that thrived on lies and deceit, death and destruction. Politically he must be at odds with everything she believed in.

What had he been feeling when he'd folded her into his arms? From their first meeting she'd sensed that he was responding to her on a basic male-female level. Just as she had to him. And each meeting had intensified the feelings as if they'd been involved for years, not weeks. But the way he'd carefully calculated the end of their kiss made her almost certain that his ardor had all been an act. A man who could manipulate his passions in that way was the worst kind of liar.

The best thing for her would be never to see him again, but that just wasn't one of her options. She already had an appointment with him for Sunday. That meant she was going to have to be on guard not only against the man's calculated moves but also the part of herself that was drawn to him despite the awful risk.

SUNDAY MORNING came all too soon, Julie thought as she parked Fitz's car in one of the half-empty lots at Casa de Campos. In deference to the day, which was already showing signs of becoming a scorcher, she was wearing a pair of pink culottes and a striped knit top. As she started up the hillside toward the lake, local artisans and vendors were already spreading their wares on blankets on either side of the gravel path. A display of painted figurines caught her eye, but she was much too anxious about her meeting with the Russian to give bargain hunting any attention.

This time Rozonov was in full view, leaning casually against a wooden railing as he watched her come up the hill. He too was dressed informally, in jeans and a pullover shirt. Again she was stuck with his ability to blend in. But if anything, the sportswear emphasized his dark good looks. She caught more than one señorita giving him the once-over.

Rozonov, however, kept his eyes fixed on her. Her fingers tightened on the strap of the pocketbook slung over one shoulder. Most men she knew were too polite to stare at a woman in that frankly assessing manner. Of course, the Russian didn't play by anyone else's rules.

"Buenos días," he said when she drew within earshot.

"Have you decided to speak Spanish after all?" she asked in that language.

"Only until we're out in the boat."

So Cal had been right about his plans.

Julie had been afraid he might take her arm as they crossed the road to the boat dock. But he kept his hands shoved in his pockets and a closed expression on his face. It was almost as though he were on guard against any feelings that might have been stirred up between them at their last meeting. She found it hard to believe that he thought he had anything to fear from her.

She waited while he rented one of the wooden rowboats bobbing next to the pier. Then he settled himself in the bow and watched as the attendant helped her down to the bench seat across from him.

They pushed off and he began to row toward the middle of the lake. It took him a few moments to become comfortable with the rhythm. Once he did, he pulled in smooth, even strokes that propelled the boat rapidly through the water. He made it look effortless, Julie thought, unable to keep from admiring the play of strong muscles in his forearms. There were other boaters already out, but he headed for a section of the lake that was relatively deserted.

"Have you rowed before?" she asked curiously.

"On the Black Sea. We used to go there on holiday when I was a boy." He paused. "I'd forgotten how satisfying it feels."

"My brother was on the rowing team at Princeton," Julie related. "But I prefer fencing myself."

He laughed, and she was surprised how much she welcomed the sound. "I've noticed."

She joined him in the private joke, at the same time realizing that in a way it was a compliment. "So what do we fence about this morning?" she inquired. Her stomach suddenly lurched and she knew it had nothing to do with the movement of the boat.

He gave her an appraising look. "At our last meeting you mentioned that you were prepared to take Eisenberg's place."

Julie nodded.

"How are you planning to do that?"

For a moment her mind went blank. Then she gathered her thoughts and tried to steady her racing pulse. "I worked with Dan in the political section. We had access to the same files."

Rozonov's blue eyes pinned her as though she were a butterfly in a specimen case. "Go on."

"Material that would be of interest to your government." By the time she reached the end of the sentence, her voice had risen half an octave.

Another boat was drifting in their direction. Rozonov unlocked the oars and rowed to a more secluded spot. He didn't speak as he maneuvered the wooden craft.

"Are you proposing the same arrangement that Eisenberg had?" he finally asked.

"No. I'd want more money." God, she had no idea what Dan had even been getting.

She watched as a dark eyebrow lifted. "The information would have to be very worthwhile."

"What about NATO troop strength and deployment for starters?" she offered, her face averted as she looked out across the lake.

"I'll have to think about it."

Her head swiveled back to stare at the man on the other side of the small boat. She had expected him to jump at the offer. For just a moment an odd expression flickered across his austere features. Had she sounded too eager and put him on his guard? Did he suspect the trap that Cal was setting?

But whatever his doubts, she had to play out her part. "When can I expect an answer?"

"Some time next week. I'll be in touch." He glanced at his watch and began to turn the boat so that he could head back toward the dock. "I think our hour rental is up."

As he rowed toward shore, a duck made a ninety-degree turn and paddled in the opposite direction.

"Not very friendly is he?" Julie observed.

"I understand the ravens here are even worse." His blue gaze was intent on her face, watchful for any sign that she put more than surface value to the cryptic comment.

Her brow wrinkled. "Are there ravens in Madrid?"

"Occasionally." From her puzzled expression, he was sure she had no idea what he was talking about. How would Bogolubov react to that?

He bent his concentration to the rowing, but his thoughts had rapidly outdistanced the water sliding past the side of the wooden craft. Julie McLean had revealed more than she'd planned this morning. He was now almost sure little Ms. McLean was a plant of some sort—probably an instrument of the CIA. All his instincts told him to walk away from this situation. But he was under orders from Bogolubov to discover her game. That meant he was going to have to make her play out her hand no matter how high the stakes.

Chapter Nine

Yuri Hramov was a disciplined man who never allowed his lean, compact frame to gain an ounce over its ideal fighting weight. Swiftness and agility were his trademarks. More than once they'd saved his life, and incidentally given him a success rate that was the envy of every other hit man in the KGB.

Over the past ten years his allegiance to that organization had been unswerving. As a kid back in Radomyshl, he'd shown a remarkable facility for lying, cheating, fighting and flouting authority. At eighteen he'd been well on his way to early Siberian exile when an astute KGB recruiter came across his records and recognized his potential.

At the isolated training camp outside of Novgorod, they'd started by pounding respect into him and then teaching him a skilled trade. What he'd known instinctively as a boy was honed to a fine art. He could pick off a mark with a high-powered rifle just as easily as he could slit a throat in a back alley or keep a torture victim on the agonizing edge of life long enough to get the information he wanted.

His mentors had also made sure he could blend into the lower and lower-middle class of almost any international setting. Although it had meant a considerable amount of pain, he'd seen the wisdom of the plastic surgery that had turned his coarse Slavic features into the blandest of European faces. When he shaved in the morning, he never failed to marvel at how unthreatening his countenance looked.

If he'd been asked to rate what he liked best about his work, Yuri Hramov would have had no trouble answering. He particularly enjoyed terrifying women and killing. The way things were going with this assignment, it looked as though he might get to do both.

When the phone rang in his downtown Madrid hotel room at seven in the morning, he picked up the receiver on the first ring and even managed to sound alert.

"General Bogolubov here," the voice on the other end announced without any pleasantries.

"Yes, Comrade General?"

"I'd like your report on the Café Sabatini meeting."

"There's nothing to report."

"What do you mean, *nothing?*"

"Nobody showed up."

The outpouring of *mat* on the other end of the line was surprisingly creative for someone as stolid as the general. When he'd stumbled on that dead drop at the Prado, he was sure he'd cornered the Raven. But somehow the son of a whore had fluttered through his fingers again. The man must have an uncanny sixth sense for avoiding traps. He'd steered clear of the San Jeronimo, and now this! Well, there was more than one way to clip a bird's wings.

Hramov waited. When Bogolubov got over his tantrum, he would issue new orders.

"Are you ready to move on the contingency plan we discussed for eliminating his new contact?" the general asked.

"I'm always ready. You tell me when, and I'll make sure it looks like an accident."

"Good. I'll be in touch soon."

The line went dead.

JULIE SIGHED and glanced at her watch. It was already late in the afternoon, and there was still one unpleasant job she had to finish before she called it a day.

Picking up a small stack of photocopied newspaper and magazine articles, she pushed back her chair and stood up. Filing Spanish media references to terrorist activities had become one of her least favorite activities. Before the San Jeronimo she'd felt somewhat removed from the reports of murders and bombings. Now every graphic account made her more aware of what could happen to innocent people who got in the way of political fanatics.

Pulling out the folder labeled ETA, she stuffed a copy inside. Then she cross-filed the same article under Barcelona, where the incident had taken place, and also under Juan Tomasa, the man suspected of engineering the murder.

She did the same for a dozen other articles. The task was also a reminder of the way Dan Eisenberg had completely pulled the wool over her eyes. She'd thought of him as a friend and a man whose loyalty to his country was beyond question. At the beginning she'd been convinced that Cal's allegations were based on some misunderstanding. Even when things had looked bad, she'd clung to that hope. But Rozonov's reaction to her offer in that boat last Sunday had been the confirmation she'd been dreading.

Julie slammed the file drawer closed. The new knowledge of Dan's duplicity made her angry—at him for being such a charming liar and at herself for being so naive. God, what a mess she'd gotten herself into by using that ticket of his. If she emerged in one piece, she'd be lucky.

She wasn't aware of the expression on her face until Paula knocked on the door and then stepped into her small but nicely furnished office.

"Julie, are you feeling all right?" she inquired.

"Do I look that bad?"

"You look pale and drawn. Maybe you're getting that flu that's been going around. Why don't you stop downstairs at the nurse's office?"

If it were only something as simple as the flu, Julie thought. "Maybe I will." She was appalled at how readily the little fib sprang to her lips.

Paula continued to regard her co-worker with concern. "You could use a little R & R. Why don't we go out to dinner this evening?" she asked.

"Thanks for the offer, but I feel more like going straight home."

"And probably having a carton of yogurt for dinner."

Julie looked down at her fingernails. There'd been so much on her mind that her appetite was almost nonexistent.

"Listen, I have the perfect prescription. We'll stop downstairs for one of those pizza mixes from the PX. Then we'll drop in at that market near your apartment and get peppers, mushrooms and sausage for toppings. How does that sound?"

Suddenly the idea of putting down the lead weight she'd been carrying around and spending the evening with a friend was very appealing. "Actually, that sounds great."

Paula grinned. "Then I'll come by for you in about half an hour."

After locking up for the day the two young women took the elevator down to the small convenience store maintained for embassy employees and then headed for the market where Julie often picked up meat and fresh produce.

She felt her mood lighten as she inspected green peppers and inquired about the freshness of the chorizo. While the spicy Spanish sausage didn't have quite the same flavor as pepperoni, it would still be a welcome pizza topping.

Paula, who had been in Madrid less than a year, stood back and let Julie do the talking. "I wish I knew the fine points of the language," she observed when they were once again out on the sidewalk.

"Oh, it doesn't take that long. The first time you bring home an overripe melon and want to make the shopkeeper understand why you're taking it back, your facility picks up."

"I already blew it on that one. I tossed the melon in the garbage and chalked up the loss to experience."

As they strolled down the sidewalk, they continued to discuss some of their more amusing Foreign Service experiences. By the time they reached her apartment, Julie was feeling more carefree than she had in weeks.

"I'm really glad you suggested this," she told Paula as they fried the chorizo and spread the sauce on the pizza dough.

"I'm having fun too. I'm sorry it's been so long since we've gotten together in the evening like this."

"Yes," her friend agreed, beginning to distribute the toppings. By the time she had finished, the tomato sauce and cheese had almost disappeared under a layer of chopped green peppers, sliced mushrooms and sausage.

"It's a masterpiece," Paula proclaimed as she opened the oven door and Julie slid their dinner inside.

They had just taken glasses of white wine into the living room and kicked off their shoes when the door knocker sounded.

Paula raised questioning eyebrows, and Julie shrugged. Eduardo usually made strangers phone up from the lobby, so it must be someone he knew.

In fact, it turned out to be the *portero* himself.

"Excuse me, *señorita*," he said in Spanish, "but a man left a message for you. He said it was important and I should deliver it right away."

Julie accepted the sealed white envelope. *"Gracias."*

"De nada." The *portero* closed the door and left.

Julie looked nervously down at the thin white rectangle clutched in her fingers. The angular scrawl across the front was unfamiliar. Had Rozonov decided to use this method of setting up their next meeting? Somehow she'd pictured his handwriting as more controlled.

After breaking the seal, Julie scanned the message. It was in an odd mixture of Spanish and English, as though the writer was trying to use her language but didn't know all the correct words.

"If you would like to uncover the meaning of Señor Eisenberg's *trabajo escondido* and find out who ordered his *asesinato* at the *San Jeronimo,* meet me *esto* evening at 573 Calle Hermosillo. Take the *pasadizo* leading to the courtyard and wait by the small shrine directly opposite. Come alone at *nueve.*" The signature was simply "A friend."

Julie slowly retraced her steps to the living room.

"My God, what's in that letter?" Paula asked, glancing at the paper in Julie's hand and then looking up to see that the blood had drained from the other young woman's face.

"Nothing."

"Don't tell me 'nothing.' This has something to do with whatever has been eating at you for the past few weeks."

"Paula, I'm not allowed to talk about it, and believe me, you wouldn't want to get involved."

"Honey, I care about you. If you're in some kind of trouble, I want to help. You've been uptight ever since Dan was killed. This is more than grief, isn't it?"

Julie buried her face in her hands. Carrying all this around was pushing her beyond the edge of her control. The temptation to lighten the burden just a little bit was overwhelming. She looked up at her friend. "I can't tell you much. But I need your help tonight."

"You know I'll do anything I can."

"I have to be somewhere at nine. You stay here. If I'm not back in two hours, I want you to call Cal Dixon."

Paula's mouth dropped open. "Cal Dixon. Isn't he CIA?"

"I told you you wouldn't want to get involved."

"And I told you I want to help. I can't let you go out to whatever this is alone."

"The best way you can help me is to stay here." Julie paused and laughed, her voice rising with an odd inflection. "Besides, someone has to take the pizza out of the oven. Keep it warm for me. I'll be back as soon as I can."

Julie slipped her shoes back on and grabbed her purse. Then she handed Paula the note. "Here's the address. But don't mess things up by calling Cal unless it's absolutely necessary."

ALEKSEI ROZONOV'S FACE showed nothing, but as he left General Bogolubov's office, he felt a queasiness in the pit of his stomach that had little to do with the fact that it was eight o'clock in the evening and he hadn't eaten anything all day.

He and the general had met twice since Julie McLean had offered to sell him the classified documents. He'd thought the toad would hop at the opportunity, but Bogolubov had stalled him. Today, when he'd proposed to set up another rendezvous, the general had said that he was going to take care of that aspect of the problem himself. When Aleksei asked for details, the general simply announced he was taking him off the case. Logically, he should have felt relief. He hadn't wanted the assignment in the first place. But he didn't like the comrade general's imperious tone of voice or the triumphant gleam in his eyes.

Instead of going back to his own desk, he took the elevator downstairs to the embassy security office. Even though General Bogolubov wasn't willing to level with him, there might be a way to get a hint of his plans. In the locked room was a book where KGB daily activities were logged, in case there was any question later about authorization for specific operations. Aleksei scanned the notations. They were a code unto themselves. He couldn't tell what was being planned, but there was an item that mentioned a message being sent to Julie's address followed by another address he didn't recognize and a time—9:00 p.m.

What the devil was Bogolubov up to? He had to find out—and fast. As though he were simply going home for the day, he signed himself out and left the building. He needed to make a phone call, but despite the urgency he didn't stop at the first booth he passed. Instead he walked to a small tobacco shop where he sometimes bought the evening newspaper. There was a phone booth in the back where he could talk in private and also watch the street.

Although he'd only dialed Julie's number once, he'd committed it to memory. But the woman who answered wasn't the one he'd been expecting. He almost hung up. Instead he asked in Spanish if Julie was home.

"I'm sorry, she had to go out to a meeting."

The woman sounded upset.

"Where is she?" The queasy feeling in his stomach turned into a knife twisting in his guts.

"Who am I speaking to?"

Her Spanish was adequate but not polished. Could he fool her into thinking he was a native speaker? "I'm with the civil guard. Señorita McLean may be in danger. You must tell me where she's gone." He made the statement with so much authority that the woman didn't question him further.

"She received a note. I'll read it to you."

After listening to the message, he responded with a quick *"Gracias,"* and hung up.

Still sticking to his expected routine, Aleksei bought a Spanish language newspaper as usual. Tucking it under his arm, he went out and looked casually up and down the street for a cab. There was one waiting for the light to change at the corner. Luckily it was empty. Once he was inside, his studied manner changed abruptly.

"I'll double your fare if you can get to 573 Calle Hermosillo in fifteen minutes."

The driver grinned and gunned the engine.

As they sped through the darkening city, Aleksei's mind was racing. The note had mentioned Eisbenberg's undercover job and an order for his assassination at the San Jeronimo. What a clever lie. Just the thing to trap a babe in the woods like Julie McLean.

He thought back over the wording of the message. It had been very specific about where Julie was to stand. That might be a setup for kidnapping. Or was someone waiting with a high-powered rifle on top of a nearby building? It would be hard to make a gunshot wound look like an accident. But maybe it could be passed off as terrorist activity like the assassination of Vice Admiral Esgrivas last year.

Aleksei glanced at the lighted dial of his watch. It was ten of nine. *"Dese pris!"* he urged the driver.

"If the police stop me, you'll really be late."

"Just drive faster."

They turned onto Hermosillo. Aleksei watched as the numbers decreased. Only three more blocks. They were in a district of renovated office buildings. It seemed deserted now. An ideal place for a trap, he thought grimly.

When the cab pulled to a halt, he shoved a wad of pesetas into the driver's hand and jumped out. The darkened sidewalk was empty of pedestrians. Traffic was sparse.

Julie was nowhere in sight, but he spotted the narrow alley the note had mentioned. Apparently it connected a courtyard with the street.

If he'd had any hard facts about what was going to happen this evening, he would have strapped on his shoulder holster under his suit jacket. Now he felt at a disadvantage without the Makarov in his hand. He forced himself not to dash down the passageway, but to move slowly, making a careful inspection as he went. When he reached the courtyard, he stopped in the shadows. Julie was standing directly opposite him, her head turned to the right, her hands immobile at her sides. She was wearing a pale yellow dress, and the light color made her slender form an easy target in the moonlight. Instinctively, he glanced up at the rooftops and windows. There was nothing that his trained senses picked up. But someone else could be cloaked in shadow, just as he was.

On the roof two stories above her was a small pillar capped by a bulbous concrete finial. Was someone crouching behind it?

He glanced at his watch again. It was only one minute till nine. Someone had been very specific about the place and the time.

Twenty feet away, Julie stood stiffly, feeling as vulnerable as a lone sentry in a field. If only this place weren't so deserted. The note that had brought her here had been signed "A friend." But what kind of person would want to meet in a dark, empty courtyard? For the last fifteen minutes her ears and eyes had tried to pierce the gloom, but as far as she could tell, she was alone. Was this a ploy to get her out of the way so that someone could search her apartment? If it hadn't been so close to nine, she might have gone to warn Paula.

Did she hear footsteps? She whirled to face the alley where she'd entered, her heart in her throat.

Aleksei saw the movement. "Julie," he called urgently from the shadows, "get away from there." He half expected his warning to draw fire.

"Aleksei?" she whispered. It was obvious she couldn't see him.

"Move away from there," he repeated, automatically shifting his position.

She didn't obey. "What are you doing here?" She paused. "Did you send the note?"

There was no more time for talking. Suddenly he was running across the courtyard in her direction, his footsteps echoing loudly in the enclosure. He was prepared for a rain of bullets around his body, but he didn't change his course. As his arm grabbed her by the waist, she screamed and tried to shove him away. Her eyes were wide with fear.

He ignored her reaction, half dragging, half carrying her away from the little shrine where she'd been waiting.

She screamed again, but the sound was drowned out by a clap of thunder almost directly over her head.

He pushed Julie against the wall and curled his body protectively around hers. The roof ornament above where she'd been standing separated from the building and crashed to the ground. It hit with a second thunderclap that vibrated through the enclosed courtyard like cannonballs ricocheting off the walls.

Aleksei didn't have to look to know that it had landed precisely where she'd been standing only moments before.

For several heartbeats, neither of them moved. Around them, cement dust swirled like a summer snowstorm.

"Julie, are you all right?" he finally asked.

She didn't answer, but he could feel her trembling against him. She started to cough and he pulled out a handkerchief and pressed it over her nose and mouth.

"We have to get out of here. Do you understand?"

She stared at him blankly but let him lead her out a side entrance to the court. When they reached the street he stopped and brushed the cement dust off his dark suit and her dress.

There were no cabs in sight. They had to walk several blocks down to the avenue before he could hail one.

When he helped her inside, she huddled in the far corner.

"Adónde?" the driver asked.

Aleksei named an address on a side street near the Palace Hotel.

It wasn't a long ride. Now and again he glanced at Julie. She sat with her body rigid, looking straight ahead. She must be in a state of shock. But he had to force his mind to keep functioning. Bogolubov had tried to get rid of Julie. The bastard would try again unless he could be convinced it was the wrong course of action. She must be hidden until he could think of what to do.

When the cab pulled up at the address he had given, he paid the man off and helped his charge out onto the sidewalk. She seemed to be coming back to life.

"Let me go."

"Julie..."

From the way she stared at him, he knew she'd made him the focus of her fears. "I'll scream if you don't let me go."

There was no time to argue with her, no time to try and make her understand what was at stake. His only hope was that she bought the lie he was about to deliver.

"You will come with me, and you will come quietly if you don't want to get hurt," he ordered, his voice like cold steel. "I have a gun, and I'm prepared to use it. Do you understand?"

"Yes."

"Walk in that direction." He pointed toward the cross street to her right. "I'll be right in back of you with the gun."

She obeyed, her shoulders rigid, her legs stiff. They approached the sprawling old Palace Hotel from the back. At the entrance to the garage, Aleksei put his hand firmly on her arm. "In here. If we pass anyone, keep still—unless you want an innocent bystander to get hurt."

He felt her shudder, but she complied.

There was no problem about slipping across the garage into the basement through a door which he knew would be unlocked. There Aleksei stopped at a service phone and made a call to a contact on the domestic staff. A few minutes later he had the number of an empty room on the fifth floor. The door would be unlocked by the time he and Julie arrived.

They took the stairs instead of the elevator and emerged in a wide hallway lighted by decorative sconces. No one else passed. As promised, 503 was unlocked and unoccupied.

After closing the door and throwing the bolt, he turned to Julie. "You're safe now."

"You mean I'm your prisoner." Her eyes were enormous as she backed away toward the window.

"No."

"Then let me out of here. I have to tell the embassy what happened."

"No."

She glanced at the phone on the stand between the two double beds.

"Don't make me rip it out of the wall."

"What are you going to do? Shoot me? Torture me?"

He winced. "I'm not going to hurt you. I want to help you."

She flexed the arm he'd grasped too tightly. "You have a funny way of showing it."

"I had to stop you from trying to get away."

They glared at each other.

"Julie, someone almost killed you tonight. They sent you to a precise spot in that courtyard and set an explosive charge to go off above your head at exactly nine o'clock." The words were meant to persuade her, but they almost tore him apart. If she had been in some kind of shock, so had he. All at once the enormity of what had almost happened hit him. "They almost killed you," he repeated in an anguished whisper.

She stared at him as though coming out of a dream. Ever since she'd gotten that note she'd been walking through some sort of bizarre nightmare. His words were like a splash of cold water in the face. They brought her back to life—and confusion. Her gaze skittered around the room, came to rest on the bed, then bounced back to Aleksei. Along with anguish, the sexual awareness that had been simmering between them was in his eyes. And God help her, she felt it too.

Closing the distance between them in two long strides, he pulled her into his arms. He had to hold her, touch her, satisfy himself that she was truly safe. But it was more than that. Her brush with death had left him icy cold. He needed to wrap himself in her warmth.

"Julie," he rasped, his hands moving to caress her hair, her shoulders, her arms. If she had shown any resistance, he might have stopped there. But her face lifted to his, and he saw the golden flecks of fire in her dark eyes just before he felt the soft whisper of her breath on his cheek. In slow motion he kissed her forehead. The contact snapped his restraint. All at once his lips were traveling rapidly over her face, kissing her cheek, her eyebrows, her nose.

He heard her speak his name too.

"You need me," she marveled.

"Yes." The admission was wrung from him. He'd thought he'd never say that to another human being again. But he'd said it to her.

As he spoke, her lips and hands began to move just as urgently as his. Their mouths collided, held. He heard her indrawn breath, felt her open to him, tasted her warmth and sweetness. She murmured something he couldn't possibly understand. It didn't matter. If neither of them spoke the other's native language it would not have been important at this moment.

When they had kissed before, he had held something of himself back. Now that was impossible. His tongue explored the outline of her lips, then slipped inside to caress the silky interior. He felt her fingers thread themselves in his hair, her body mold against him. Her breasts, pressed against his chest, made him ache to increase the intimacy. His hands traveled down her back, cupping her bottom and pulling her hips more firmly against his own. He knew she must feel his arousal, yet she made no effort to move away.

Julie's senses reeled. This man had denied she was his prisoner, but he couldn't have been more mistaken. She was totally captivated by the strong arms that held her close, the hungry mouth that ravaged hers, and the hoarse confession he had made. More than that, he had cared enough about her to save her life.

She realized she had never felt more alive, more exhilarated than at this moment. Fiery threads seemed to weave themselves through her body, building an unfamiliar tension that threatened to consume her. She was a creature of sensation now, burning for Aleksei as she had never burned before.

Her passion intoxicated him and almost made him lose all reason. He drank in her essence, sealing her mouth more tightly to his. He felt her hands in his hair tighten beseechingly. Shifting her body slightly, he cupped one soft breast in the palm of his hand. He heard her moan deep in her throat. Somehow, the tiny noise brought back a measure of sanity. How could he take advantage of her vulnerability like this?

To let her go would be to die a little. For one electric moment he allowed his hips to move against hers, savoring the ache inside him. Then his hands went to her shoulder, gently pushing her away so that a few inches of space separated their bodies. He lifted his head.

Her eyes snapped open. They were large and dark, the pupils dilated. Around their rims the golden lights seemed to dance.

"Julie, *lyubovochka,*" he murmured. "We have to stop."

Her face registered confusion, hurt. "You're playing with me again. The way you did at Casa Mendoza."

"Playing?" His laugh was harsh. "Is that what you believe? Do you think a man can fake his reactions to a woman?"

Unwillingly, she shook her head.

"Julie, listen to me. The kind of brush you had with death tonight is the most powerful kind of aphrodisiac. You are very vulnerable right now. No matter how much I want to make love to you, I can't use that to my own advantage."

Deep inside, she acknowledged the truth of what he said. But she couldn't attribute her longing only to that. "Is that why you think I . . ." She couldn't finish.

"That's part of it, certainly."

"So you're protecting me?"

"Yes."

"Since when does a major in the KGB protect an American spy?"

"When he cares about her very much."

Chapter Ten

Aleksei crooked his finger under her chin. "Julie, if you're a spy, I'm a Russian Orthodox priest. And nobody has ever accused me of that." From the first he'd sensed her discomfort with the role someone was forcing her to play. Now he was determined to find out what she really knew.

But she seemed just as determined to unmask him. "Just what have you been accused of?"

The question struck chords she couldn't be aware existed.

"The less you know about me, the better."

"Why?"

In frustration, he ran a hand through his thick black hair. "We must talk, and there's so little time." Taking her hand, he drew her to the couch that occupied an alcove across from the two beds. Before releasing her fingers, he pressed them tightly.

"I think we could both use a drink."

Like most European hotel rooms, this one was equipped with a minibar. It was locked, but that didn't bother Aleksei. Julie watched in fascination as he hunkered down, pulled out something that looked like a Swiss army knife, and selected a tool. In a moment he had picked the lock and opened the door. He turned and looked back at her. "A brandy, I think."

"I can't drink on an empty stomach."

"Did you miss dinner too?"

"Yes. But why didn't you eat?"

"I've been too worried about you." The admission should never have left his lips. He looked down quickly and began inspecting the contents of the small refrigerator. "We can share a bag of corn chips, some salted almonds, and a candy bar for dinner."

After bringing the snacks and two brandies back to the coffee table in front of the sofa, he sat down next to her.

"So we both know you're not a spy. Then how are you involved in this?"

With slow deliberation, she opened one of the packages and took out a salted almond. The feeling of trust for him had been growing. But was that confidence misplaced? Was she being carefully led down a path that he had chosen? Or even worse, had this whole evening been staged to gain her confidence?

"Look at me," he demanded.

Unwillingly, she raised her dark eyes to meet his blue ones. They had deepened to the cobalt color she had come to associate with strong emotion. "Julie, you are still in a great deal of danger. *T'fu!*" He spat out the Russian expletive, using it as an outlet for his frustration. "And I can't do a damn thing about it unless you help me."

"You're asking me to betray my country."

"No."

"Then what?"

He sighed. "Let me start with a very basic assumption. You know absolutely nothing about what Dan Eisenberg was involved in. Am I correct?"

She nodded almost imperceptibly.

"Then someone—presumably a CIA operative—is using you to try and get information about Eisenberg's activities. But he can't care very much about your welfare if he gave you that ticket and sent an innocent like you to the theater on a fishing expedition."

"That's not right. I found the ticket in Dan's desk after he died."

His eyes narrowed. "So our CIA man was just taking advantage of your naïveté. That's not much better. And he's not—" he hesitated as he fumbled for the American idiom "—playing straight with you, either."

"What do you mean?"

"Either he's a bumbling idiot or he already knows that the San Jeronimo bombing wasn't directed at Eisenberg. If he had shared that piece of information, you wouldn't have gone over to Calle Hermosillo this evening, would you?"

"Cal knew?"

"Calvin Dixon?"

"Oh, Lord. You're right. I'm not very good at this."

He reached for her hand. "It would have saddened me if you were."

Julie took a sip of her brandy. It burned all the way down.

"Why did you use the ticket in the first place?" the man across from her finally asked.

"Dan and I were friends. I wanted to prove to myself that he wasn't . . . that he wasn't involved in anything illegal."

"But you thought he might be?"

"Cal thought so. And then there was Dan's calendar. There were cryptic notations . . ."

Aleksei interrupted her. "No, don't tell me anything that's going to compromise you. It's obvious that your Cal Dixon is swimming out of his depths in shark-infested waters and doing his best to pull you under with him."

She raised her eyes to his. "You seem to know a great deal more than I do about what's going on. What can you tell me?"

"Nothing."

"But I thought . . ."

"You can't make assumptions."

"So I really can't trust you, can I?" The words were spoken with vehemence, sadness.

"Only so far."

"You must be enjoying this."

"You have a strange idea of what gives me pleasure."

She put her glass down on the table. "I think I should go home now."

He shook his head. "I wouldn't advise it."

"Why not?"

"Because the person who wants you eliminated is going to be very upset when he finds out the attempt failed. He will try again. I can guarantee it."

The only way to get through this was not to surrender to the terror building inside her. Her thoughts flew to Paula. She only hoped that she had indeed left the apartment at eleven and that nothing had happened to her. "Then I'll go to the embassy."

"You might not be safe even there."

"Are you telling me this hotel room is my only sanctuary in Madrid?"

"Tonight, yes."

"Are you trying to frighten me?" It was impossible to keep her voice steady.

"I wish it were only that." He reached across the sofa and pulled her against him. His arms went around her shoulders, and he cradled her head against his chest. One hand stroked her thick brown hair. Neither of them spoke. The feeling of strength she'd felt that first time he'd held her enveloped her again. For the moment she felt protected in his embrace, but she understood just how false the sense of security was.

"Aleksei?"

"I can buy you some time." For her sake, he said the words with confidence, but inside he knew it would be a miracle if he could pull it off. "But you're going to have to do exactly what I tell you."

Her face was still pressed against his chest. "Why should I trust you?"

"It's your only option." He held her close for a little longer and then shifted her body so that he could see her face once again. "I have to leave you." His strong hands caressed her hair, her cheeks.

Several emotions registered in her eyes. Surprise, fear, regret.

"I want you to promise me that you will stay here tonight. Don't answer the phone if it rings. Don't make any calls. And don't open the door for anyone. Will you do that?"

"Yes," she whispered as she realized now she couldn't call Paula to be sure she was safe.

"At the lake you offered me NATO documents. Was that just a bluff, or did you mean it?"

"Cal told me to stall, but he had something for me to give you."

"I may need it."

She didn't expect him to tell why, so she simply waited tensely in silence.

"You're due to go home next month," he said.

She was past surprise and only nodded her confirmation.

"You must leave Madrid by the end of the week."

"What do you mean?"

"I said I could buy you a little time. But after that you won't be safe until you're back in the States." If then, he thought, but he couldn't say it aloud.

"They won't let me go just like that. My tour's not up."

"They'll let you go if you threaten to make a public statement."

"What do you mean?"

He laughed mirthlessly. "You might start by letting the ambassador know what the enterprising Mr. Dixon has been up to. I doubt he's been fully informed. Don't hesitate to use whatever you can. Put in a call to your uncle the senator if you have to. He has a lot of influence with the White House."

He stood up and glanced at his watch. "It's 4:00 a.m. in Moscow. I'm going to have to get some people out of bed.

But you should be able to report back to your embassy to-morrow morning at nine." He crossed to the door. "Put the chain on after I leave."

"You could lend me your gun for protection." She tried to make her voice light.

"I wish I could. But I didn't know I'd need one this evening when I left the office."

"Then back there on the street . . ."

"I was using your assumptions about me to my own advantage. Good night, Julie."

Before she could answer he was gone.

ALEKSEI ILIYANOVICH had done his share of things that he'd regretted. But one point of personal ethics he'd prided himself on was never using his father's political connections for his own advantage. Now he searched his memory looking for members of the premier's staff who would remember the son of Iliyan Alexandrovich and be willing to pull a few strings for him. There was another criterion in his search, as well. He also needed someone who'd welcome an opportunity to put the ambitious Slava Bogolubov in his place.

He finally settled on Deputy Foreign Minister Misha Panov, who had been his father's friend and superior as head of the Soviet delegation to the U.N.

Aleksei glanced at his watch. It was still the middle of the night in Madrid. But if he timed things right, he could catch the minister after he'd awakened but before he'd left for the office.

He didn't like placing the call at the embassy, where it would be recorded. But if he were going to pull rank on Bogolubov, he had to make damn sure the general couldn't find any fault with the procedure.

When it came to actually placing the call, his hand hesitated over the red phone. He had only one chance to get this right, and he didn't want to think about the alternatives.

He listened as the phone rang thousands of miles away, imagining the heavy overstuffed furniture in Panov's Moscow apartment and the grandfatherly-looking man who complemented it so well. Panov was a study in contradictions. He might look soft, but his aging exterior concealed a mind as sharp as a military saber.

The minister himself picked up the secure phone on the fourth ring. He sounded as though he'd already had a cup of coffee.

"Aleksei Iliyanovich here," the younger man began.

"My boy, how are you? I thought you were in Madrid."

"I am, Misha Davidovitch."

"Then this must be an important call."

"Yes. I'd like your advice about a problem I'm having."

"Go on."

"I was assigned to cultivate a particular information source. Things had been going rather well and she had offered us a look at some NATO planning documents."

"Ah, a woman," Panov remarked knowingly. "But you can't have come to an old man at six o'clock in the morning for advice about her."

"No, it's about the information. I believe our comrades at headquarters would be very interested in these documents."

"Oh, very interested I'm sure."

"That's what I'm distressed about. General Bogolubov has taken a strange about-face. After I've spent weeks on this assignment, he's decided to abort the mission just when my work is about to pay off."

Panov snorted. "Slava does things like that. There are times when I suspect he's more interested in one-upmanship than in doing his job effectively."

"Yes, and that sometimes makes it hard for those under him to serve the motherland."

Panov laughed. "So you really called to get me to tie his hands behind his back while you complete the assignment."

"Are you making that offer?"

"Actually, I owe Slava one myself. How urgent is this?"

"Very."

"Then I'll wake him up as soon as we get off the phone. But remember, an old man can take chances and it won't really matter one way or the other how it turns out."

"You provide good counsel."

"Bogolubov is a dangerous enemy. You're putting your neck on the chopping block if it turns out you can't produce."

"I'm prepared to take the consequences. Thank you for your help, Misha Davidovich."

After hanging up the phone, Aleksei reached for his pocket handkerchief to wipe the perspiration off his brow. The white cloth was the one he'd lent Julie. It was covered with cement dust. He couldn't use it on his face. Instead he dropped it into the bag designed for sensitive documents that were to be destroyed. Before he went home to change and shave, he dropped the bag in the incinerator.

IN AN APARTMENT not far away, Feliks Gorlov was also caught in the grips of a night sweat. Throwing off the covers, he got out of bed and went to the cabinet where he kept his vodka. A stiff drink might help him get back to sleep.

He should have stuck to grain deals, he thought morosely, as he poured the colorless liquid into a heavy crystal tumbler. They might be tedious, but they were certainly a lot safer than the clandestine dealings he'd been engaged in lately.

Taking the glass to an easy chair by the window, he looked out over the sleeping city. The peaceful view didn't do any more than the vodka to calm his nerves.

He'd been trying not to think about it, but he could damn well have gotten killed that night at the San Jeronimo. On the other hand, maybe that would have been less painful than what was going to happen if the KGB found out about his extracurricular activities.

Right now, thank the devil, he had that pup Georgi Krasin running interference with his sanitized reports of the incident. But that wasn't enough. He was going to have to come up with something better, and soon. Maybe, once he'd made good on this present commitment, he could get out of the whole thing. Or was he simply fooling himself? His covert activities had set some powerful forces in motion. Lately they'd developed a momentum of their own, like a snowball rolling down a hill in icy Gorki Park, getting bigger and bigger as it picked up speed. It wasn't difficult to picture who was going to get smashed when the damn thing reached the bottom.

Was there any way out of this? He certainly couldn't outrun the snowball. But maybe he could develop a good story to explain what it was doing there and how the Kremlin could use it to its advantage.

The thought made him feel a bit more confident. Setting the glass down, he leaned back against the comfortable cushion and clasped his hands behind his head. There were other avenues he should be pursuing too. Project Topaz, for example. That certainly had the old toad hopping right now. Perhaps there was a way to use what he knew about the operation to buy himself some more time.

A POLICE CAR was parked in front of the main entrance to the embassy when Julie's cab pulled up. As she climbed the steps to the door, she looked at her reflection in the one-way mirror and cringed. She'd been afraid to get undressed, so her yellow dress looked as though it had been slept in. That was something of a misconception since she'd done little more than toss restlessly on the soft mattress, her ears straining every time footsteps passed in the hall.

Though she'd washed her face and run a comb through her hair, she hadn't been completely able to remove the cement dust. What's more, she didn't have any makeup to cover the dark circles under her eyes.

The marine guard inside had orders never to leave his station unattended. But he was at the door and pulling her inside before she could ring for admittance.

"She's here," he shouted into his walkie-talkie.

"I'll be right down to get her," Fitz's voice answered almost at once.

She was waiting on the other side of the metal detector when the elevator opened. Fitz's freckled face looked ashen. "We've been very worried about you," he said, taking her arm. She expected to be ushered into his office; instead he pushed the button for the ambassador's floor.

"Are you all right?" he asked as the car moved upward.

"Shaky."

He nodded. "I feel guilty as hell about this, if that does you any good."

"I'm not going to tell you it's all right and try to make you feel better."

Fitz slanted her a sympathetic look. "I deserve that."

She didn't reply.

He changed the subject. "Ambassador Thomas isn't in this morning, so we can use his office."

"All right."

At the door he turned to the secretary. "Bring us two cups of coffee, with cream and sugar." He turned to Julie. "Do you want a roll or something?"

"Not now."

The person who came in five minutes later with the coffee was Cal. It was obvious that the man had been up all night, and a good bit of the starch had gone out of his demeanor. But he wasn't above trying to put Julie McLean on the defensive immediately. "What the hell is the idea of going off on a wild-goose chase in response to a cockamamie note?"

"If you had leveled with me about the San Jeronimo, I wouldn't have gone."

"What do you mean?"

"You know perfectly well. I don't have to tell you."

"You didn't have a need to know."

"Apparently, I did! And I'd like to know if Paula is okay."

"She's fine," Cal answered in a clipped tone.

Fitz interrupted. "I hate to break in on this friendly interchange, but I want to know where Julie spent the night."

"With the man who saved my life."

"And who was that?"

"Aleksei Rozonov."

Cal muttered a curse.

Julie closed her eyes for a moment and took a deep, calming breath. She had passed long sleepless hours thinking of what she was going to say this morning.

"Maybe you'd better tell us about it," Fitz said.

"What do you know?"

"Only that you got a note sending you to an ambush. We've made some discreet inquiries. The police aren't aware you're involved. They think the explosion was just a piece falling off a building like the one that almost hit the king last month. Whoever did the demolition must have been an expert."

Julie's gaze flicked to Cal and then back to Fitz. She was going to try to stick as close to the truth as she could. "Rozonov wouldn't say much. I gather there was a difference of opinion about how to handle whatever operation they think I'm involved in. Somebody wanted me killed. Rozonov wants those NATO plans. He says he can guarantee my safety if I give them to him. Last night he took me to a room at the Palace Hotel and left me there while he went to cancel the orders." She paused. "The orders to have me killed."

Fitz's face had gone even grayer.

"But any information we pass to Rozonov won't stand up to close scrutiny," Cal pointed out.

"Then maybe I'd better not be in Madrid when he finds out."

"I don't know," he mused.

Julie gave him a direct look. "Perhaps if I fill in Ambassador Thomas, he'll see things differently."

Cal's head snapped up.

"I thought you cleared this with him," Fitz cut in.

"I don't answer to the ambassador," the CIA man pointed out.

The head of the political section swore. "Julie, you don't know how sorry I am that I didn't talk to Thomas about this myself."

"Just start writing up my exit papers."

"Wait a minute! Who's going to give that NATO stuff to Rozonov?" Cal questioned.

"You'll find a way," Fitz assured him.

Julie looked at the consular officer. "I'd like to see Paula and let her know *I'm* all right and then go home and get some sleep now, if you don't mind."

Cal nodded. "All right. But you know what all this proves, don't you?"

When she didn't answer, he continued. "It proves that true-blue friend of yours, Dan Eisenberg, was passing information to the Russians."

THE PHONE was ringing when he stepped out of the shower. Aleksei grabbed a towel, wrapped it around his narrow hips, and crossed the bedroom floor. He left a trail of wet footprints on the wide wooden floorboards. It wasn't hard to guess who would be on the other end of the line.

The caller didn't bother with a greeting. "You must have had a busy night."

"What makes you say that, Comrade General?"

"I received a top priority call from Moscow—from the office of the foreign secretary—this morning. I have never received such a call before. It was not a request, it was a *demand* that I alter my course of action."

Aleksei waited.

"How dare you presume that a major can get away with countermanding a general's orders!" Bogolubov bellowed into the phone.

"You believe I..." he began.

"*Ay-ay-ay!* Don't play dumb with me."

"Comrade General..." A pool of water was beginning to collect on the floor by the bedside table.

"Aleksei Iliyanovich—" the general's tone was uncharacteristically direct "—let me speak plainly. I have thought for some time that you were occupying a position far beyond your limited abilities. I can see now that you must have been trading on your father's reputation to advance yourself. But this time you have gone too far. When you get those NATO papers—*if* you get those NATO papers—I will be going over them with a fine-tooth comb. And if they are not the genuine article, the *very* genuine article, you will be on your way to Siberia in the next rail shipment of prisoners. Do I make myself clear?"

"Very clear."

"Now, I want you down here on the double. We will continue this discussion in the privacy of the embassy."

The line went dead.

Aleksei hung up, feeling a strange mixture of elation and rage. So Bogolubov was coping with humiliation by threatening him. The bastard! The only consolation was that he had bought Julie the time she needed to get out of Spain. But at what cost to himself?

Chapter Eleven

The Raven knew that the third phase of Project Topaz was drawing to a close. He had pinpointed the planting of disinformation at various locations around the world and he knew who was coordinating the effect back in Moscow. The last—and most classified—phase was a Quadrozine field trial, to make absolutely sure the assumptions about its properties were true. He was fully aware that the top-secret report on such a trial could not be trusted to even the most secure satellite link.

The data would be sent home as hard copy. Since at least one report was being couriered from Afghanistan, it would probably pass through Madrid. That was his best hope—maybe now his only hope—of getting proof of the Kremlin's very nasty scheme.

The Kremlin wouldn't send something so important without prior warning. So his customary check of the communications traffic took on a sense of urgency. But day after day the Raven left the noisy communications center with nothing to show for his efforts but a headache.

He had almost given up hope when the message he had been looking for surfaced. It was sandwiched between two other communications from field stations to their central offices back in Moscow. Most observers would have pegged it as ordinary military correspondence. Only the "from" and "to" notations gave away its link to Project Topaz. Of

course, it might still be just a piece of routine business. He
had to hope that it wasn't.

The actual communiqué would be in the next diplomatic
pouch. Finding out when it was coming through was simply a matter of alerting one of the junior officers in the
communications office that he wanted to send a priority one
dispatch to headquarters. She informed him that a courier
would be arriving the next afternoon, staying the night in
Madrid, and taking an early morning plane to East Ger-
many, where he could get a connecting flight to Moscow.
That meant the diplomatic pouch would be in the building
for approximately fourteen hours.

The Raven's face betrayed none of his thoughts as he
headed back to his office, but his mind was frantically ex-
amining and discarding possibilities. The pouch would be
locked in the basement vault, and unfortunately he had no
official reason to need access to that area at this time. He
might be able to make up a story that would sound plausible to the guard. But when the book was checked the next
morning and his signature was noted, he would be asked for
an explanation.

The plan he finally decided upon was hazardous in the
extreme. The KGB dirty-tricks department had been testing
a gas designed to gain its agents entry to guarded facilities.
When inhaled, the compound—which had been labeled with
the code named RG-52—caused a temporary state somewhere between unconsciousness and amnesia. Anyone who
wished to pass through the effective area could inject himself with a blocking agent. Although it was reputed to sting
like the devil, it had been proven effective.

There were limitations to the new product. Since the gas
dissipated quickly, it could be used only in enclosed areas.
And the effective time was short—only about twenty minutes. That meant you had to plan on getting in and out of
the area quickly.

There was, of course, one more factor that had to be
considered. Using RG-52 inside his own embassy bordered

on insanity. But since it was his only hope of getting the last piece of Topaz information, he had to take the risk.

"Borrowing" the key to the safe was only a minor problem. It was kept in a locked drawer in one of the third-floor offices, and he had the combination to that lock. There was little chance that the key would be missed in the early hours of the morning.

In preparation for his raid on the vault, the Raven stayed late at his desk readying the material bound for Moscow he had told one of the communications officers to expect. It was a status report on his present undercover assignments—with some manufactured details that made it seem urgent enough to include with the diplomatic dispatches.

He waited until after midnight to lock his office door, rolled up his sleeve, and swabbed some alcohol on the inside of his left arm. The rumors had been correct; the blocking agent for the gas felt like sulfuric acid as he injected it into his arm. A scream would have released some of the agony, but he could hardly chance that.

After counting off the required ten minutes for the antidote to take effect, he readied the small canister of gas and took the elevator to the basement. Because the guard station was around the corner from the elevator, he was able to discharge the canister in the hall without being seen.

He'd been half afraid the stuff wouldn't work properly, but the guard promptly slumped over with his head on his desk. The Raven glanced at his watch. He now had about fifteen minutes to get into the vault, find the report in the diplomatic pouch, and photograph it.

It was one of the smoothest operations he'd ever pulled off, and he'd known from the start that it would be one of his last. Topaz was a heavily guarded state secret. That meant there was almost certainly an infrared seal on the all-important envelope being sent from Afghanistan to the Kremlin. It would probably pass a visual inspection tomorrow morning, but back in Moscow the recipient would know at once that someone had tampered with the material. The investigation into what had happened would likely start in Madrid. If he were very lucky, that meant he had perhaps forty-eight hours left as a trusted servant of the USSR.

ALEKSEI ILIYANOVICH turned to look at the lighted dial on the clock on the bedside table. It was only ten-thirty. Though the adrenaline pumping through his system urged him to get on with the evening's business, he forced himself to clasp his hands behind his head again and relax. There was a lot to think about before he went out.

Long ago, as a schoolboy in New York, he had developed considerable skill at a card game called poker. It was a contest in which bluffing counted as much as holding the right cards. The trick, he'd quickly learned, was to keep your opponents off balance so they never knew whether you were holding a pair of twos or a full house. The strategy of the American game had appealed to him on an intellectual as well as a sporting level.

Although they certainly weren't sitting across a felt-covered table from each other, Aleksei could imagine that he and Slava Bogolubov were playing poker now. The rules, however, were a bit modified. Aleksei knew the general had prudently slipped a number of extra cards up his sleeve. The best way to neutralize them was to pull out a couple of additional aces of his own.

Luckily he had already collected the material he needed and stashed it away for just such an emergency. Bogolubov's career had included a number of unsavory episodes that would be highly embarrassing, even to an organization as liberal in its interpretation of the law as the KGB. If the general knew detailed reports of his past indiscretions were in danger of surfacing, he just might switch priorities from an attack to a fold.

Of course, bluffing wasn't enough in this case. Aleksei must be able to convince the comrade general that the proof of his allegations was tucked away somewhere very safe.

And he couldn't do that unless he were convinced himself. That was what he had to take care of next—and quickly.

Cursing in impatience, he glanced at the clock again. Maybe it was late enough to get started. Swinging his long legs off the bed, he stood and looked for a moment at his reflection in the closet-door mirror. First he made a conscious effort to relax his tense features. Then he carefully inspected his clothing. Already dressed in a navy jogging suit, he slipped into a pair of dark running shoes and tied the laces. He might be just another Madrelino returning from an evening's constitutional, he thought, as he crossed the room and picked up a nylon fannypack. In it was a small package wrapped in white tissue paper, a flashlight and some tools. After securing the pack around his waist, he headed for the back stairs.

Not until he was absolutely sure he wasn't being followed did he hail a cab on a nearby avenue. Then he gave an address more than half a mile from his ultimate destination. The building was one with a lazy *portero*, who was seldom at his post in the lobby. Aleksei was able to walk in the front door and out the back without being seen. Once in the alley, he headed north, then west on a side street, then north in the next alley. The roundabout route was essential for his own safety—and that of someone else.

He approached the redbrick apartment building from the back. With his customary thoroughness he had checked it out weeks before. The pedestrian door to the garage was secured by a lock that was easy to pick. Less than two minutes later he was standing inside the service courtyard under the shadow of a kitchen balcony. Each apartment had one, and in between ran clotheslines where tenants could hang out freshly washed laundry. He paused for a minute, inhaling the cooking aromas of saffron, olives and onions. Then his eyes sought the third-floor balcony across the court. It was dark, and he could see only a dim light beyond. According to his best information, no one should be home. He hoped it was true.

Back stairs brought him to the third floor unseen. He passed up the front door to the apartment he wanted in favor of the entrance to the balcony. It gave way easily to his expertise, and the kitchen door lock was no better. His running shoes were silent on the white tile floor. But when he stepped onto the wide boards in the dining room, the wood creaked. He froze, his ears straining, but there was no response.

He waited a few moments, letting his eyes become accustomed to the dim light. Piles of plates and cups covered the dining room table. Cardboard boxes were strewn about the room, some empty, some filled with newspaper-wrapped household goods. Others were crammed with books. He took in the disorder and then looked over toward the shelves on the living room wall, hoping to see a collection of small china animals. It was still there, waiting to be packed.

He had just taken off his fannypack and was crossing to the shelves, when the door at the end of the hall was suddenly thrown open. For a moment Julie McLean stood framed in a rectangle of luminescence, her dark hair burnished by the light behind her. She was wearing a thin white robe, and with the back lighting he could see the shadow of her body as she tiptoed down the hall on bare feet.

Julie peered uncertainly into the darkness. Though Paula had wanted her to spend the night, she'd insisted on coming back to the apartment to pack her china and other breakables. After everything that had happened this week, worrying about her Limoges was ludicrous. But until a couple of minutes ago she'd been happy to focus on the task of packing. The creak of a floorboard had brought her out of the bedroom. The noise was probably nothing, but her heart was pounding nevertheless. In the last few days her imagination had become overactive. Now it was conjuring up a dozen different demons.

For a moment Aleksei wondered if he might fade into the shadows near the wall. Before he could move, Julie had switched on a small lamp beside the sofa. Her eyes found him almost immediately. She gasped. He was the demon she had feared the most.

Before she could call out he was across the room, one hand closing tightly over her mouth, the other catching her firmly by the shoulder and pulling her away from the living room windows and back into the hallway.

Her body went rigid.

"I won't hurt you."

She didn't move.

"I can take my hand away if you promise not to scream. Do you agree?"

She nodded.

Slowly he loosened his fingers, ready to clamp them down again if necessary. "Why aren't you with your friend Paula?"

In the semidarkness she glared at him, her eyes raking over the dark knit clothing. "Why are you dressed like a burglar?" she countered, trying to make her voice harsh. It came out thin and reedy.

The answer he had prepared just in case it might be needed came easily to his lips. "I wanted to give you something."

Her eyes mirrored her disbelief. "So you picked a time when you thought I wouldn't be here and broke in."

He nodded tightly.

"Why?"

He was very conscious of the warmth of her body just inches from his, the softness of her skin where his hand still gripped her shoulder through the thin robe, the familiar scent that was hers alone. He had wanted to avoid something like this at all cost. "You know why."

She looked down, turning her head away slightly. "I'm leaving the day after tomorrow." The words were barely above a whisper.

"Then it went well with you at the embassy?"

"Yes."

Without any conscious thought on his part, his fingers slid across the silky fabric of her robe and down her arm in a long, stroking caress. "I'm glad."

She turned her face up toward him again, her dark eyes fathomless. "Who sent you?"

"No one."

Her lips were trembling, and the most natural way in the world to steady them was with his own.

"Julie." The syllable was lost as he turned her in his arms, pulled her close, and lowered his head to hers.

His mouth moved hungrily back and forth against hers, but it was no less hungry than her own. She felt his hands gentle on her face, steadying her frantic movements so that his tongue could breach the barrier of her lips and find the moist warmth beyond. She opened to him with a sigh of arousal, her hands clutching at his shoulders, her body melting against him.

She had thought she'd never see him again and had almost convinced herself that it was for the best. Now she recognized the self-deception.

This time it was almost impossible to restrain his greed for her. His tongue teased the sensitive inner lining of her lips, stroked more deeply, tasted, coaxed. When he finally lifted his head, they were both trembling.

His lips sought the line of her jaw, the soft skin of her neck. She arched backward, giving him better access. But she needed more of him too. Her hands moved across his back and shoulders, kneading the firm muscles through the knit fabric of his running suit.

She felt his fingers skim her ribs and then the sides of her breasts.

"Oh, yes, please, yes."

She sensed the subtle change in him even as his lips left her face.

"Aleksei . . ."

His hands dropped to his sides, fists clenched. "Julie, you must understand—I didn't expect—didn't want to find you here." His eyes were veiled in the darkness. "I can't stay."

So here was the truth between them—finally. He really didn't want this. She looked up at him with as much dignity as she could muster. "Then I believe you can leave the way you came in—whatever it was." Turning, she started back down the hall.

Behind her, she heard him utter a savage curse. Catching up in seconds, he whirled her around and pulled her back into his arms, pressing her hard against him. The hands that ranged up and down her back trembled in betrayal of his desperation. "Never think that I don't want you—or that I don't need you. There have been too many times I've wakened in the night from dreams of making love to you." The words were torn from his mouth unwillingly.

With a little sob, she pressed her face against his neck. "Then why must you go away tonight?"

"Simply being here puts you in danger. Staying puts you in more."

"I'm willing to take that risk."

His hand found her chin, tipped her face up so that his intense blue gaze could meet her dark one.

"Julie, I can't ask that of you."

"It's my decision."

Tenderness, passion, and admiration welled inside him, but still he held a part of himself in check. Gazing down at her, he reached up to stroke back a strand of the thick dark hair that he loved to touch. "*Lyubovochka,* there's another risk to you. I didn't expect that we . . . I mean I'm not prepared to . . ."

The hesitantly spoken words, coupled with the desire he was so obviously struggling to rein in, told her more about the depth of his feelings. A man with only superficial interest in a woman would simply take his pleasure with her and damn the consequences.

This time it was she who gently covered his mouth with her fingertips. "You're worried about pregnancy?"

He nodded. Under the circumstances leaving her with a child would be unthinkable.

"I'm protected against that."

Still he held back, searching her face. Sadness was mixed with the passion smoldering in his eyes. "You know that I will have to leave before morning." As he spoke, he couldn't prevent his lips from caressing the fingers that still rested against his mouth.

"*Alyoshenka,* let's not talk of that again."

He looked down at her in wonder. She had uttered a very personal sort of endearment, embroidered on the name Aleksei in the Russian fashion. It had been a long time since anyone had spoken to him that intimately. "You think about me that way?"

"Only in the middle of the night when I can't sleep from wanting you."

She didn't know if a curse or a benediction came from his lips this time, but it didn't matter. The important thing was that he had folded her into his arms once more.

"Come into the bedroom," she whispered.

She turned, and he followed her back down the hall, his hand possessive now on the curve of her hip. At the entrance to the room, he paused, holding her gently against himself as he looked around. His lips feathered the side of her neck, his hands combed through her hair as he took in the room, glad that her packing had disturbed only one small corner. There was so much of her here, and he wanted to know her through that as well as the pleasure of knowing her body. The lamps on the tables beside the double bed were unlit, but soft light streamed into the room through the open bathroom door.

The woven rug was South American, the wall decorations prints of some of the most romantic landscapes from the Prado. But inevitably, his eyes were drawn to the carved mahogany bed with its lacy coverlet.

The whisper kisses of his lips on her neck as he stood behind her and the gentle tug of his fingers in her hair were arousing powerful feelings. Julie took a step toward the bed, and his hands came around her shoulders in gentle restraint to pull her back against him.

"I've longed to hold you like this," he confessed, his strong fingers making a contrast against her white robe as they traced down the wide strip of lace that adorned the front.

Julie held her breath, watching as his hands cupped her breasts and weighed their fullness before beginning to stroke them in a way that was all the more erotic for the silky fabric that separated his skin from hers. Through the almost translucent material her nipples budded, and waves of pleasure shot through her body.

He felt her strain against his hands, needing to increase the contact. The response was so elemental that it threatened to break through his tightly held control.

"You're like a drug that's seeped into my soul." He could no longer fight the addiction.

"And what of mine?" she questioned, her voice deep and throaty.

"Dushenka!" The soft Russian endearment was a word that meant soul, and never had it had more meaning to him.

His hands were at the buttons of her robe then, releasing them quickly so that he could slide the slippery fabric off her shoulders. When his hands found her unencumbered breasts again and his thumbs stroked across the hardened nipples, she gasped. Suddenly her body was on fire, every nerve ending alive and sending urgent messages to her brain. Though she was standing with her back to him, she wanted and needed to touch him too. The strength of the need surprised her. The realization suddenly hit her that always before in a man's arms she had held something of herself back. Now she felt compelled to give and take everything she could.

Slipping her hands from the sleeves of the robe, she reached up and behind her, her fingers touching the thick silk of his hair. The robe would surely have slid to the floor except that there was not a millimeter of space between their tightly pressed bodies. She felt his lips on her cheek, and her head strained sideways against his shoulder. She ached to feel the pressure of his mouth on hers.

"Is this some sort of Russian torture?" The words slipped from her mouth before she knew she'd said them.

His laugh was husky and not altogether steady against her ear. "No, an American plot for bringing the Kremlin to its knees."

As he spoke he turned her in his arms. For a moment they smiled into each other's eyes. Then, as the silky robe slipped slowly down her hips, his blue gaze darkened.

The passion she saw there fueled her own. Her fingers slid under the waist of his running jacket and upward across the bare expanse of his back, feeling with pleasure the taut skin and hard muscles.

"Such clever hands," Aleksei murmured.

The words made her bold. One palm moved to the front of his body and journeyed slowly across his chest to stroke his flat nipples and wring an exclamation of pleasure from his lips. When she touched the line of a scar that descended downward from his breastbone, she felt him suck in his breath.

"Did I hurt you?"

"No, that was from long ago." He turned his face to nibble at the lobe of her ear. The endearments he whispered were half in Russian, half in English. The words and the emotion in his voice sent another wave of longing through her.

The hand on his chest turned to grasp the neckline of his jacket from the inside. The other found the zipper closing and pulled it down. Pushing aside the knit material, she pressed her breasts against his naked chest. This time his gasp of delight mingled with her own.

It was several moments before he released her to shrug out of the jacket.

Even covered by his usually conservative clothing, the lean but muscular lines of his body had been impressive. Now she had a better idea of how magnificent he really was. The long scar only added to the fascination of his masculinity.

"You're beautiful," she sighed, her hands settling at his waist.

"Not compared to you." His fingers traced over her shoulders, down the line of her spine, and slowly up again. Then quickly he lifted her in his arms and carried her to the bed, where he laid her gently down. In a moment he had shed the rest of his clothing and joined her.

The pleasure of his body covering hers was almost unbearable. She had dreamed of this. But reality was far more potent than the fantasy.

"*Alyoshenka,*" she crooned, glorying in the intimacy of the name. At least now, for this moment, he belonged to her. No one could ever take that away.

Could a man live a lifetime in one night, he wondered, not realizing that he had spoken the thought aloud in Russian.

"*I can,* with you," she promised in the same language, her lips close against his ear.

"Julie. Oh, God, Julie." The freedom to touch and caress her as he had longed to was almost overwhelming.

"Oh, yes, please, now," she begged. Her hands on his body were urgent, imploring.

He braced himself on his arms above her. Never had pleasing a woman been more central to his own satisfaction. "No, *dushenka.* Not yet." Slowly he bent to kiss her face, her shoulders, her breasts. "So soft, like velvet. So wonderful to touch," he murmured, shifting so that he could stroke up the inside curve of her thigh to the warm, moist center of her femininity. His smoldering gaze followed the progress of his hand.

She trembled beneath him, pressing her face against his chest. She was overwhelmed by the sensations he was creating. But he would not be hurried. Not until the skillful coaxing of his hands and mouth had lifted her up on wave after wave of pleasure did he enter her.

The heat and hardness of him stunned her. Then her need for fulfillment became the only truth in the universe. She was helpless to do anything but move with him, cling to him, call his name. Up and up he carried her as though she were caught in the spiral of a tornado. And then suddenly she was there in a tight, blinding whirlwind of sensation that brought her to the edge of frenzy before she surrendered to the rapture of it.

He waited, poised on the brink, feeling her deep contractions of pleasure around him. Her ecstasy shattered the last barrier. And in the glory of his own fulfillment, he felt his soul fuse with hers.

For a long moment neither one of them moved. When Aleksei finally rolled to his side, he brought her with him, cradling her body tightly against his.

She felt his lips move lovingly against her cheek, her hair.

"Was that as good for you as it was for me?" she asked hesitantly.

He laughed softly. "I thought you could tell, but in America is that what the women ask?"

She angled back slightly so that her solemn gaze could meet his. "*Alyoshenka,* until a few moments ago I didn't know it was possible for a woman to feel anything that intense."

He stared back at her in surprise. "Truly?"

"Yes, truly." The thought that she would never see him again after tonight almost tore her heart in two.

He saw the pain flicker in the depth of her brown eyes. "Don't think about tomorrow. Just give me tonight." What they had found together was so incredible. But their hours together were so few.

She pressed her face against his chest again and clenched her eyes shut. She'd had years of experience masking her emotions. Surely until dawn she could hold her despair at bay.

His hand stroked across her shoulders, the gesture comforting and sensual all at once. "When I couldn't sleep, I'd lie awake at night thinking of questions I wanted to ask you."

"Like what?"

He hesitated for a moment. "The most intimate kind of questions. Like how you sleep—on your back or curled up on your side? What are your fantasies? When do you prefer making love—in the morning or the evening?"

She couldn't help smiling. "Were they really in that order?"

"No."

"Well, the first one is easy, I sleep curled on my side." As she spoke, her hand burrowed into the thick hair of his chest. She couldn't deny the need to keep touching him.

"And the rest?" His fingers stroked the indentation at her waist.

She felt her cheeks redden slightly. Even when she'd been so afraid of him, he'd still haunted her dreams like an incubus offering her heaven and hell if only she would surrender. Now she tried to make her voice light. "I think you know what my fantasies have been lately."

"Tell me."

"A dark, dangerous Russian, with arms like bands of steel and lips that take my sanity away."

"Such power this man has," he murmured, his mouth teasing hers as he spoke. "But your Russian is captive as well as captor."

The kiss lengthened, and she felt her arousal, so recently satisfied, beginning to build again. But he seemed to relish the slow sensuality of the tempo. "And when do you prefer to make love?" he prompted.

"Ask me in the morning."

"Early in the morning."

They were skirting close to dangerous ground again.

"I've wanted to tell you, I love the way my name sounds when you say it," she said quickly.

"It's not quite right, is it? That's because we don't have the *J* sound in Russian."

"You make it seem beautiful and exotic."

"The way you are to me, beautiful and exotic." His warm gaze caressed her face.

She lifted his free hand and kissed the fingertips. "Do I get three questions too?" she asked. If only they were three wishes.

"Of the same type, yes."

"Can I be a bit more serious?"

He nodded cautiously.

"Are you happy with your life?"

His grip tightened on her shoulder. "Not happy, but there are certain satisfactions."

The regret in his voice made her chest tighten. She wanted to ask what it would take to make him happy, but that was beyond the boundaries of this bedroom. "What do you do for fun?" she asked instead.

"When I'm at home, I like to take long walks in the woods."

"That sounds very solitary."

"Oh, no. In my country, we do that with friends or as a family."

"I'd like to know about your family."

A shadow crossed his face. "I have no one left."

"I'm so sorry."

"It's better that way." His finger stroked the side of her face. "You've had more than your three questions. It's my turn again. Tell me something about your childhood."

She searched her mind and brought back a warm Christmas memory of the first time her mother had let her cut out the sugar cookies. The episode sparked a story from Aleksei about a pair of cross-country skis Grandfather Frost, the

Russian version of Santa Claus—who came on New Year's Eve—had brought him.

Each had access to dossiers on the other filled with the cold facts. But only now were they learning the truth about one another. Eagerly they exchanged recollections of treasured moments and insights into two childhoods that were worlds apart.

As they talked, they continued to stroke and touch each other's bodies, the caresses becoming more intimate as the hours of night flew toward dawn. Though each was fully aware of the other's arousal, both were reluctant to bring it to its logical conclusion because it must be for the last time.

Finally, there was no option except to grasp the short moments of joy they had left.

Julie felt tension coil inside her until she found herself moving against Aleksei with a frantic urgency—an urgency that could be assuaged in only one way. It was the same for him. A few hours ago they had found the heights of ecstasy together. Now the joining took them even higher. As the first streaks of dawn stole through the window, Julie cried out, overwhelmed by a fulfillment that was all the more intense because it was tinged with anguish.

Chapter Twelve

Slava Bogolubov had also spent a sleepless night. But the reasons were quite different, though no less pleasurable. He'd finally gotten the proof he needed to put the Raven in a steel cage, and he'd spent the small hours of the morning documenting his facts.

Leaning back and lighting a thick Havana cigar, he allowed himself to savor his victory. It was all the more sweet because—though he would never admit it publicly—the Raven was a worthy opponent. The man was crafty, with an uncanny ability to sniff out traps—like the dead drop at the Prado. But he had finally made a fatal mistake by tampering with the infrared seal on that diplomatic pouch. The lab in Moscow had pinpointed the hour when the seal was broken. The only suspect staffer who was still in the building was the Raven.

Reaching for the phone, the general dialed Yuri Hramov's hotel. "I have the authorization I need. The Raven's identify has been confirmed. Go pick him up."

Hramov's steely eyes lit. Getting even with a bigwig who had thwarted him in the past was always gratifying. Shifting the phone to his shoulder, he opened the bedside table and took out a set of brass knuckles. "You don't mind if I settle a few scores of my own before I bring him in?"

Hramov was a barely controlled savage, the general thought. While savages had their uses, they weren't known for thinking through the consequences of their actions. "You're underestimating the man," he snapped. "He's hidden his identity for this long because he's a crafty son of a bitch. Be very careful or he's going to slip through your fingers."

The henchman patted the automatic pistol in his shoulder holster. "I never knew a man who could run very far with a shattered ankle."

"I want the bastard alive and wishing you'd sent him to hell. He's going to give me some answers if it's the last thing he does," Bogolubov shot back, already anticipating the interrogation to come.

"Understood, Comrade General."

ALEKSEI DRESSED quickly. He had already stayed here with Julie dangerously long, yet there was still some unfinished business between the two of them.

Turning back from the doorway, he caressed her with his gaze. Though her body was covered by a sheet, he knew its contours intimately now. The pleasure of holding her in his arms would have to warm him for many a long night. But at this moment the pain in her eyes made his breath catch in his chest. "Do you remember that I came to leave you something?" he asked softly.

She nodded, not trusting herself to speak, because she knew she would ask him to stay.

"I'll get it from my knapsack."

She was propped up against the pillows when he returned from the living room with a small tissue-wrapped package. Sitting down on the side of the bed, he placed it gently in her hands. With shaking fingers she unwrapped the paper. Nestled inside was one of the exquisite Russian wolfhound figurines they'd seen the day they'd met for lunch.

"Oh. It's beautiful."

"I bought them both and kept the other one."

She clutched his hand, knowing that in a few moments he'd walk out of her life forever. "I don't have anything for you."

"You've given me more than you can ever know." He looked down, unable to meet her gaze. The impulse to lie to her, to tell her that there was some chance they might meet again, was overwhelming. Yet he understood that false hope was more cruel than no hope at all. There was one more thing, however, to leave her with—something that might bring her some measure of peace.

He turned his hand up to grasp her fingers. "You were drawn into danger by your loyalty to your friend Dan Eisenberg. Julie, the trust in Dan wasn't misplaced. He was an honorable man, not a traitor to his country."

"How do *you* know?"

"I can't tell you, but it's true nevertheless." Leaning over, he brushed his lips against her forehead, knowing that if he dared to kiss her mouth he wouldn't be able to leave her at all. "Goodbye, *dushenka*. I leave part of my soul with you."

"And mine with you," she whispered.

He stood up, turned away, and walked rapidly out of the room.

She strained her ears, listening for the sound of the door closing. It was very faint. But when she heard it, the tears she'd held back through the night began trickling down her face one by one.

AMHERST GORDON put down the Teletype printouts and slapped his hand on the leather arm of his desk chair. "The crafty son of a bitch did it," he chortled.

"I take it the Madrid crisis has finally broken?" Constance McGuire inquired evenly, swiveling from her computer screen to face her employer.

She might look calm, the Falcon thought, but he knew she was just as eager as he was for any news of their beleaguered operative.

"According to my information sources, all hell broke loose at the Russian embassy early yesterday morning."

"Has the Raven made his move?"

"Yes, he flew the coop and he left a mess of chicken feathers flying."

"Oh?"

"Well, we can start with Yuri Hramov. He was admitted to a Madrid hospital with a bullet in his ankle. The official reason was 'an accident cleaning his gun,' but if you believe that, you'll believe the Soviets have just dismantled their nuclear arsenal."

"So he *was* in on this." Connie grimaced. "The comrade general likes rough company."

"Well, he's not going to enjoy the company he's keeping now quite so much. Our sources report he was called back to Moscow to explain how the diplomatic pouch that was in the Madrid embassy safe for fourteen hours was tampered with."

"Do we have any further word on the others who were supposed to be closing in on the Raven?" Connie questioned.

"Yes." He permitted himself a grin as he held up a Kremlin report U.S. intelligence had just intercepted and decoded. "Aleksei Rozonov is also officially listed as being detailed back to headquarters. The agricultural attaché, Feliks Gorlov, is another one who's in trouble," he continued, his voice tinged with something that was close to glee. "It seems that besides dealing in wheat, he was also turning quite a personal profit in the Iberian drug market. Our sources now believe he was the real target for the San Jeronimo bombing. One of the local distributors wanted to get even for the Russian's muscling in on the action. Eisenberg's being there was nothing more than a tragic coincidence after all."

Connie's face registered a mixture of regret and relief. "It's a damn shame they got Dan in his place. But at least the news on Gorlov clears up the drug connection."

"Thank God, yes. That's another one we owe the Raven."

"I still can't believe Gorlov was the ringer in this. The man was really taking chances."

"Yes. The Raven must have ferreted out his underworld involvement and used it as a diversion to cover his escape. I think he also raised some questions about Georgi Krasin having had an affair with a British agent. But I'm not sure what that's all about yet."

Connie studied her employer's face, knowing he was keeping back a critical piece of information. "Do we know the Raven is safely away or are they secretly holding him somewhere for interrogation?" she finally ventured.

Gordon's expression became serious. For a few minutes he'd allowed himself the luxury of enjoying the Russians' embarrassment. Now he could no longer ignore his own problems. He sighed. "Dammit, Connie, there's no way to know for certain yet. There was no escape tunnel in Madrid. If he makes it out of Europe, it's going to have to be by a circuitous route. We'll have to keep the contacts open and pray that he surfaces soon—and with the Topaz documents."

HE WAS ON THE RUN and he knew how a lone wolf must feel hunted across the tundra. Of course, he wasn't in the frozen north, but still, at night, there was simply no way to keep himself warm.

The first thing the hunters would have done was lay traps at all the obvious routes out of Spain. That was why he had headed cross-country for the mountains.

The Raven had been prepared to disappear almost since the moment he'd put the Topaz material back in the embassy safe. But he hadn't expected to find Yuri Hramov tiptoeing across the main room of his apartment quite so early in the morning. On the other hand, Bogolubov's thug didn't know his target had taken the precaution of installing a silent alarm at the front door. The sixty-second warning had determined who ended up on the floor writhing in pain.

After tying up the intruder, he'd even had time for a little question-and-answer session. Hramov had gasped out a very interesting piece of information about one of the Raven's fellow embassy employees that fitted in perfectly with his plans to leave in a cloud of thick Madrid smog. Even though every second counted now, he'd stopped to put in a call back to KGB headquarters that would give them another quarry to chase besides himself.

It had always struck him how quickly modern civilization vanished in Spanish countryside. The hilly terrain northeast of Madrid was crisscrossed with goat and sheep trails. Now, dressed in a well-worn peasant outfit, he was following a trail to Navarra and the Pyrenees. The rough clothing made him look like a local. In addition, he had used other tricks to change his appearance. He'd stopped shaving, and his heavy beard had already begun to conceal his strong jaw. The dark bangs he had combed downward almost met his thick eyebrows, making his forehead disappear.

His plans were flexible, but the first step was to get out of Spain. During his tour in Iberia he'd made some contacts in the ETA, the Basque separatist group, and cultivated them on a personal level. He wouldn't turn his back on the Basques for a minute. But he knew the terrorist organization had ways of getting people across the border and even out of Europe entirely. They also needed funds. His passage could be bought with some of the money the Falcon had transferred to his secret Madrid bank account.

Of course, the transaction ate at his conscience. Giving money to terrorists was tantamount to buying them guns and ammunition so they could kill someone else. He wasn't sure his hide was worth it. But the information he had was. Even though he'd left a copy of the Topaz report in a safe place, he couldn't be sure it would make it out of the country. With his most reliable Peregrine links broken, his only way to alert the Falcon that something was coming had been to mail an encoded letter to a post office box in Virginia. But he had no way of knowing whether that route was still open.

Night turned into day, and the June weather was hot. Pausing to wipe the sweat from his forehead, he took a drink from his canteen. He could have walked the whole two hundred miles in about eight days if he'd pushed. Luckily, he had the offer of an occasional ride on a hay wagon.

There was still plenty of time, however, to think about his predicament as he hiked the uneven terrain, his few possessions in a canvas rucksack slung over his shoulder. He'd told himself for years that he wouldn't be leaving anything behind, but now that he'd actually made the break with everything he'd known, his heart was heavy. He didn't really know what kind of life he was going to. Right now he wasn't even sure how he was going to contact the Falcon. But that would be of no importance if he failed to get out of Spain alive.

He avoided the towns, except for brief forays to replenish his food supply. Any contact with civilization made him jumpy. It was no paranoid delusion that the KGB had informers in the most unlikely places. The reward for turning him in was probably more than a peasant's yearly income. So he slept in the open on the hard ground, not daring to allow himself the comfort of a campfire. His daily ablutions were made in the icy water of mountain streams.

The inhabitants of the ETA encampment he found on the eighth day might have dismissed him as a tramp to be robbed of any valuables and disposed of—except for his manner of arrival. Because he knew the clandestine community's approximate location, he discovered the position of the southwestern sentry before the man discovered him. They came walking into camp together, the lookout moving carefully to avoid being shot by the automatic pressed firmly against the small of his back. The bravado entrance was a gesture calculated to win instant respect among men who lived as outlaws in the rugged mountains on Spain's northern border. It had the desired effect.

Not long after demanding to see the leader of the group, he was sitting in a snug mountain cave eating his first bowl of hot stew in over a week. Between bites of goat meat and onion he explained what he needed. His major disappointment was that the head man he'd met with in the past had been killed by the Spanish civil guard during a raid on Pamplona just weeks earlier. His short, fair-haired replacement was a stranger who obviously viewed this new arrival with extreme mistrust.

At the mention of ample payment for services rendered, the expression in the blond man's calculating gray eyes changed for the better. Yet he still failed to inspire any genuine trust. For a moment the Raven considered walking out of camp and trying to find another group of rebel Basques. But he suspected he might well be tracked and his throat quietly slit the moment fatigue forced him to close his eyes. These were men who dared not trust the location of their camp to a hostile stranger.

The Raven repressed a sigh. With his ties to the Peregrine Connection temporarily severed, coming here in the first place had been one of his very few escape options. He was a man hunted by his own people—and for all he knew, hunted by the other side as well.

Tipping his stool back against the wall of the cave he wiped up the last of the stew gravy with a piece of coarse bread and chewed it thoughtfully. He had been in worse situations and come out alive. His best strategy—probably his only strategy—was to play his cards as though he dealt from a position of strength, and hope that there was some honor among thieves.

SPECIAL AGENT Richard Borman took off his tortoiseshell glasses, set them on the desk beside him, and gave the woman across from him a level look. "Ms. McLean, you've been fairly cooperative in contributing to the State Department's investigation of the Eisenberg murder.''

Fairly cooperative! Julie thought, looking curiously back at him. There was something about his close-cropped ash-blond hair, fair skin, and rigid posture that reminded her of Cal Dixon. The comparison did nothing to make her feel at ease. He wasn't trying to help her relax either.

The tone of his voice implied that she had been anything but helpful. Yesterday she'd been led to believe that the questioning sessions were drawing to a close. But this morning Borman had taken the place of the two investigators she'd talked to for most of the week since her return to Washington and had started picking away at details she'd thought were already a matter of record. As she'd talked, his half-lidded gaze made her feel like a suspect rather than a trusted employee being debriefed at State Department headquarters. Was she going to have to go through the whole thing again for him? And why?

They had moved from yesterday's conventional-looking office to a matchbox-size room that was already starting to give her claustrophobia. She had lost track of how many hours she had spent being grilled. Since security had made it clear that she wouldn't be released from the State Department until they'd evaluated her part in the Madrid affair, she'd been desperately dredging up every piece of pertinent information she could think of.

She'd gone into detail about her relationship with Dan, her association with Cal, her conversations with Aleksei, and her narrow escape from death the night she'd received the note. The only thing she'd held back was her personal involvement with the Russian agent. In retrospect, that wasn't so difficult to accomplish. The experience had been incredible, but so intensely private that she had wanted to lock it in a secret place in her heart like a finely cut, perfect white diamond nestled in a velvet-lined box. Only when she was alone did she dare take it out and admire its beauty.

She leaned back in the padded steel chair and straightened her shoulder. "I've been cooperating as best I can, Mr. Borman," she said.

"But perhaps you haven't told us everything."

She stared back. His voice was mild enough. But something in the way his mud green eyes regarded her like a mutant cell under a microscope made her mouth go suddenly dry. "What do you mean?" she managed.

He paused and took out a government form. "Oh, yes, I'd better have your signature consenting to have this interview recorded and videotaped."

That had been standard procedure throughout the week. Julie had read the form carefully the first few times. Now she scribbled her signature impatiently on the line indicated and pushed the paper back in Borman's direction.

"Let's continue." His voice suddenly took on a hard edge. "Ms. McLean, we have reason to believe that you and Rozonov were involved in a sexual relationship."

Julie's heart stopped for a moment, then restarted in double time. Her first impulse was to grab back and tear up the consent form she had just signed.

"Is that correct?" Borman persisted.

"You have no right to ask me anything about that," she shot back.

"Then you admit that there is something to discuss."

"I admit nothing." She started to stand up.

"Just a moment, Ms. McLean. I don't have to remind you that collaborating with known enemy agents is a felony punishable by imprisonment."

"Then I don't have anything to worry about. I haven't collaborated with an enemy agent." Underneath the bravado, she could hear fear creeping into her voice.

"Maybe you had better let me be the judge of your involvement."

Instead of continuing immediately, he rested his chin on his thumb and forefinger and regarded her speculatively. Under the scrutiny, Julie felt each breath become a pain in her chest. Why didn't he go on? She forced herself not to ask.

Finally he cleared his throat. "Let's try a slightly different tack. Did Rozonov ever touch you?"

Julie stared back. Under the table she clenched her hands together and tried to make herself think calmly before answering. God, was the hidden camera recording every play of emotion on her face? Touching someone was not a crime, she reminded herself.

"Ms. McLean, you're taking a rather long time with your answer," Borman observed, leaning toward her.

"Yes, he touched me."

"When?"

"He pushed me away from the falling stone ornament. And—and—he put his arm around me to comfort me afterward."

"Ah... And in the hotel room where he took you, did he touch you intimately?"

There was a roaring in her ears. "What do you mean by that?"

"Well, while he was—um—comforting you, did he try to physically arouse you? Or for that matter, did he try at any time to gain your loyalty through sexual involvement?"

"My God. You have a filthy mind. The only contact I had with Rozonov, that would have any relevance to you, was when I was carrying out the orders of Calvin Dixon." She'd phrased the statement so that it wasn't a lie, but her eyes remained fixed on a picture of the President in back of Borman.

"Mr. Dixon thinks otherwise."

Julie's eyes widened. So this was Cal's parting present. "That bastard! he has no reason to think that, except for his own overactive imagination."

Borman took a minute to look through the folder in front of him. "When was the last time you had sexual relations with anyone?"

"That's entirely irrelevant. I don't have to answer that." What right did this stranger have to be probing into her sex life like a dentist drilling into a cavity without bothering to use Novocain?

"I'm afraid it is relevant. According to Dixon, your sexual contacts in Madrid were very limited."

"You mean I'm damned if I did and damned if I didn't?" Had the CIA been watching her bedroom door for three years?

"Ms. McLean, I have to assume from your psychological profile that you're a normal woman with normal needs. If you were sexually inactive, that might have made you very vulnerable to the advances of a skilled foreign agent."

Julie's nails dug into the flesh of her palm. The idea that making love with Aleksei could be reduced to "the advances of a skilled foreign agent" was unthinkable. Or was it? Had that been what had happened, or was Borman intentionally tying her up in knots?

He pursed his lips. "Of course, there is this one fact that has me puzzled. If you weren't sexually active, why did you have a standing order with the post pharmacy for birth control pills?"

Julie took a deep, steadying breath. "Mr. Borman, I'm surprised that you haven't been over my medical record with as much care as you spent on my psychological profile. If you'd perused it, you would have discovered that I had monthly menstrual cramps that were interfering with my ability to do my job." The very clinical explanation was issued between clenched teeth. "And now that I've satisfied your prurient interest, I think that's all I'm going to say."

"Then you'll be willing to swear to all this under a lie detector test?"

"Yes," Julie replied evenly. God, what if it came to that? She'd just have to pray that it didn't.

Borman studied her for more than minute. She forced herself not to flinch under the scrutiny.

"Well, then," he finally said, "I think we have all we need from you for the time being. You can go on leave-of-absence status as long as you stay in the Washington area."

"I presume this means I'm free to go now?"

"Yes." He had enough clout to pull her back in if he needed her. But he had the feeling that the best thing to do now was to give her enough rope and let her hang herself.

Another special agent came in to witness her statement and Julie went through the motions of signing the second set of forms. Twenty minutes later she was standing on the sidewalk in the muggy air of Foggy Bottom, blinking in the strong sunlight.

The interview with Borman had made her feel dirty. All she wanted was to head back to her town house and scrub herself in the shower, as though that could cleanse her of his lewd accusations. She'd hoped this nightmare would be over when she'd come back to Washington, but they still wouldn't believe her. She had wanted to handle this by herself. Maybe she was going to have to turn to her uncle for help after all.

AFTER JULIE MCLEAN had left, Richard Borman picked up the phone and called his office at CIA headquarters in Langley, Virginia.

"I think Cal Dixon's right on the money," he reported.

"You mean she's involved with the Russian?"

"Yes. He must have been dynamite in the sack. Her face brightens like a neon light every time you mention his name. Too bad I can't put her under hypnosis and get the details. She'd never agree to it. And we can't do that to an American citizen."

"Well, as soon as she does something we know is illegal, she's going to lose her protection under the law."

"I wish we could put her under twenty-four-hour surveillance."

"Yeah, but it could be months before anything breaks. Let's just put a tap on her phone and sit tight."

"Agreed."

"I'd like to know what she's told Rozonov and how he expects to use her now."

"I have the feeling we'll get it out of her—with her cooperation or not."

Chapter Thirteen

He leaned back in his contoured cockpit seat, adjusted his earphones, and listened to the captain's chatty tour guide spiel to the passengers. They were over Long Island and would be starting their approach to Baltimore-Washington International Airport soon. The weather at BWI was overcast and muggy, with a chance of thunderstorms. But Captain Leoni promised it would be clearing up by the weekend.

Would the 475 travelers in the belly of the Air Italia jetliner panic, the Raven wondered, if they knew the third officer was a last-minute replacement with no cockpit experience? And would good old Captain Leoni be fired for taking eight million lira under the table for signing the personnel switch? He had his own reasons for hoping the deception wouldn't be discovered—for a while anyway.

The plane taxied to a smooth landing. Third Officer Mario Sabatino cleared customs with the rest of the crew. But when he changed out of his uniform in a staff men's room, he burned his passport and took its replacement from the false bottom of his flight bag. When he emerged from the washroom cubical, he was wearing a baggy Windbreaker over a blue oxford cloth shirt and faded jeans. Scuffed Adidas completed the unassuming costume. The gun in the shoulder holster under his arm didn't show, of course. It had nestled in his flight bag, protected by the assumption that a member of the crew wouldn't bring a weapon on board.

He'd shaved off the scraggly beard he'd grown in the mountains just before he'd accepted the temporary third officer's billet. But he'd kept a droopy mustache so out of character for his personality that it made him blink every time he caught sight of his face. The strenuous journey coupled with the skimpy diet in the rebel camp had taken more than fifteen pounds from his already lean body, giving his face a hollow look. Pausing in front of the mirror, he ruffled the longish hair he'd slicked down for the airline role. He hoped he could pass for a writer or artist. He certainly didn't look like an American businessman.

The Raven glanced at his watch. It was after seven. If he spent an hour in the bar, it would be almost dark when he went to get the car that was supposed to be waiting for him in the satellite parking lot with its keys taped under the left front bumper. The whole time that he sipped his Scotch and soda—he didn't dare order vodka—he inspected the other men in the room, and also the women. Most looked like bored travelers killing time between flights. But there was always the grim possibility that one of them might have orders to kill him.

The Ford Escort that had cost him double its legitimate price—in cash—was supposed to have been delivered several days ago. He hated having to rely on a long-distance arrangement, but he would compensate by proceeding with extreme caution.

After paying for his drink with some of the American money he'd gotten on the black market, he picked up his nylon tote bag and took the escalator downstairs. Instead of catching the shuttle bus to the parking lot, he watched it pull away and then started up the road on foot. The thunderstorm that Captain Leoni had forecast was approaching rapidly from the west. Nevertheless, instead of heading directly for the car, he circled the lot and climbed over the back fence. The Escort was supposed to be between the seventh and ninth rows about a quarter of the way from the end. Crouching behind the station wagon, he studied that section of the lot. Though it was almost full, it contained only one small blue sedan.

The evening shadows were very welcome as he slipped slowly from car to car. The bus had discharged its passengers ten minutes ago. It wouldn't be back until it had made a circuit of the airport. Though the parking lot looked deserted enough, there was a tense prickly feeling at the back of his neck that had nothing to do with the large pellets of rain that were starting to hit his Windbreaker. The torrent that he had been expecting, however, held off.

He was within three vehicles of the blue car when a brilliant flash of lightning was followed by a loud clap of thunder. In the instant of illumination he saw something that made his blood run cold. A head had popped up in the back window of the Escort and then disappeared again. *Chyort!* So his misgivings had not been unfounded. The renegade Basque leader had taken his money and then turned around and sold his travel plans to the KGB.

Forget the car. Get the hell out of here while you still can, his mind screamed. But the decision had already been taken out of his hands. Something whizzed past his right ear and embedded itself in the side of a small pickup truck in back of him. It was a bullet. He ducked before the next one zinged through the patch of empty air where his head had been a moment before. The guy in the car wasn't the only one waiting in ambush. He had company—someone whose gun was equipped with a silencer.

A crack of thunder shook the parking lot. At least the impending storm would mask his return fire. Pulling out his Makarov, he dropped to a crouch and zigzagged his way through several lines of cars. As he rounded a fender, he was greeted with two flashes of gunfire in the dim light and the spit of two more bullets. One deflated the tire next to him. The other slammed into his upper arm. The pain was like a hot slash of lightning. For a moment his vision blurred, but he managed to get off three shots of his own and was rewarded with a gasp of agony from the direction in which the fire flashes had gone. Gritting his teeth against his own pain, he moved forward. His aim had been lucky. The fading light revealed a man writhing on the ground, his hands pressed to his abdomen. Between the fingers, dark blood oozed.

Kicking the assassin's gun out of reach, the Raven turned back toward the car. The interior was still dark, but some sixth sense told him it was now empty. The other man must be in the parking lot. He heard a low whistle. Then silence except for the rising wind. The sound was repeated. Still there was no reply. If he interpreted correctly, there were only two of them and he'd gotten one. Or maybe it was a trick to throw him off.

His left arm throbbed. It was like a foreign body, hanging uselessly at his side. The inside of his shirt felt wet and sticky. He wondered how much blood he had already lost.

Teeth still clamped together, he began to drag himself across the parking lot again. Lightning split the sky, spotlighting his position for an instant. The roll of thunder that followed masked the spit of three more bullets that spattered into the blacktop of the parking lot, sending chips of pavement flying. Instinctively he rolled, the pain in his arm multiplied a hundredfold by the pressure of the macadam surface. Hot fire skimmed against his body, this time over his hip. Holding his breath, he lay absolutely still on the ground between two cars. It was a calculated risk. But he knew that in his weakened condition he couldn't keep up the battle much longer. His ears strained. At the barest crunch of leather on gravel, he rolled again and squeezed off four rapid shots. The man who had been coming forward to finish him off sagged to the pavement. He was dead before he hit the ground.

On a hunch the Raven felt through the man's clothing. In the right front pocket was a set of car keys. Before turning away, he looked at the face. No one he knew. Perhaps the next one who came to try and kill him would be familiar.

After retrieving his flight bag, he staggered to the car. Once inside, he closed the door and took a damage assessment. The left arm was no surprise. He quickly made a tourniquet to stop the bleeding. He swore vehemently when he felt the skin over his right hip. That was where he had taped the vital Topaz film. The flat metal envelope had deflected a bullet. In the process, its contents had been destroyed. So now he no longer had the report. He would have to get the backup copy.

Chyort! He knew where it was—in the last place on earth he'd pick to visit. He was going to have to get in and out of there fast, no matter what the personal cost.

In his flight bag was a bottle of capsules that contained a powerful stimulant. After choking two down he waited for several minutes. The drug made him feel better, but he knew the effects were only temporary, and that it would be dangerous to repeat the dosage again too soon.

While he was marshaling his strength, the airport bus discharged another group of passengers, and the rain picked up in earnest. Convenient, he thought, as he started the engine, flipped on the wipers, and maneuvered into the line of cars waiting to pay the attendant. A few minutes later he was heading down the Baltimore-Washington Parkway toward D.C., fervently giving thanks that he was familiar with the city.

JULIE SHIFTED the heavy paper sack to her left hip and unlocked the inside door that connected the garage of her Georgetown town house to the kitchen. She was exhausted, but that seemed to be her natural condition these days. A good therapist could have told her that the physical symptom, along with her lack of appetite, was caused by depression. But she didn't want to see a therapist. Her nerves were just too raw, her emotions too vulnerable to open herself up to any more strangers. She'd had enough of that recently to last a lifetime.

To the outside world she'd presented the image of a woman adjusting to past trauma. When she allowed herself to think about her mental state, she admitted privately that she felt as though she were existing inside a dead, gray cave. Somehow she was going to find a way out. She just didn't have the strength to do it yet.

The couple who had been renting her house had vacated the month before, so she was able to move in as soon as some of her household belongings arrived. Instead of hiring a cleaning company to put the place back in order, she'd elected to do the polishing and scrubbing herself. The physical labor sent her to bed every night so tired that she was asleep almost as soon as her head hit the pillow. But that was what she wanted.

This evening she'd gone out to the Safeway to lay in a supply of scouring powder and bathroom cleaner so she could get started again first thing in the morning. In the bottom of the bag there was some canned soup and two of her favorite gourmet cheeses along with crackers. She gave herself two brownie points for that.

She walked into the dining room and stopped in horror. The box of dishes she'd left on the table was turned upside down, newspaper and broken crockery scattered about the room. But there was something else that made her heart stop and then leap into her throat. In the center of the gray rug were several small congealing red puddles. Blood.

She had started to back out the doorway when the glint of light on gray metal caught her eye. Her unwilling gaze lifted toward the archway that led to the living room, and she screamed.

Propped on the couch was a rumpled, desperate-looking man, his dark hair shaggy around his haggard, mustached face. The blood that had stained the dining room rug had made a little trail to the couch and soaked into the white velvet cushion beside his left arm. The gun in his other hand was pointed at her stomach.

"Don't scream again."

The face was contorted. The voice was the one she still heard in her troubled dreams. "Aleksei! My God! What—?"

"Just give me the wolfhound figurine and I'll be on my way."

The voice she remembered? No. A trick. A mistake. This voice was as cold as the dead of a Siberian winter.

"The wolfhound," he snapped. Talking to her like this was tearing him apart. But he must leave quickly, for her sake.

"I—I don't have it."

"You're lying."

"No. It's in the luggage that's been delayed."

"Sweet mother!" He tried to raise his left arm. The look of agony that crossed his features made her stomach lurch. Then he seemed to remember where he was. The gun leveled at her once more. At all cost he must keep her from sympathizing with him and just get the hell away from here.

She stared at his red-rimmed eyes, feeling something between despair and numbness. The void he'd left behind had almost destroyed her. Now here he was breaking into her life again, a wounded animal ready to strike out. Would this man who'd once held her so tenderly really shoot her? She honestly didn't know. But if he were capable of that, maybe it was the best way to end her misery.

Slowly she began to advance across the carpet.

"Stay back."

"No." She reached his side and knelt. For a silent moment his blue gaze locked with her brown one. Then he muttered a curse and dropped the gun onto the sofa cushion.

Vitality seemed to seep out of him even as she watched. "I have to get out of here, Julie. If I could find you, others can too." His voice was barely above a whisper.

"Oh, God. Aleksei, tell me what this is all about."

"Anything I tell you puts you in more danger."

"Dammit! I've heard that line before. You said Cal was using me. You're using me too!"

"Yes." He was so tired. He didn't have the energy for any more pretense.

"What did you hide in the wolfhound?"

"Can't tell you." The words were slurred.

"Did you make love to me so I'd take it out of the country for you?"

It seemed to require a tremendous effort for him to make his eyes focus on her. Slowly, slowly the hand that had held the gun moved up so that the fingers could tenderly touch her lips. "No." The hand fell back. His head slumped to the side. She realized that he had passed out.

Dear Lord, what was she going to do now? She slid up beside him on the sofa, cradling his head against her chest, stroking his face, his hair. Her fingers clutched his good hand, warming the chilly flesh. In a few moments she felt him stir.

"How long?" he whispered.

"How long were you unconscious?"

He nodded.

"Not long. Let me call a doctor."

"No!" The syllable was edged with panic. It seemed to bring more adrenaline to his system. "No doctor. Have to get out of here."

She eased him back against the cushions again. "You can't. You must know that."

"In my flight bag. Stimulant capsules."

She looked at his gray skin. "A stimulant would probably kill you."

"Julie..."

"Tell me. Give me some information. Aleksei, in the name of God, play fair with me just once." He was so weak. The demand wrenched at her insides, but she had to make it. She had to know. Her fingers pressed over his. She needed to maintain the contact.

He closed his eyes, gathering his strength. Finally his voice rasped, "Dan and I were working together."

Julie sucked in her breath. "You told me he wasn't doing anything against the interests of his country."

"He wasn't."

"Then . . . ?"

"*I* was."

She stared at him, her mind suddenly processing information in new ways. Aleksei Rozonov, a KGB agent giving away his country's secrets. It still didn't quite compute. "Why didn't Cal know? He's CIA, for God sakes."

"Not the CIA. Another organization. More secret. Can't . . ."

"You must have a code name. Tell me that."

He hesitated, made a decision. "Raven."

Dan's calender. The *R*s. "Was he supposed to meet you the night he was killed?"

"Yes."

"And the theater?"

"We always had . . . backup meeting."

"Then that's why the notations on the calendar came in pairs?"

"Yes."

"What did you hide in the wolfhound?" she asked gently.

"Vital information . . . for your government."

Her eyes swept over his ravaged appearance. He had gone through hell to get here. "You're in the country illegally?"

He closed his eyes, not bothering to answer.

"Who shot you?"

"KGB."

She had made her own decision. "Can you walk a little way if I help you?"

"Don't know."

"We're getting out of here."

AMHERST GORDON tossed the FBI report he'd been scanning onto his desk. His thin lips were set in a grim line.

"What do you think about this evening's shoot-out at the OK Corral?" he asked his assistant.

"You mean the mysterious murders in the BWI satellite parking lot?"

"Um-hum."

"Those two dead men aren't from the Clayton gang. I'd say they were Soviet agents."

"My thought exactly. And I'd be willing to bet that they were looking for the same person we are."

Connie nodded. "The fact that *they're* dead and he isn't is a hopeful sign."

"Marginally. We still have a lone agent on the loose whose chances of getting through to us are almost nil. We don't know if he got out of Spain with the information we need, and we don't know if he's been wounded. The only thing we do know for sure is that Moscow is trying to kill him." He paused and stroked his chin. "That does make it more likely that he has the Topaz material. Unfortunately, it also means that he's better off shooting first and asking questions later—which certainly doesn't make the job of contacting him any easier."

"You forgot to mention that if the American authorities find out he's here, they're going to consider him a threat—and fair game."

Gordon's expression darkened. "Yes, we mustn't leave out that little detail. So what would you do if you were in Aleksei Iliyanovich Rozonov's shoes?"

"Find some help."

"Too bad Conti is out of the country on that damn opera tour. If he weren't, I'd bet on the Raven showing up at his New York apartment. I thought about trying to get him back—with a fake appendicitis or something. But by the time he'd get home, it would probably be too late."

"So who else would the Raven trust with a secret that could change the balance of world power?"

Gordon laughed harshly. "No one I know of off the top of my head. That's why I want you to start cross-checking our data bases.'' He paused and looked thoughtful. ''And get those McLean debriefing tapes from State. Dixon's cockamamie operation threw her into contact with Aleksei several times. Maybe she learned something from him that will give us a clue.''

Connie looked doubtful.

''Dammit,'' the Falcon rasped, ''I know it's a long shot. But long shots are all we have at the moment.''

''I'll get right on it.'' She turned back to her computer, a feeling of urgency making her usually steady fingers tremble slightly. There was not a doubt in her mind now that some operative of the KGB was going through the same kind of search she was about to initiate. It was just a question of who found Aleksei Rozonov first—the Falcon or the assassins.

JULIE DUMPED the cleaning products out of the bag onto the kitchen floor and opened the kitchen cabinets. Into the bag and another one went some food. It took her only a few minutes more to throw a few changes of clothes into a suitcase. The gun she stuffed gingerly back into the flight bag.

After loading the few supplies in the car, she cranked the right front seat down so that it was in full reclining position. If only she could make Aleksei more comfortable. But it was the best she could do with a Toyota.

When she reentered the living room, his head was thrown back against the cushions and his eyes were closed.

Sitting down beside him, she touched his face tenderly. His skin was cool and damp. But his lids snapped open.

''It's only about thirty steps to the car. We'll take it slowly.''

''Where are we going?''

''My uncle has a little place near Solomon's Island. I've been there before. It's very private, very secluded. He suggested that I use it to relax and gave me the key.''

''Julie, you don't know what you're...'' In his weakened condition, the long speech was too much.

"I love you. That's all I need to know." As she said the words, she realized their truth. *She loved him.* She had known for a long time but hadn't been able to admit it, even to herself.

For a moment his expression registered shock mingled with an intense joy that he had no right to feel. He tried to speak again but she silenced him with her palm.

"We can talk about it later. You're the one who said it was important to get out of here."

"All right." The gravity of their situation took precedence over any emotional considerations.

She looked at his arm. Thank God there was no more fresh blood. "Do you need anything before we go?"

"Water."

She brought him a large glass and helped him drink. He was terribly thirsty but even swallowing seemed to sap his energy.

The walk to the car was agonizing. Though he leaned heavily on her shoulder, he could barely stay on his feet. The way he sank into the seat made her want to cry. But she couldn't allow herself that luxury.

Julie headed east out of the city through Upper Marlboro and then south along the Chesapeake Bay. Her hands gripped the steering wheel so tightly that they ached. She drove with one eye on the road, one on the rearview mirror. No one set of lights seemed to be constantly behind her. She had so little experience in this kind of thing, but Aleksei's life—and hers—might depend on that judgment.

It was a two-hour ride that seemed more like ten. Every time the car hit a bump, she glanced anxiously over at the man beside her. Mercifully, he slept.

The beach house loomed dark and silent at the end of a winding private drive, but it looked like a haven after the harrowing ride. As they pulled to a stop in the gravel parking area, Aleksei stirred.

She put a reassuring hand on his shoulder. "We're here, safe and sound. You wait in the car. I'll open up and come back for you."

He nodded.

Julie turned on a few lights and raised the windows. The house felt stuffy, but the decor was pleasantly rustic, with white wicker furniture and sisal rugs. After bringing in the luggage, she opened Aleksei's door. To her surprise, he pushed himself to a sitting position with his good arm.

"Don't..."

"I'm a little better. I must have needed the sleep."

Still he had to lean on her as they climbed the wooden steps to the wide front porch and made their way to the living room couch.

"I should get you into bed," she murmured, gazing down at him with concern. "You need rest."

He shook his head. "Not yet. Sit beside me."

She looked at him questioningly but obeyed.

He searched her face for a moment before starting to speak again. "Julie, there's a bullet in my arm. It has to come out, and I don't think I can reach it."

Her eyes widened. "You want *me* to do it? You can't be serious."

"I'm perfectly serious. Bring my flight bag over. There are some things in it that you're going to need."

"Aleksei, we must call a doctor."

"I can't explain a gunshot wound to a doctor."

She had to knit her fingers together to keep her hands from trembling. The hot, close air of the house seemed to press in around her.

"First, we have to cut my shirt off."

"Aleksei..."

"I'm not going to get better until the bullet is out!"

He was right, of course. "You insist that we have to do this alone?"

"Yes."

"How do you know so much about this?"

His laugh was harsh. "Part of my training. Now get the bag."

The note of command in his voice made her obey. She wondered vaguely if he'd ever used that tone to force a squadron of troops to follow him into a hail of machine-gun fire.

"This could be messy. Maybe we'd better go into the kitchen."

She helped him to the Formica table. Just removing the blood-encrusted shirt made him grit his teeth and brought beads of perspiration to his upper lip. It made her sick to her stomach to hurt him, but she followed his instructions. The arm looked mangled, bruised, and swollen. Julie brought warm water and clean towels to sponge off the dried blood.

"You've lost weight," she whispered, gently running her fingers across his chest.

"I'll tell you about my adventures tomorrow."

"I want to hear them." She was putting off the inevitable.

He told her how to check for arterial damage by taking his pulse. It was fast and weak. He flexed his fingers to show her that the nerve pathways were intact. Then he examined the arm with the fingers of his right hand. The bullet was on the outside near the shoulder. She could see where it had tunneled through lean flesh.

"Well, I don't think I'm going to lose the arm."

Julie swallowed convulsively. Was it a grim joke, or had that been a real fear in the back of his mind?

"Lucky. It's only lodged in muscle tissue," he continued. "Look. You can see it under the skin."

She closed her eyes for a moment, gulping in oxygen. When she looked at the purple bulge, her stomach lurched.

"You won't have to probe. There's a sharp knife and alcohol in the bag."

"You came prepared."

"A necessity. I brought antibiotics too. I should probably start them now." Getting the tablets and a glass of water bought her another few minutes. Finally she could no longer put off the inevitable.

She studied his face. "It's going to hurt."

"I know. I promise not to faint again."

She turned quickly away and made herself busy. After finding a strong light and bringing it into the kitchen, she sterilized both the knife and her hands. But still she hesitated.

"Do you want a drink first? I think that's what they do in the cowboy movies." Her voice was shaky.

"My blood pressure's probably too low for any kind of depressant."

She lifted her eyes to his.

"Julie, do it."

He didn't move, didn't flinch, didn't call out as the sharp point of the knife pierced his flesh. Now she couldn't risk looking at his face. Out of the corner of her eye she saw his good hand gripping the edge of the table. The knuckles were bloodless. She bent her concentration to the job, as though she were simply cutting into raw meat and not the man she loved. Only when the sweat from her forehead threatened her vision did she pause. Automatically she wiped it away with her forearm. Red blood welled in the incision, making it difficult to work. She hadn't been prepared for that. But somehow, after what seemed like hours, she got the bullet out and dropped it with a loud clank onto the table.

"Thank you," he whispered between gritted teeth, reaching up to press the bleeding incision together with his fingers.

"Oh, God, Aleksei."

"That was perfect. Now you just have to sew the wound together and put on a bandage."

If she had done the first part, she could do that.

By the time she finished, his skin was clammy, his brow covered with cold perspiration. He was starting to shiver, and his lips were tinged with blue. The ordeal must have sent him into shock.

"Let me put you to bed."

Leaning on her shoulder again, he allowed himself to be taken to a downstairs bedroom. After folding back the covers, she eased him onto the bed and began to loosen his belt. In a few moments she had stripped him to his white briefs. There was another extensive bruise on his hip and several recent abrasions. Her earlier appraisal was confirmed. He looked like a man who had taken a terrible amount of punishment to get this far. Quickly she pulled the covers back over his trembling body. He didn't open his eyes, and she wondered if he had drifted off to sleep as she brushed a kiss across his cool forehead.

"*Dushenka,* stay and warm me," he whispered.

"I will."

After taking off her own jeans and shirt, she slipped into bed beside him, turning on her side so that she could press herself against him and share her warmth.

Shaky fingers grazed her waist, her hip, the line of her leg. "I thought I'd never feel you lying next to me again."

"*Alyoshenka,* I'm here—for as long as you need me."

Chapter Fourteen

Yuri Hramov opened the door of the small office three levels beneath the main floor of the Soviet embassy in Washington, D.C. He and General Bogolubov had slipped into North America disguised as an elderly Swiss invalid and his devoted companion bound for a Toronto clinic and had quietly crossed the border in upstate New York. For the last week they'd been waiting anxiously for the Raven to surface. Two hours ago, an alert on the police radio band had brought some mixed news. Their quarry had landed. But he'd also escaped the airport reception committee.

As soon as Hramov had gotten the word, he'd put their fallback plan into operation and headed for Georgetown. Now once again, he hadn't been quite quick enough.

"His blood was all over the carpet and on the sofa. It was fresh."

"So you just missed the son of a whore." Bogolubov's voice was harsh, the knuckles of his beefy hands white.

"He leads a charmed life. But his luck will have to run out soon."

Yuri Hramov's deep-set eyes shone with an intensity that almost frightened the general. If he hadn't despised Aleksei Rozonov so much himself, he would have felt sorry for the man. He'd seen what Hramov had done to others he'd been sent to bring in. What would he do to someone who had humiliated him?

"What else did you find?"

"They got out of there in a hurry. She left her bedroom drawers open and cleaning supplies scattered all over the kitchen."

"The film he smuggled out. What about the film?" The general's tone had taken on a note of desperation. Back in Moscow he'd talked himself out of the mess the Raven had left him in. But it was only a temporary reprieve. Along with the Topaz report, Rozonov had included a secret dossier on his KGB superior. If any of that muck was made public, Bogolubov could kiss more than his dacha goodbye. He shuddered. He was too old to survive many Siberian winters.

"There was nothing that could be a Kremlin report, Comrade General. And I tore the place apart."

Bogolubov strove to keep the note of authority in his voice. "How far could she have taken Rozonov?"

"It depends on the severity of the wound. From the stains on the couch, I'd guess he took a bullet in his arm or shoulder. The blood loss will slow him down. But I assume he can stand a lot of pain. Maybe we'll be lucky and he'll develop blood poisoning or gangrene. Then he'll have to check into a hospital."

"If so, the CIA will get him."

"Don't count on it."

Again Bogolubov thanked the devil that Yuri Hramov was on his side.

"I spotted his car on the street," the hit man continued. "So they must have taken hers."

"Find out what kind it is—and the license number."

"Right." Hramov stood up and moved toward the phone, the lines in his forehead deepening every time his foot hit the floor. He knew something about standing pain himself. Almost anyone else would still be convalescing after the injury to his ankle, but he had asked specifically to be brought along on this assignment. He would get his revenge.

"Check the personnel roster," the general continued. "Find me someone with a good American accent stationed in D.C."

"Do you want Midwestern or Brooklyn?"

"Either, just so he can pass for a State Department employee when he starts calling McLean's friends and relatives. If we make it sound as though they need to get in touch with her right away, maybe someone can give us an idea where she's gone."

THE MORNING AFTER the impromptu surgery Aleksei's warm gaze followed Julie as she moved about the bedroom adjusting the window shades and straightening the covers. There was no longer any doubt of his absolute trust in this woman. But while she lightened his burden, he knew what kind of jeopardy was being shifted to her slender shoulders. Telling her about his espionage activities had been bad enough. He was also aware that by drawing her into his life he was making her as vulnerable as he to the likes of Yuri Hramov.

He pushed himself to a sitting position in bed. "Julie, I have no right to involve you in this any further."

She set down the tray of tea and toast she'd brought him for breakfast. "I thought I made it clear that I *want* to be involved."

Her dark eyes told him of the emotion behind the words. He sighed. "The key to getting myself out of this mess is to contact the Peregrine Connection, the intelligence organization Dan was working for. They're the only ones who can intervene on my behalf."

"I presume it's not as easy as simply calling them."

"No. For obvious security reasons, I don't even know where their headquarters is located, except that it's somewhere in the Washington area. The only thing I have is a post office box in Virginia that I can't be sure is still active, and a mechanism for setting up a mutual meeting."

"Which is?"

"An ad in the classified section of *The Washington Post* — under 'Animals and Pets for Sale.'"

"But you don't want to call it in from here. And you're in no shape to drive."

"Can you do it for me? You'll have to find a pay phone that's at least thirty miles away."

Her eyes flicked to the bandage on his arm. "I don't want to leave you for that long."

"I'll be all right."

Suddenly she realized she was adding to his problems by voicing her concern. "Are you selling a raven?" she asked lightly.

"Actually a mynah bird."

She brought him a pencil and paper and he wrote out the exact wording. "Get it for the next possible day."

"I will."

She left after she'd cleared away the breakfast tray and tended to his wound again. Because the injury was extremely painful, he showed her how to make a sling to keep the arm immobile.

THE MOMENT she returned two hours later, he wanted to know when the ad would appear. "Not till Monday," she admitted, aware that he was going to be disappointed. "The weekend deadlines are early. But while we're waiting, let me help build up your strength. I've even gotten some fresh beets at a produce stand. You can give me a critical opinion of my borscht."

He smiled and allowed her to fuss over him. There was no point in adding to her burden by dwelling on their precarious situation.

It had been a long time since someone had ministered to him like this. He knew that the soothing comfort carried its own danger. Devotion to a cause had brought him this far. Now at the edge of his mind was the tantalizing possibility of abandoning the weary chase and taking the personal comfort he knew he'd find with Julie McLean.

It was so tempting to say to hell with the rest of the world. He had plenty of money. Together he and Julie could find a hiding place in the Canadian wilderness. He wanted that so badly that he could picture their life in startling detail. The Canadian north would be something like the land he remembered, bitter cold in the winter, warm and tranquil in the summer. They could have a garden, raise vegetables, read the books he'd never had time for, listen to music. She was a good cook. She could learn the rich Russian dishes he loved. And in the nights . . . His face softened as he remembered again the taste and feel of her body.

He was still playing with the fantasy three days later.

"What are you thinking?" she asked gently. He had insisted on staying out of bed as much as possible during the day. They were sitting in wicker rocking chairs on the back veranda, watching distant sailboats skim by on the Patuxent River.

He turned to her, his gaze a warm embrace. Then his expression sobered. "Dangerous thoughts. I want to take you away with me somewhere safe and just live a normal, peaceful life. But the only thing that will buy us any permanent safety is to get the Topaz report to the Falcon."

She had seen him gain strength every waking hour, though she knew he was still in pain. During the days and long nights, he had given her a good idea of the peril through which he had maneuvered and what had been at stake. "Aleksei, haven't you done enough?"

The question firmed his own resolve. He must live in a world of realities, not fairy tales. "Don't you see, I haven't done *anything* unless the Topaz plot is exposed." The vehemence in his voice was as much for himself as it was for her.

She reached out and clasped his hand, knowing in her heart that he was right. "What turned you into such an idealist?"

His mind raced back over memories from his youth. "My father, for one. He spent his whole career trying to ease tensions between my country and the West. He couldn't move a mountain by himself. In the end, the disappointment killed him."

He had told her something of Iliyan Alexandrovitch Rozonov already. Although the father had given the son his values, she doubted they alone could have been enough to trigger his total rejection of his country's policies.

"There's more, isn't there?"

"*Dushenka,* you read me so well." A shadow crossed his face. "There was only one person I could ever talk to about it."

She waited, her chest tightening even though she didn't know the cause of his pain. "Can you tell me?"

He nodded. "I had two choices when I was young. I was from the privileged class. I could have carved out a comfortable life by turning my back on the problems. Instead I chose to try and make a difference. I joined the diplomatic corps. When the KGB offered me a commission as well, I accepted, knowing that many of the decisions that counted were made by them."

She twined her fingers with his and felt him respond to the contact.

"It was a disillusioning experience. You can't imagine the corruption, the deceit, the striving for personal gain and power that takes precedence over national interests."

"Like the game Cal Dixon was playing with my life, you mean?"

"No, much worse than Dixon. It's a difference in the way he was raised, what he was taught to expect out of life. In the Soviet Union it's different. My country's leaders act as though we're under siege—guns take precedence over butter. There isn't enough of anything to go around. Food, clothing, good jobs, decent housing, prestige, self-esteem." He hesitated for a moment. "Competent medical care." The last was said with such disgust that she saw some of his hidden anger.

He disentangled his fingers and stood up. She saw the restlessness in his expression as he walked to the porch rail. Enough questioning for the afternoon, she thought. He would tell her the rest in his own good time.

"Dushenka." He turned back to look at her. "We can't stay in this house much longer."

"Why not? No one knows we're here."

"Someone can find out. It's not safe to remain anywhere too long. Tomorrow we'll leave. It doesn't really matter where we are when we get the Falcon's reply to our advertisement."

"Aleksei, are you strong enough to travel?"

"Thanks to you, yes."

IN THE AVIARY'S small projection room, Connie ran the videotape back to the previous question. "Now, look at her face," she requested. "She's trying to keep her features neutral, but when anyone mention's Aleksei's name, they soften for just a second."

"You're right, I can detect the slight variation. How deep do you think the emotional involvement is?"

Connie didn't answer immediately. "Let me put up the last McLean tape, the one with Borman." They waited while she removed the previous cassette and inserted the new one.

As it played, the Falcon shook his head. "I'd say Borman's enjoying making her squirm. Sadistic son of a bitch, isn't he?"

"She's avoiding his eyes, and her breathing is shallow," Connie pointed out. "That could just be a reaction to being forced to discuss intimate sexual details with a stranger. But in this case, notice how carefully she's choosing her words, even under the obvious stress."

"So what's the bottom line?"

"I'd guess that she's in love with Aleksei Iliyanovich."

Gordon was thoughtful. "He's quite a man. She could do a lot worse—if circumstances were different. But she thinks he's on the other side. The real question is, if he came to her would she protect him?''

"Or would he risk going to her in the first place?"

The Falcon's brow wrinkled. "I just don't know. He's been a loner for so long, he might not trust anyone." He paused, gathering his thoughts. "Have you been able to reach her?"

"Negative. Her phone just rings."

"Then send someone down there. And do me another favor—run a check on Borman. He just doesn't hit me as a State Department type."

Later that afternoon they had a great deal more to discuss as they sat in the tropical warmth of the solarium having tea and watercress sandwiches. In an open cage in the corner a pair of rare cockatoos were grooming each other.

"So he's been there," Connie mused, looking at the photograph of the sofa and rug.

"And probably the KGB too," Gordon added. "But at least we know what they're looking for." He was holding the letter that had just been brought by courier from a post office box in Falls Church, Virginia. The envelope looked as though it had come via the Amazon jungle. "Damn incompetents," he muttered. "You'd think a letter could get from here to Madrid in less than three weeks."

A parrot fluttered to his shoulder and he paused absentmindedly to offer the bird a small sandwich.

"Well, we have the information now," his assistant said.

"I hope it's not too late to do us or the Raven any good."

"If McLean brought the figurine back with her, either she's still got it or the Russians do. But there's a chance it's still in her freight. Find out if the shipment's still on a boat or if it's arrived. I'm going to put in a call to the Director of the CIA." He stood up and flexed his bad leg. "One more thing, I need to buy a mynah bird. Let me know the minute an ad for one hits *the Washington Post*."

Connie nodded. "What agent should I tap for the meeting?" she asked.

The Falcon looked thoughtful. "Now that Dan Eisenberg's dead, there's probably no one Aleksei would recognize by sight. No, wait a minute," he added, remembering
an incident almost a year ago in Berlin when KGB Major
Aleksei Rozonov had helped save the life of another Peregrine agent. "Maybe there is."

"Are you thinking of borrowing Mark Bradley from the
Pentagon?"

"Yes, get the colonel down here right away. If Aleksei is
going to trust anyone on sight, it's Mark Bradley."

"I already took the liberty of alerting him. He's in a heli-
copter on his way now."

"Connie, you're damn efficient for a woman of your
age."

"And you don't seem to have lost your way with words."

JULIE DIDN'T QUESTION his decision to leave. That night she
packed her suitcase again before slipping into a light cotton
gown and getting into bed. They were still sharing the
downstairs room where she had taken him that first night.

"What were you doing?" he asked. He was lying on his
back, a pillow propped behind his head, another one easing the position of his arm. The white sling stood out against
the darker tones of his skin.

He had turned out the light, but the room was lit by the
silvery radiance of the moon. She smiled down at him.
There was a special intimacy to their nights together. In the
dark hours they had exchanged confidences, come to understand each other better.

Reaching out, she stroked her fingers lightly against his
naked chest. He preferred to sleep that way, she had discovered. She was more modest. "I was getting ready to leave
in the morning."

"Do you always take me at my word?"

"Yes, now."

"You remember when you were afraid of me?" His voice
was husky in the darkness.

"A lifetime ago."

"It hurt to see that in your eyes. But I didn't dare let you know what I really was—or how much I loved you. The night in Madrid when you brought me to your bed, I wanted to tell you then. Very badly."

"Alyoshenka." She turned to him in the moonlight, her lips seeking his. She had meant it to be a gentle kiss, but it flared into passion like a spark hitting parched kindling. His right hand came up between them, finding her breasts. Through the cotton gown he stroked first one and then the other, groaning as he felt the peaks bead beneath his fingers.

Her breath was ragged, her heart pounding wildly, as she pulled away. "Aleksei, you're still not well. You can't."

He laughed softly, taking her hand and carrying it lower. "I believe I can."

She closed her eyes, feeling his hot, hard potency. "You shouldn't."

"Dushenka, let me be the judge of what will speed my recovery. I need to bury myself in your softness, feel you tight around me, holding, clinging, loving."

She made a little sound of mingled pain and pleasure deep in her throat. What he needed, she needed too, had been needing as she'd lain beside him these past few nights.

Her hand closed around him, stroking, caressing. He felt like steel tipped with velvet. When he trembled in response to her touch, she knew a surge of desire and satisfaction at her power.

"Do you like that?" she whispered.

"I told you once before you have clever hands. Tonight they're too clever. Come back up here."

She released him, turning to look down into the cobalt of his eyes, her own expression serious and sensual all at once.

His hands stroked her dark hair. "You're going to have to take the initiative tonight." He gestured toward the sling on his arm.

"*Alyoshenka,* it will give me great pleasure to give you pleasure."

"Take off your gown." His voice had roughened with urgency. "I want to see your beautiful body, touch you, taste you."

In truth the gown had been a shield, to prevent their bodies from brushing in the night. Now he was telling her there was no need to hold herself away from him. His words made her feel radiant, desired, sexy. She sat up and faced him, pulling the shift over her head with deliberate eroticism. When her eyes met his again, his passion-filled gaze made her shiver with anticipation.

"Come here." His tone was husky and caressing.

She moved forward, knelt over him, looking into his eyes as her fingers played across his face, his hair. Lovingly his hand drifted over her breasts. Then he took her shoulder and pulled her gently forward so that his lips could continue the caress.

"Oh . . ." The wiry brush of his mustache lightly scoured her tender skin. Her exclamation of pleasure turned into a little sob as his mouth found one nipple.

He tasted, stroked, sucked—and felt her fingers tangle more urgently in his hair.

"I see you like that," he whispered.

He turned to the other breast, repeating the moist caress while his hand stroked down her ribs and tried to reach farther. She felt him start to sit up, heard him wince, sensed his frustration as he fell back.

"Let me come to you." She slid forward until he could reach the curve of her hip. She felt his fingers move inward, find the warm, dark place that was her womanhood.

His knowing touch set her body on fire, making her ache for a closer joining. She could feel his readiness. Gently she moved up onto the cradle of his hips and lowered herself on him. As he entered her, a soft gasp left his lips.

"Ahh, I can tell *you* like *this,* my love," she laughed softly.

"You are magic," he replied, reaching up with his good arm, pulling her closer.

Her own little cries mingled with his as she moved above him. Each new stroke brought its own thrill of discovery. She reveled in the control and power she felt and the electric response of the man beneath her. The potent sensations they created together urged her to a faster rhythm. His hand and then his mouth caressed her breasts, intensifying her need for more of him.

The long weeks of separation had made her ravenous for the joy that only he could bring her. A fine sheen of moisture glistened on her olive skin as she strove for release.

Below her she felt his body stiffen.

"Julie! I love you." The words were a hoarse cry on his lips.

His shudders of gratification triggered her own shattering climax. She had felt ecstasy with him before. Now their spoken love for each other brought the experience new meaning.

She drifted back to earth slowly, her head on his shoulder, her hair a damp tangle around them.

"Until I met you, I didn't know what love was," she murmured.

His hand trailed across her shoulders. Love. Until a few months ago, he had told himself he would never feel that emotion again. After years of desolation, finding it with Julie was all the more sweet. He pushed her hair gently aside and kissed her face.

"I'm selfish enough to be glad that you were waiting for me," he admitted. "But, Julie, I am a hunted man, a man without a country. There is nothing I can offer you." His expression was melancholy.

She pressed her fingers to his lips. "Don't say that. This is your country now. You've already given more to preserve our freedom than most men born here."

He held her close against his side. There might be a home for him here, if he lived long enough to claim it, but for the present, the only haven he could imagine was in her arms.

For long moments neither of them spoke, then he stirred slightly. "This afternoon you asked me what turned me into an idealist," he finally said. "I didn't tell you the whole story. I couldn't deal with all of it then. But you have the right to know."

She could see the grief of past memories etching his features. "You don't have to say anything more."

"It will help you understand." He turned to her, his eyes questioning. "Julie, did my dossier say that I had been married?"

"Yes."

"It was a long time ago. We loved each other very much. She was the only person I dared share my real feelings with, the person who made the kind of life I led tolerable."

Her fingers sought his. "What happened?"

"She died bearing our child. They couldn't save the baby either."

"Oh, Aleksei." The pain in his voice tore at her heart.

"I might have accepted it if it couldn't have been prevented. Have you ever heard the Soviet establishment proclaim that our medical care is the best in the world? Don't believe it. Like every other national system in my country, our health care is riddled with incompetence. Anna developed diabetes during her pregnancy. But they didn't find out until very late. By that time the baby was huge. Some fool of a midwife let her go into labor when she should have had a Caesarean. She was in agony for hours, and all my political connections couldn't do a damn thing for her. Our son suffocated. Anna hemorrhaged. Even then, they could have saved her with the right injection or even surgery, but..."

"Oh God, Aleksei, what a terrible nightmare."

Tenderly, so as not to press his injury, Julie put her arms around him. She wanted to take away the sorrow he'd buried inside himself for so long and envelop him with her love.

"For a long time it made me hate." His voice was harsh. "Then it strengthened my resolve to do something to change things. When a man who had known and respected my father—an American who called himself the Falcon—cautiously approached me, I was ready to listen." He had told her that part of the story earlier. Now he closed his eyes and let her comfort enfold him.

"Are you all right?" she asked gently after a time.

His lips grazed her brow, her cheek. "I feel better. Sharing the memory makes me feel closer to you."

"I'm glad. The more I know about you, the more I understand why I was drawn to you from the first."

"*Dushenka,* I don't deserve you."

"You deserve anything that brings you happiness."

"And you, Julie. So do you. I've taken so much from you."

She drew back so that her eyes could meet his. "Aleksei, you've given me more than you can possibly realize. You've taught me how to share myself with another human being."

Still his eyes told her of his disbelief.

"It's true, *Alyoshenka.* My parents gave me everything that money could buy, but they didn't teach me about love. It wasn't that they meant to be cold, exactly. But there was a stiff formality in their relationship with people and a high value placed on controlling their emotions. I grew up thinking that was the way I was supposed to be."

"I assumed your cool exterior was just for me."

"No, for the whole world. I think now that's why the turmoil you stirred up in me was so disturbing. It was something I couldn't ignore and couldn't control."

"I didn't know how to fight my reaction to you either. Even knowing the risks to both of us."

His hand stroked the silky skin of her lip. With his new understanding of the special gift she'd given him alone, it was impossible not to luxuriate in her closeness. He had been isolated for so long that loneliness had become part of his existence. The years had muted it into a dull background ache—until he met this woman. Then suddenly the knowledge of what he lacked had swelled into a fierce, piercing agony. He pressed his face against her soft breasts, almost shutting out the knowledge of what it would be like to exist without her now.

She sensed his need, and again it mirrored her own. Even when she felt him drifting into sleep, she kept her arms around him.

It was close to two in the morning when the phone rang. Her eyes open, she turned automatically to reach toward the bedside table. His hand shot out and grabbed her wrist.

"Don't answer it."

The ringing stopped, then started again.

He sat up and flung the covers off them. "Get dressed. Someone suspects we're here. We have to leave—right now."

Chapter Fifteen

Instead of heading directly for the southeastern edge of the city, they took the beltway around to Rockville. By the time they arrived at the park-and-ride Metro station, the first wave of early commuters had already filled the closest rows of the lot. Though there was a risk of discovery if they stayed in the Washington area, Aleksei had insisted on remaining near the capital.

"The Peregrine Connection has to be somewhere close by," he'd argued. "I must stay here."

She looked at him with concern as they made their way to the station. To help fade into the crowd, he'd sacrificed the comfort of the sling. If someone on the train jostled his arm, it was going to hurt.

But no casual observer would know what he'd been through recently, she thought with satisfaction. Even in just a few days, she'd been able to put some of the weight back on his spare frame. The July sun had given him the beginning of a tan. And she'd trimmed his longish hair, making it more respectable. The mustache she'd left alone, because she found she liked it for a number of reasons. When she looked at him, she felt a surge of possessiveness. To the outside world his features might be hard. But she knew they could melt to infinite tenderness when she took him in her arms. He belonged to her in the most elemental way, and she belonged to him.

He was wearing slacks and a sport jacket she'd purchased over the weekend at a shopping center near the beach. They were a good fit, she noticed as she gave him a quick inspection out of the corner of her eye. Her own bright sundress, wide-brimmed hat, and sunglasses had been acquired at his suggestion. "Find an outfit you'd never buy, something that's completely out of character," he'd advised.

On the drive back to D.C., he'd suggested they stay in a large, prominent hotel. "It's arrogant. Like Poe's 'Purloined Letter.' Hide something in full view where no one will think to look," he pointed out.

She laughed and he raised a questioning eyebrow.

"Back in Madrid, when I felt caught between you and Cal Dixon, I thought of Poe, too," she explained. "Only it was 'The Pit and the Pendulum.'"

"I see. Which was I?"

"The pendulum, I think."

From her list of candidates he selected the Mayflower, which was centrally located just a few blocks from the White House.

But as the subway train sped along the tracks into the city, she felt her anxiety rising. KGB agents might be waiting for him here. Suppose he was delivering himself into their clutches?

Despite his calm, matter-of-fact manner at the registration desk, she had to clasp her hands behind her back to keep them from trembling as he signed in a Mr. and Mrs. James Gunderson and left a cash deposit.

It wasn't until the bellboy had set her suitcase on a luggage rack and closed the door behind them that she felt a small measure of safety. The room was beautifully appointed with a dark wood Queen-Anne-style armoire, desk, and bed. The velvet sofa and chairs that formed a conversation group in an alcove by the window were done in green and mauve. The same color scheme was picked up in the drapes and bedspread.

"Capitalist luxury," he observed dryly as he noted the phone and hair dryer in the bathroom. But when he saw her tense expression, he quickly crossed the room and put his arm around her shoulder. She pressed her face against his chest, letting his familiar scent and warmth envelop her.

"Our second time in a hotel room together," he murmured.

"Yes."

"I ached to make love to you then."

She tipped her face up so that her dark eyes could meet the cobalt of his. There was a basic, unalterable honesty between them now that no one could ever take away.

She smiled. "Even then, even when I was afraid of you, I went to pieces every time you touched me."

"I felt it. It drove me wild with need for you."

Their lips met in a long, lingering kiss. Their lack of any other liberty made the freedom to love each other all the more sweet. His fingers were sensuously stroking the back of her neck when a knock at the door made her jump in alarm. Though Aleksei's body stiffened, he didn't remove the arm that clasped her to him.

"Yes?" he called out, his now steely blue eyes focusing on the painted wood as though he could pierce it.

"Housekeeping. Do you need any extra towels in the bathroom?"

"No. Thank you."

There was a pause and they heard a knock at the next door down the hall.

Julie let out the breath she'd been holding.

"It's all right," he said. "We're both jumpy." His fingers stroked her shoulder. "But maybe you should get ready to leave. The sooner you finish the business we discussed, the sooner you'll be back."

She closed her eyes for a moment, resisting the inevitable. But he was right—tracking down her missing shipment of household goods was probably going to take some time. She couldn't make the calls here.

"Will you rest while I'm gone?"

He nodded and turned to fold down the bedspread. Then he took off his jacket, and she saw him wince as he moved the injured arm. She tried not to watch as he unbuckled his shoulder holster and transferred his gun to the drawer beside the bed.

After adjusting the pillows, he lay down. It looked like a lazy pose, but his eyes were alert as he studied her appearance.

She noticed his appraisal and pirouetted. "Will I do?"

"Very well. I'd have to look twice to know you were Julie McLean."

"I was taught the art of disguise by a crafty Russian."

"Your lover?" His light tone matched hers. He was determined to send her out into the city feeling confident.

Her eyes locked with his. "Yes. Definitely my lover."

"When you get back, he'll order room service—champagne and caviar for two."

"And what for dessert?"

"Something very delectable, I'm sure."

The moment the door closed behind her, his manner changed. After securing the safety chain, he picked up the early edition of *The Washington Post* he'd purchased at the subway station.

When he turned to the classified section, his lips thinned. At the top of the page was a notice explaining that due to an unrecoverable computer error, a number of ads called in on Saturday had been lost. The management apologized for any inconvenience this might have caused and offered to run any ad that was lost for an extra day.

Quickly his eyes scanned the "Animals for Sale" section. No mynah birds. *Chyort!* He couldn't wait another day.

Getting off the bed he started to pace the room. Every minute wasted meant the Topaz documents were more likely to fall right back into KGB hands. He had to get to them first. The fact that he didn't even know where they were made him feel as impotent as a Soviet negotiator at the

SALT talks. The walls of the expensive hotel room seemed to close in around him. His first instinct was to get out of there and *do something*. But until he found out where that Russian wolfhound was, there was really nothing he *could* do. Hopefully, Julie would find that out for him. Then her part in all this would be over. Once he knew where the film was, he was going to leave her here so she wouldn't get caught in any cross fire.

AFTER STEPPING OUT into the muggy Washington air, Julie walked to a nearby Metro stop. Picking a destination at random, she got off at Van Ness Center. Then, armed with several dollars in quarters, she found a phone booth and started making calls. As she'd expected, she was shuffled from office to office. No one seemed to have the information she wanted. But each secretary was sure that another department would be able to help. On the tenth call she reached the supervisor at a warehouse in Newport News.

In her best State Department manner she inquired about the status of the missing shipments. A rough voice on the other end of the line said "Just a minute," and she was put on hold. Five minutes later the voice said, "Part of McLean's stuff has arrived. Part of it's still in transit. That's why it hasn't been sent. So tell the pushy broad to stop bitching that her stuff wasn't waiting on the doorstep when she arrived home early."

"I wasn't aware of a prior complaint."

"Well, someone up there must be raising bloody hell. This is the third call we've had today about her damn stuff."

Julie stared at the receiver, her face gone white.

"No one else has been authorized to follow up on the shipment."

"Like I told the rest of them, honey, if you want any of those boxes before they're scheduled to be delivered, you're going to have to show me a signed SB34G."

"Just exactly where are you?" Julie probed, trying to keep her voice steady.

"Are you new at this or something? It's always Building Seven."

Hanging up, Julie gave in to a few moments of panic. Suddenly she realized that despite all Aleksei's elaborate precautions to hide their whereabouts, she'd been hoping that the men he had battled in the airport parking lot were the only ones after him. Now here was cold hard evidence that they weren't. Before she realized what she was doing, she had dialed the private phone number in her uncle's Senate office.

"Julie, where are you? Are you all right?" His tone was strained.

"I'm fine," she lied.

"The State Department's frantic to get in touch with you."

"What's wrong?"

"Your town house has been vandalized. Julie, I was down there. It's a mess. And there's blood all over the living room. What kind of trouble are you in? Whatever it is, I can help."

The offer was so tempting. Maybe he could give them sanctuary. But then she remembered the way Aleksei had looked when the knock on the door had penetrated their hotel room. It was better not to trust anyone, even her uncle. "This is something I have to work out by myself."

"Don't hang up."

"I've got to. Your line may be tapped."

"In the Senate Office Building? It better not be!"

"I'm sorry, Uncle Bill."

"Please let me help," he said.

"If you want to do something, don't talk to anyone about me. All the people who are showing concern may be the same ones who tore my house apart."

"Good God, what do you mean?"

She wanted to tell him. But anything she said could be just as dangerous to Aleksei as the KGB agents after him. With a sick feeling, she realized that she never should have made the call. Instead of giving away anything more, she simply hung up.

SLAVA BOGOLUBOV set down the sheaf of reports that had arrived that afternoon and turned from the desk in his temporary command post under the embassy. "Good," he murmured. "Very good. Our inquiries have paid off."

Yuri Hramov, who had been shuffling a pack of cards at a square wooden table, paused. "So we're going to make our move," he observed quietly. The calm control in his voice belied the feeling of power that suddenly pumped through his body. He'd been cooped up in this hole with the general for days now, and he'd quickly found he couldn't stomach the man. But he'd also learned to read the old toad. Slava had acquired caution in Madrid. He wouldn't risk defeat now. So he must think the odds were in his favor.

Bogolubov's gaze flicked to Hramov's large, square hands and the blue-and-white deck that now rested between them on the table. The slapping, almost gurgling noise of shuffling cards had come near to driving him mad. He'd tried to close his eyes and pretend he was listening to a babbling brook deep in a cool pine forest. It hadn't worked. How could a human being sit there mindlessly shifting and manipulating little pieces of shiny cardboard? More than once he'd pictured himself jumping up and knocking them to the floor. He'd been stopped by the certain knowledge that he'd end up down there too. But the ordeal was almost over now. With an air of command, he handed the assassin a sheet of paper and watched as his eyes flicked across the lines of Cyrillic, amazed once again that the big gorilla could actually read.

"Has transportation been arranged?" Hramov asked.

"Naturally."

"And you authorize me to proceed as I think best."

The general hesitated. Before he could speak again, Hramov stood up and walked toward him. It took every ounce of will to hold his ground against the maniacal look in those close-set eyes. "Don't you think I want to bring him in alive?" Hramov grated. "Don't you think I'd rather take him on with a knife instead of a gun? Or perhaps a length of piano wire slipped over his head from behind. I wouldn't choke him to death. At the last minute I'd let him gasp for breath. Then I'd turn him so that he could see my face."

Bogolubov swallowed convulsively. For a moment he felt that wire around his own throat.

"I will bring him to you alive," Hramov promised. "Unless it's a choice between him and me. And what about the girl?" he asked. "Do you want to question her too?"

"Yes."

"I know how to make women talk."

The general had a strong stomach, but he didn't want to hear the details behind the icy assurance in those words.

THERE WAS A STRANGE feeling of elation at being back at the Aviary, Colonel Mark Bradley, USAF, thought as he pulled out a wrought-iron chair and sat down. As always, the lush tropical foliage and the squawking parrots seemed so out of place at the headquarters of an intelligence operation. Yet as soon as Amherst Gordon's silver-headed cane hit the flagstones of the solarium, Mark could feel that familiar surge of excitement associated with a new mission. Ever since his narrow brush with death in Berlin had earned him a promotion and a new assignment in the situation room at the Pentagon, Mark had been itching to get back to field duty with the Peregrine Connection.

"I'm glad Eden accepted my job offer," Gordon began affably. Mark was glad too. Eden Sommers had put her life on the line to free his mind from control of the East German sadist Hans Erlich. Mark was now married to Eden. There were few women who would be willing to stand by him through the dangerous episodes that would always be a part of his life. Her acceptance of a job as staff psychologist at the Aviary was just more evidence of her commitment.

"Yes. But frankly I've been a little jealous lately."

"Oh, nothing exciting happening on your watch at the Pentagon?" Gordon asked as he pulled out a chair and sat down.

"Not much. Hijackings, terrorist attacks." His dark eyebrows lifted. "Two KGB agents illegally in the country who decide to shoot it out at a local airport."

Gordon hid a grin. "Funny you should mention that last."

"I've seen the CIA reports. They can't explain it. I have the feeling maybe you can."

At that moment Constance McGuire came in with a tray bearing a silver coffee service and a thick manila folder. She set the pot in front of Gordon and handed the dossier to Mark.

"One of you can pour while the other reads," she explained.

Mark had read only a few paragraphs when she heard him whistle between his teeth. "So Rozonov was working for you all along."

"You understand why I had to keep that information under wraps."

"Of course."

"Well, now you have the opportunity to return the favor he did for you during that gunfight in Berlin."

"He saved my life by drawing Erlich's fire. What can I do for him?"

Quickly Gordon briefed him on the recent developments in the Topaz affair and what role he wanted Mark to play.

"Have you gotten the CIA to lay off?" the colonel asked.

"I tried. I don't know. Once they get a deep cover operation going, it feeds on its own momentum. I suspect the people in charge lose control."

"I suppose you have a way to give me the authority I'll need."

"The secretary of defense is working on that now."

"How do we bring the Raven in?"

"I'm waiting for an ad in *The Washington Post*. Meanwhile, I want you to familiarize yourself with Aleksei's and Julie's files."

Early that afternoon Mark was still in the library reading when the critical-message alarm sounded.

Connie was tearing the message off the computer terminal as he and Gordon arrived in the shielded office.

"This has got to be the break we're looking for. A woman whose voice matches McLean's pattern called Warehouse Seven in Newport News and located part of her shipment. She called back an hour ago to ask them to have it ready tomorrow morning."

The Falcon turned to Mark. "That means that Aleksei must be planning to get it out of there tonight, so you're going to have to hustle."

"Did you get me the authorization papers?"

"They're supposed to be on their way. You'll leave the moment they arrive."

JULIE EYED the packed bag beside the hotel room bed. "You were going to leave without me, weren't you?"

"Yes. It's better that way."

"It's more than a four-hour drive to Newport News. How were you planning to get there with only one good arm?"

"I drove from BWI to Georgetown with a bullet still in it."

She made a derisive noise. "And collapsed on the sofa in a pool of blood."

"Don't you understand, *dushenka?* I don't want anything to happen to you."

"Yes." Her tone softened. "I have equally strong feelings about you. That's why I'm going to be your chauffeur. You need every advantage you can give yourself. If you rest instead of driving, you'll be in much better shape to face whatever we find down there in that warehouse tonight."

"A Russian woman wouldn't give such back talk."

"Too bad you had to get mixed up with the likes of me."

Though he tried to keep a stern face, new admiration for her shone in his eyes. Despite the tension of the moment, he laughed. "All right, prove your worth and pay the bill while I collect the rental car I've ordered."

She eyed him suspiciously. "I'm not letting you out of my sight. We'll settle up at the front desk together and get the car together too."

RICHARD BORMAN rubbed his hands together with ill-concealed excitement. "Julie McLean's made her move," he announced, looking across the small cinder-block room at Gary Conrad, the agent who was working with him on this case. Conrad was a good man—cool and precise. What's more, his electronics skills were going to be invaluable.

Conrad put down the circuit diagram he was studying and glanced up. "You don't think she'd try anything alone, do you?" he asked.

Borman had already considered that question. "No. I'm willing to bet Rozonov arrived at her town house the night she disappeared, and she took him to some sort of hideout to recuperate." He paused and laughed. "She must have some bedside manner. If they're on the move again, he's put himself back on the active-duty list."

The other man snorted. "The R & R might have been fun. But I don't envy him that welcoming reception his friends in the KGB arranged."

"True," Borman admitted.

Conrad hesitated. There was something that didn't feel right to him in all of this. He couldn't put his finger on it, and he really shouldn't question a seasoned operative like Borman, so he voiced his doubts cautiously. "From over here, it looks like a power struggle in the KGB, but I thought those guys didn't break ranks."

"Rozonov must have stepped on someone's toes."

"Bogolubov?"

"We know the general's had a grudge against him for years. That makes it interesting that both he and Rozonov have dropped out of sight as far as the Soviet grapevine is concerned." He glanced at his watch. "Let's grab some supper before we settle in."

Conrad bowed to the inevitable. "Shall I take the first shift?"

"We'll flip for it after dinner. I have a feeling it's going to be a long night."

HE TRIED TO GET HER to register at a motel near the interstate highway and wait for him. She shook her head. "I'm staying with you."

The adamancy of her voice told him an argument would simply be a waste of precious breath. The only way he was going to leave Julie McLean behind tonight was to tie her up, and he didn't have the heart for that.

As a compromise, they both checked into a Quality Inn, where they could change and leave their luggage. He knew he should rest before the evening's mission. Instead, the moment the door closed behind them, he pulled her body against the tense length of his. Her arms came up to hold him even closer; her hips moved against him. His mouth on hers was urgent, seeking, plundering. She was no less rapacious. The fire between them reached flashpoint in seconds.

He cursed when the injured arm got in his way. She tore off his clothes and hers as well. Then they were on the bed, their bodies a hot, desperate tangle against the quilted spread. He felt the first shudders of her climax almost as soon as he had entered her. A few more hard, driving strokes brought his own release. Then he was cradling her damp, panting body against his.

"Did I hurt you?" His eyes were grave, his voice unsteady.

"God, no."

"I've never needed a woman that badly."

"I've never needed *anything* that badly."

They clung together, fingers stroking, lips caressing. "Will you stay here?"

"No. I love you too much to let you go alone."

"And what if I love you too much to let you come with me?"

"I'll rent another car and follow you."

He sighed. "We might as well leave as soon as it gets dark."

"Tell me I'm going to be some help to you, not a hindrance."

He stroked her face. "You'll be able to unpack the boxes a lot faster than I will." And if we have to run for it, maybe one of us will get away, he thought silently, not allowing her to hear his fears.

Though she tried, she couldn't control the shiver that raced across her suddenly cold skin.

An hour later they both changed into jeans, dark T-shirts, and jogging shoes. It was almost frightening, Julie thought, the way his manner altered as he dressed for the night's activity.

Her heart was beating wildly as they approached the warehouse complex near the docks. She stole a sideways glance at his profile. His face seemed perfectly calm.

She had known he was a trained professional. But he proved it now. As she waited where he'd parked half a block away in the shadow of a wall, he made his way noiselessly toward the corrugated steel building that was designated Warehouse Seven. Total concentration went into the task at hand. He noted doors and loading docks as he circled the structure. He'd made Julie ask about the layout of the interior when she'd put through her second call. Now he wished he had a floor plan.

When he came back, his expression was grim. "I don't like it."

"Why not? It seems quiet enough."

"That's the problem. It's too quiet. Where's the night watchman?"

She shrugged. "Maybe they have an alarm system."

"No. If they do, it's without bells and wires."

"Do you want to leave?"

"No."

She opened the car door. "Then let's get it over with."

He'd selected a side door into what he judged was the storage area. It yielded rather easily to the tools in his flight bag. Before he opened the door, he drew his Makarov.

They paused to get their bearings in the dim light. Somehow she hadn't been prepared for the size of the place. Or the air-conditioning. Cold storage, she thought, unable to keep from shivering. The sudden image of a sheet-covered body laid out on a slab in the morgue flashed into her mind. She didn't want to lift the sheet and see the face. Resolutely she forced her thoughts back to the task at hand.

Boxes and packing crates were stacked on massive shelves all the way to the metal rafters. Now she understood why Aleksei had told her to arrange to have her shipment brought to the front of the building. Only the very bottom crates were accessible without a fork lift.

Julie fought the impulse to back out of the enclosure. Aleksei had been right; the silence was ominous. He stood for a few moments listening intently and probing the darkness with wary eyes. Finally he motioned with the gun for her to follow him.

It was impossible to control her wayward imagination. Each time they reached a cross aisle, she pictured a hairy arm whipping out and grabbing Aleksei by the neck.

The office was supposed to be near the front and walled off from the rest of the storage area by a metal and glass partition. As they came to the end of the long aisle down which they'd been creeping, she saw the little room bathed in dim light. Fifty feet from the door was a stack of four cardboard boxes.

Aleksei pointed and raised a questioning eyebrow. Julie nodded and moved forward. On the side of a large crate she could see a stenciled notation. It said "McLean" and "dining room." She looked on the back of another. Its legend was "living room."

The illumination coming from the office was enough in which to work. Aleksei laid the Makarov on the floor and, one-handed, helped her move the "living room" box to the cold concrete. From his bag he produced a knife and slit the thick tape along the top seam.

Julie knelt and reached for a newspaper-wrapped object. It was a brightly painted Spanish pottery plate. She'd packed several like it, but she didn't remember this particular design. After glancing quickly at Aleksei, she went on to the next package. Inside the newspaper was a miniature Toledo sword. Holding it in her hand, she studied the engraved metal, a sick feeling rising in her throat.

"What's wrong?" Aleksei whispered.

"This isn't mine."

"Are you sure?"

"Positive."

"Try something else!"

Dutifully she unwrapped a crystal vase. She had never seen it before in her life.

A flicker of movement from the corner caught his attention. Before he could reach for the gun on the floor, a warning rang out across the darkened building.

"If you move, I'll kill the girl." The voice was guttural, the words in Russian.

Chapter Sixteen

Julie watched in horror as a lean but muscular man moved forward from the shadows. With his own gun trained on Julie's abdomen, he kicked Aleksei's Makarov under a forkloader. Every detail about him impressed itself on her consciousness. His face had a bland smoothness, as though someone had taken a sharp knife and planed away all the rough edges. Yet the eyes, like dead slag, conveyed a malevolence that was terrifying. As he moved, he favored his left leg slightly. When he reached her side, he grabbed her arm and jerked it behind her back.

Both the physical contact and the stab of pain made her gasp. Out of the corner of her eye she saw Aleksei grimace as though the pain had been his. He took a step forward.

"Stay right there, Major," the muscular man warned, still speaking in Russian. "Or she gets it now."

"Your business is with me, not with her," Aleksei replied in the same language.

Julie strained her ears to catch the rapid exchange of dialogue.

"No, both of you," the man who held her arm in a vise snarled.

"She's useless."

"But apparently quite valuable to you."

Aleksei shrugged. "She's been very cooperative. A pleasant diversion. But I was through with her anyway."

Hramov laughed. The sound was like a file scraping across a sheet of metal. "Save your breath, Raven. Lies won't do her any good now. But maybe I'd be willing to give her a quick death if you fork over some information."

Aleksei's eyes flicked to Julie's ashen face for just a second. "What do you want?"

"The Topaz material and whatever you stashed away concerning the general."

"It's not here, Hramov."

The hit man gave Julie's wrist a half turn and she screamed. "You can do better than that," he grated. "You wouldn't have risked breaking into this warehouse unless you knew you could get it."

Torturous sensations shot up Julie's arm and into her shoulder. Yet through the agony something tugged at her memory. What was it? It was hard to think straight when she was on the verge of passing out from pain.

"The Topaz material," the assassin persisted. "If you don't tell me where it is, I'll break her arm for starters and then go on to all the other bones in her body."

"You bastard. I should have finished you off in Madrid," his opponent gritted.

"Your mistake."

As the upward pressure of her arm increased, it was harder to hold unconsciousness at bay. The temptation to give in to oblivion was almost overwhelming. Yet that wouldn't help her or help Aleksei.

Think, she commanded her brain. Hramov. She'd heard that name from Aleksei. This was the cold-blooded killer who had come after him the morning he'd left her in Madrid. And then suddenly an important detail snapped into place. In the scuffle Aleksei had wounded Hramov in the ankle. That was why the man was limping. Dare she use that weakness to her advantage?

Her gaze skittered down to the gun. It was still pointed at Aleksei. Anything she tried could tighten Hramov's finger on the trigger. But if she didn't act, he was surely going to kill them both.

"I'll tell you where the film is," she panted.

"Where?" Hramov demanded.

"You're hurting me. Let go of my arm."

The pressure slackened and Julie twisted a few inches away, glad her captor could not see her face. Her eyes sought Aleksei's and blinked twice rapidly. It was the best she could do. There was no way he could know what she had in mind, but she hoped he'd be ready to take advantage of the opportunity she was going to give him.

"If you're lying, you're going to regret it, bitch," Hramov snarled.

Aleksei watched her, his face neutral. She had told him the goods in the box weren't even hers. What was she up to? Whatever it was, he had better be ready.

"I wouldn't fence with you," she meekly countered, hoping Aleksei would pick up on the phrase they had used that day in the boat. But his expression gave away nothing.

She didn't allow herself any more time to think. Calling upon skills she hadn't used since college fencing class, she made her move. In one smooth motion her body shifted to the side as though dodging an opponent's thrust. At the same time, her foot shot out and caught Hramov's injured ankle, scoring a direct hit. Though the KGB agent bellowed in pain, his finger still squeezed the trigger of the gun. But Aleksei was already dodging and ducking, even as she moved. The bullet missed his hip by inches.

He was across the space between them before she could let out the breath she'd been holding. Shoving her out of the way, he sprang at Hramov and wrestled the gun to the cement floor. The two men went down. She could see Hramov go for Aleksei's injured arm and heard an answering groan.

Both men had been hurt recently, but on the floor with the weight off his foot, Hramov had the advantage and he had had longer to recuperate.

What could she do to help, Julie thought frantically as the two men rolled back and forth, each struggling to incapacitate the other.

Hramov went for his opponent's throat. Somehow Aleksei broke the hold and flipped the assassin over, banging his head against the cement floor. But the cost of the effort was tremendous. She could see a dark red stain spreading across the fabric of Aleksei's shirt. Shuddering, she pictured the stitches she'd used to close the wound now ripped apart, exposing raw flesh. Though Aleksei fought with a strength that must have come from desperation, she knew he couldn't keep it up.

She had to find a way to help him. Aleksei's pistol had disappeared under the crates. Hramov's lay forgotten on the floor. Silently she inched toward it. In a moment her fingers closed around the hard grip. She'd never fired a pistol before. She didn't dare aim at Hramov as he rolled back and forth on the floor with Aleksei. Instead, she pointed the weapon at the ceiling and pulled the trigger. The recoil sent her stumbling backward, but she kept her footing. She also got the attention of the struggling men. Almost reflexively, they both rolled away from the sound of the fire. Hramov turned to face her, saw the weapon, and ducked behind a crate. She pointed the pistol in his direction, but she simply couldn't pull the trigger again. She heard the sound of running feet. Hramov must be escaping, but the only thing she felt was relief.

Crossing rapidly to Aleksei, she knelt beside him and put down the gun as he struggled to sit up.

"Hramov may bring reinforcements. We must get out of here," he rasped, his face contorted with pain.

"Can you make it?"

"I'll have to. Give me the Makarov."

"Don't touch that gun!" another voice commanded. Her hand froze in the act of reaching for the weapon. Oh, God, what now?

Her eyes lifted, afraid of what she was going to see, yet helpless to stop herself from finding out. To her stunned disbelief, she saw special agent Borman. For a moment her mind clutched at relief that the Russian assassin hadn't returned with reinforcements. But one look at Borman's uncompromising face and the automatic pistol in his hand told her he wasn't the cavalry arriving in the nick of time. His stance announced that rescue was the last thing on his mind.

"Ms. McLean, how interesting to find you here, and in such unsavory company," he drawled, and then turned to another agent with a sharp order. "Handcuff them."

Gary Conrad knelt to comply. A cold circlet of metal clicked around Julie's wrist, fastening her to Aleksei.

She felt as though she'd awakened from one nightmare to find herself in the middle of another. The double jeopardy was almost too much to cope with, but she forced her mind to keep working rather than simply skittering away from the new horror. "You've got the wrong man. Hramov's the enemy. Aleksei's a defector. He's on our side."

"Aleksei, is it. I thought the two of you barely knew each other. But don't worry about his buddy. I'm sure he won't get too far. You can all have a reunion down at the Navy brig."

"You said you were with the State Department."

"Actually, that was *your* assumption. We're CIA."

"CIA?" It took a moment for Julie to assimilate the new information. "I thought the CIA didn't conduct operations against American citizens," she finally managed.

"This business started in Madrid, and we're tracking KGB agents illegally in the U.S." He looked pointedly at Aleksei.

She turned to him. "Tell them what's going on," she begged.

An emotionless mask had settled over his features; his blue eyes were icy. They seemed to drill into hers, but he said nothing.

"You see, your Russian lover doesn't have anything to say in his own defense," Borman gibed. "But maybe later he'd like to comment on the tapes we've made here this evening."

Tapes? These cold-faced agents had calmly watched the scene with Hramov and recorded it on tape? Julie's mind rebelled from such mercilessness.

With no regard for Aleksei's injury, Borman pulled the wounded man roughly to his feet. Julie was yanked up with him. She wanted to whisper some reassurance to him, yet there was simply no comfort she could give.

In her present condition, walking with her wrist bound to his was difficult. When she stumbled she heard him draw in his breath and knew she must be causing him pain. She wanted to seek his fingers with her own, but that would just make it worse.

Outside in the moonlight she saw two brawny men shoving Hramov into a waiting van. It pulled away, and Conrad spoke into a two-way radio.

"The other one will be along directly," he told Borman. "We might as well search them first."

The agent in charge turned to his captives. "Get over against the wall." He gestured with his automatic pistol. "Spread your legs and raise your arms."

Though the command was humiliating, Julie knew it was useless to protest. However, when she tried to raise the wrist cuffed to Aleksei, he groaned and staggered sideways.

"Damn," Borman said, his eyes flicking to Aleksei's bloodstained shoulder. "Rozonov's in worse shape than I thought. Cover me while I take the cuffs off."

Aleksei waited, willing his body to remain relaxed until there was a chance of making his move. From the beginning, he'd decided there was no way he would let these men take him in. A corner of his mind admitted that it was partly Soviet indoctrination. For years it had been drummed into him that the CIA was the ultimate evil on earth. But it was more than that. There was also his instinctive reaction to the hard-faced Borman, who was probably disappointed that he didn't have a KGB assassination on videotape. Like Calvin Dixon back in Madrid, he was obviously ignorant of the Peregrine Connection's existence. As far as this CIA operative knew, he had a hostile enemy agent and an American traitor under his gun. Without proof, he wouldn't believe a word either of his prisoners said. The only one around who could corroborate the fantastic story was Yuri Hramov, and he'd cut out his own tongue before he'd help a Soviet defector.

Aleksei glanced to the right. He could see the lights of another car in the distance. It was probably CIA reinforcements. If he waited another minute, the odds would be a lot worse. His heart rate accelerated. His arm hurt like the very devil again, but he couldn't let that slow his reflexes. The key turned in the lock of the steel cuffs, but still he forced his body not to betray his readiness.

The metal bracelet seemed to come off in slow motion. When his arm was finally free, he raised his good hand to his forehead, as though disoriented. Then he slumped sideways against the metal wall.

"Oh, good. Just what we need," Borman groaned, stepping forward to take the weight of Aleksei's sagging body. It was the move the Russian had been waiting for. With the speed of a panther, he turned, grabbing Borman around the throat and pulling him hard against his own chest.

"My ring has a poison dart in the center," he informed the other agent in thickly accented English. "Toss your gun over to the side or your friend has an instant heart attack."

The junior man hesitated. He knew the KGB had such poisons. Still, it could be a trick.

Julie's eyes flicked to the ring with its serpentine pattern and sapphire stone. She'd noticed it in Madrid, but she'd never imagined its being a deadly weapon.

As she watched, Aleksei brought the sapphire stone up to Borman's line of vision before slowly moving it toward the artery pulsing in his neck.

"Do as he says!" Borman hissed, a bead of sweat rolling down his brow.

The gun clattered to the pavement at Aleksei's left.

"Quick, get Borman's pistol," he instructed Julie, "then pick up the one on the ground." His English had returned to its normal level of precision.

Aleksei's manner had taken her completely by surprise. For a moment she stood paralyzed.

"Julie, move," he ordered.

The tone of his voice snapped her body into compliance. Turning toward the senior agent, she pulled the pistol from his belt and handed it to Aleksei.

As he pushed Borman to the ground, he straightened. "Crawl over there with your friend so I can cover you both."

Breathing heavily, the agent complied while Julie went for the other weapon. As she bent down to get it, her eyes were blinded by the headlights of the van screeching to a halt in the gravel lot. Dimly, she saw a tall man jump out, and she raised the gun in his direction.

He hadn't expected to be looking down the muzzle of a service revolver, Mark Bradley thought as he stepped out of the van and took in the tense situation. Two men, CIA agents he assumed, were on the ground. Above them stood another man with a gun. The weapon pointed at his own stomach was held by a woman.

The man in charge had to be Aleksei Rozonov, also known as the Raven. With the mustache, haircut, and weight loss, the Peregrine operative was barely recognizable. But his air of command was unmistakable. The dark-haired woman must be Julie McLean. In the State Department photographs he'd studied, she'd looked cool and aristocratic—and hardly capable of shooting anyone. But from the distraught expression on her face now, he suspected that if he went for his own weapon, she might well pull the trigger of the gun she held.

That wasn't the only problem however. He'd expected to find Borman in charge. With Aleksei running the show, his executive order wasn't going to be worth a counterfeit ruble unless the Russian was willing to cooperate with him. They'd only met once—in the middle of a gun battle. Would the man really remember him?

"Aleksei Rozonov," he called out. "It's Mark Bradley. The Falcon sent me to pay back that favor I've owed you since Berlin, but it looks as though you have things under control."

"Move over into the light. Let me see your face."

Aleksei waited as the new arrival complied. His hair was darker, and the scars on his face were less evident but still there. It could be a clever makeup job.

"Berlin, you say? Give me more details."

"The auction gallery, the Ludendorf diary, Hans Erlich."

The touch of self-accusation in Bradley's voice when he said that last name was more convincing than the words themselves. Erlich was the megalomaniac East German doctor who had come within inches of controlling Bradley's mind.

"So we were working for the same organization all along, Colonel."

"Yes."

"Let's get out of here."

Julie found her voice. "Aleksei, who is this man?"

"A friend."

Borman had been watching the interchange with disbelief. "Wait a minute, what in the hell is going on here?" he challenged, pushing himself to a sitting position on the ground.

"I'm taking over this operation," Mark said.

"The hell you are." The CIA man seemed to forget that he wasn't in a position to demand anything.

"I have an executive order that gives me complete authority over these prisoners," Bradley informed him. As he spoke, he withdrew a paper from his breast pocket and tossed it into Borman's lap.

The agent hurriedly scanned the words. "You think I'm going to accept this?"

Mark glanced pointedly at the gun Aleksei still held. "It looks to me as though you don't have any choice. Besides, it will go down a lot better than trying to explain how an unarmed man got the drop on you."

"He had a ring with a poison dart," Conrad interjected.

Aleksei shrugged. "A small deception."

Borman uttered an oath. Before he quieted, Mark was standing over him with a spare set of handcuffs.

"I'm sorry to have to do this, but we can't take any chance of being followed." Quickly he chained the two agents together. Then, pulling them to their feet, he marched them off toward a storage room in the warehouse. "I'll make sure someone comes to get you out in a couple of hours."

As their footsteps faded, Julie circled Aleksei's waist with her arms and buried her face against his chest. His good arm came up to cradle her head, his fingers stroking lovingly the thick waves of her hair.

"So cool in the face of danger, so courageous," he murmured.

"No, I was terrified," she contradicted.

"What matters is that you didn't panic. If you hadn't tricked Hramov—" He felt her shudder against him, and his arm tightened protectively. "*Dushenka,* did you understand what I said to him?"

She nodded against his chest. "Yes. But I realized why. You were trying to save me."

"I shouldn't have wasted my breath. Even Hramov could see how much I cared about you."

They clung together in silence, each comforted by the steady beat of the other's heart. Finally, Aleksei spoke again. "Julie, I was terrified too. I've never been so terrified as when I saw him grab you."

She knew the admission didn't come lightly.

"Thank God it's over," she whispered. Then she realized she was drawing on his strength again, and he was the wounded one, not she.

"Why don't we get in the van," she suggested.

A few moments later, Mark Bradley reappeared and slipped behind the wheel. Two miles from the warehouse, the threesome abandoned the CIA transportation and climbed into the back of an ambulance. "I figured we could exceed the 55-mile speed limit in this without being stopped," Mark explained as he pulled a white jacket over his dark clothing.

He turned to Aleksei. "There's a doctor waiting for you at the Aviary, but it's a three-hour ride. Do you need medical attention before that?"

"I can wait."

"You're going to let me look at your arm and then lie down," Julie countered.

Mark laughed as he helped the Raven into the back of the vehicle. "I can see who's really in charge of this operation."

The two men exchanged glances in silent acknowledgment of the critical role Julie had played.

Mark showed her where to find the supplies she needed and then started the engine as she began to delicately cut away Aleksei's bloodstained shirt. He heard them talking softly, heads close together as she worked. It was impossible not to see how deeply they cared about each other. They were well out on the highway before Julie brought him back into the conversation.

"Maybe you can talk some sense into him," she called out. "He wants to sit up front."

Mark grinned silently, understanding full well the other man's reaction to reporting to his new headquarters flat on his back on a stretcher. Yet he knew what the Raven had already been through. "Aleksei, I promise to warn you when we're getting close to the Aviary, so you can get up. But right now, I agree with Julie. Try to get some rest.''

"You will tell me before we arrive?"

"Yes. Now get some sleep if you can. You're going to need your strength." Mark laughed a knowing laugh. "The old bird's been waiting a long time to bring you over here, and patience isn't one of his strong points.''

Chapter Seventeen

The Falcon and the Raven clasped hands, then embraced like veterans of a difficult military campaign meeting to commemorate the battle. When the gray-haired man stepped back, his eyes were moist.

"Aleksei Iliyanovich, at last. You don't know how much it means to me to have you arrive safely."

"Sir, it's good to be here." He stood up straighter, struggling with his own emotions, trying not to look terribly disheveled.

Constance McGuire came forward to repeat the embrace. "Welcome," she said simply. Then she held out her arms to Julie. "We all owe you so much," she murmured.

The young woman felt herself warmly enfolded. "I wish I could have done more."

"No one could have," Connie assured her quickly.

The sun was just breaking the crest of the mountains behind the Aviary, painting the eastern sky a warm gold shot through with vibrant pink. Not just a new day, Julie thought, a new beginning.

Right now, however, she was bone weary and a bit disoriented. While Aleksei had slept on the drive up, Mark Bradley had told her a bit about Amherst Gordon, Constance McGuire, and the Aviary. But the reality of the Peregrine Connection was still overwhelming.

There was a moment of panic when she and Aleksei separated in the front hall. The idea that they might really be safe was simply too new to cope with.

Gordon's assistant seemed to understand. "It's all right," she soothed. "He isn't going to leave the building. But he needs to see the doctor, and then Amherst wants to talk to him."

"Yes, of course."

"Let me show you to your room. You can catch a few hours' sleep, and then we'll all have brunch down in the solarium."

Julie allowed herself to be led upstairs to a double bedroom beautifully decorated with colonial antiques. "I've put a few things in the closet for you and Aleksei," Connie explained, opening wide mahogany doors to display a varied selection of outfits. "But you can pick some clothes of your own later."

After her hostess left, Julie treated herself to a hot shower, then dried her hair and donned one of the satin gowns hanging in the closet. By then she was so tired that she simply turned back the brocade spread and crawled between the pastel blue sheets. She was asleep almost as soon as her head touched the pillow.

A slight shifting of the mattress awakened her several hours later. When her dark lashes fluttered open, she found herself staring up into the deep cobalt of Aleksei's eyes. He was sitting on the edge of the bed, dressed in a dark terry robe, his hair wet from the shower. Despite his recent ordeal, he had never looked more content, she thought.

"*Dushenka,* I'm sorry I woke you."

"I'm glad." She raised her arms to him, and he bent to gently brush his lips against hers, before going on to explore her cheeks and forehead. The bristly line of his mustache was a pleasure she had come to enjoy.

"How are you?" she asked softly.

"Better than I've ever been."

She clasped him more tightly, feeling the strong wall of his chest, the steady beat of his heart, the quickening of his body as it pressed more snugly against hers.

"Did you come up here to make love to me?"

"Um-hum." As his lips traveled down her neck and then found the upper curve of her breast above the satin of her gown, her body arched into his caress.

Later, hand in hand, they came downstairs to brunch. Gordon was waiting in the solarium with its shiny green tropical foliage and brightly colored birds. Julie looked around in amazement. Aleksei watched her reaction with amusement. He'd had a similar one when introduced to the parrots earlier.

"A rest seems to have done wonders for you," Gordon observed drily.

"Yes. Thank you," Julie returned politely, looking away so that he couldn't see the warm flush of reaction spreading across her cheeks.

"There have been some interesting developments this morning, so I hope you don't mind if we cover some business while we eat."

Connie came in with briefing folders, which she laid beside the napkins while they filled their plates with eggs, country ham, and blueberry muffins at the buffet.

After everyone had been seated again, Gordon filled them in on what had happened in the early hours of the morning.

"You probably noticed," he began, turning to Julie, "that the box you were unpacking didn't contain your household goods."

She and Aleksei exchanged glances. That had been all too obvious.

"Well, the box you were unpacking was a decoy. Your goods were impounded by the CIA, and Borman and Conrad did the unpacking." He paused and carefully spread butter on his muffin.

"And—" Connie prompted.

"And one of the items they inventoried was the wolf-hound."

"Does the CIA know what they've got?" Aleksei questioned, putting down his fork.

"Actually, they don't have it anymore. The film was delivered here this morning and developed."

"It's hard to believe Borman went along with that," Julie observed.

"He jumped at the chance. As far as the official records show, he and Calvin Dixon get credit for recruiting a top-level Russian defector and acquiring the Topaz report," the Falcon told her.

Julie shook her head. It wasn't fair for Borman and Dixon to come out shining in glory after the way they'd treated her and Aleksei.

The man in question reached over and covered her hand with his. "It's better this way," he said. "It puts them on our side and keeps the Peregrine Connection out of the spotlight."

Gordon nodded his agreement. "Julie, you've earned the answers to any questions you might have about this whole operation. What points can I clarify for you?"

Aleksei had risked his life to get the Topaz material to Washington. She only had the sketchiest idea of its significance. "Tell me about Topaz," she said.

Gordon laughed. "I like a woman who understands the bottom line." He turned to Aleksei. "Why don't you fill her in."

The younger man paused, finding it hard to believe that he was finally in an environment where he could express his opinions about Topaz without being shot.

Connie caught the expression on his face. "Despite the comfortable surroundings, this place is as secure as NORAD headquarters," she said.

He laughed. "Old habits die hard." Then he turned to Julie. "In your job, I'm sure you were aware of at least some Soviet disinformation efforts."

"Yes. Even in Madrid we had to funnel considerable resources to countering them."

"Well, imagine a lie so convincing that it could dupe the top U.S. military strategists into thinking they had a foolproof deterrent to an important new Soviet weapon."

"What do you mean?"

"First, secret documents wind up in U.S. hands confirming Soviet reliance on a new chemical weapon. Next, the U.S. is given the opportunity by the Soviets to capture samples of the antidote to that weapon—a chemical called Quadrozine, along with substantiation for its effectiveness. Naturally, the U.S. is delighted to get the secret information. They analyze the compound, manufacture their own test batch, and run some field trials. Initial results confirm that Quadrozine works as claimed. So the U.S. produces millions of units of the stuff and dispenses it to all its troops, and to all NATO troops as well."

"How does disinformation figure into this?" Julie questioned.

"Except for the fact that the Kremlin is putting a new chemical weapon into production, it's all an elaborate hoax. In reality, Quadrozine is not an antidote, but a death trap. It's highly unstable. Over an eighteen-month period it breaks down into something about as effective as water."

"Then any troops using it as a defense to the new chemical weapon would be wiped out," Julie interjected. "But I can't believe we'd be that gullible."

"Unfortunately, our top military strategists *wanted* to believe in it. So they bought it lock, stock and vial," Gordon informed her. "Aleksei had only given me the most general of warnings about the plan before our communications link was severed. Without proof, the Pentagon went right ahead putting out competitive bids for the billion-dollar Quadrozine contract—and cut off funds for research into finding a real antidote."

"You see, they thought it was easier and cheaper to go with something the Russians were already using, rather than do their own research," Connie added.

"But now I have facts that will stop them," Gordon continued, tapping the Topaz report. "Aleksei's brought me the whole Soviet disinformation strategy on Quadrozine. It includes documentation of recent field trials in which captured Afghan troops were injected with eighteen-month-old Quadrozine and then gassed with the new chemical weapon. They died in agony."

Julie shuddered.

"That report was what Aleksei risked his life to bring us," the Falcon continued. "That and the formula for the real antidote."

Julie looked at the man she loved, her eyes full of even more respect for him. "I see now why you couldn't trust me or anyone else in Madrid after Dan was killed," she murmured.

"Topaz had to be my highest priority."

"I understand."

"Once the Kremlin knows the West has the real antidote, they won't use the weapon," Connie added. She didn't go on to spell out the implications for the cause of world peace. But the foursome at the table knew.

Brunch ended with the arrival of the assistant secretary of defense who had come down to talk to Aleksei and the Falcon. Julie had her own debriefing with Constance McGuire. Though thorough, it was certainly a lot less stressful than the sessions at the State Department.

In the afternoon they talked about the future.

"What do you want for you and Aleksei?" Connie asked gently.

Julie thought for a moment. "I want to make a home for him, bear his children, spend the rest of my life with him."

"It may not be so easy," Connie pointed out. "He'll have a lot of adjustments to make. Russians have a different— more rigid—view of the world. Sometimes they find our

open society confusing. Their choices at home are so limited that they have trouble making decisions about things we
take for granted. And even if he disagrees with his country's policies, he's going to be homesick for Mother Rus-
sia."

"I can help him deal with that. Besides, he's lived in the
West. It won't be quite so strange."

Connie gave her a direct look. "What if he won't let you
have children?"

"What do you mean?"

"He told you about his wife?"

"Yes."

"He's lost so much. He may be afraid to take the risk of
losing you that way."

"That wouldn't be rational."

"But he may not be able to help himself."

"I hope I can change his mind," Julie insisted.

"Helping him change will take a lot of love and a lot of
understanding."

"Two things I have a lot to give."

IN DEFERENCE TO Aleksei's injury, the schedule included a
long rest period before dinner. Julie came into their room to
find him lying on the bed, a brooding expression on his
chiseled features.

"Were the discussions difficult?" she asked softly, remembering her own frank conversation with Connie.

"No."

She sat down beside him and took his hand. "Then what
is it?"

He looked away.

"Aleksei, don't shut me out, not after what we've been
through together."

"What if that's the best thing for you?"

"You arrogant bastard!"

His head whipped around to find her brown eyes fierce,
the golden lights in their depths fairly sparking. His own

gaze was equally telling. For a moment they were locked in silent, mental combat.

"Let me make my own decisions," she finally whispered.

"What if I told you Bogolubov isn't going to rest until he knows I'm dead."

"I'd say it was the job of the U.S. government to protect you from him."

"And if they can't?"

"Just exactly what are you getting at?" she countered.

"The Raven has to die—and very convincingly."

Her face went pale. "Stop fencing with me."

The ghost of a smile played at the corners of his lips and his fingers tightened on hers. "Any man who fences with you is likely to get cut to ribbons."

"Is that a compliment?"

"Yes." His expression grew serious again. "Julie, Gordon and the CIA are working together on a plan to make it look as though I've been killed. Afterwards, I'm going to have to assume a new identity."

"And what about me?"

"Bogolubov doesn't really want you. You could go back to your family and your new job. In a few years, after things have settled down, we could get back together."

"Is that what you *really* want? Or what you think is best for me?"

He didn't answer.

As she stared at him, one of the things Connie had said came back to her. Gordon's assistant had speculated that Aleksei might be afraid of losing her. Was his behavior now a manifestation of that fear?

Moving closer to him, she bent to press her cheek against his. "*Alyoshenka*, I love you," she whispered, turning to caress his face with her lips. "We're not going to be separated. If you go underground, so do I."

"I can't ask that of you." She caught the raw edge of pain in his voice.

"Aleksei, I told you, I make my own decisions. Where you go, so do I."

His fingers tightened almost painfully around hers, and for a moment he shut his eyes. "There's one more thing you have to know, then. The Falcon's plan involves a high degree of risk."

"Like what?"

"Placing me in a vulnerable position and then letting Yuri Hramov escape from CIA custody so he can come after me."

"Oh, God, Aleksei. He might kill you."

"Precisely."

HARMONY, VERMONT, population 105, was a picture book little town of clapboard houses nestled in the shadow of Bald Mountain. The only turnoff from the highway was almost ten miles away, so there was little traffic on Main Street and almost no business activity. The U.S. Post Office was in the back of the dry-goods store, the filling station got by with a delivery of no-lead gasoline once every three months, and the grocery carried only one brand of toothpaste.

It was a perfect hiding place, Julie thought, as she paid for her canned and frozen food at the cash register.

"You take care now," Mrs. Carter, the short, plump proprietor said as Julie picked up her two brown paper sacks.

"Oh, I will."

Outside, Hank Sutton and Sam Allen, the two unemployed laborers who usually occupied the chairs by the front step looked up lazily.

Julie nodded to them as she opened the door of her battered red Mustang and set the grocery bags on the seat.

Bert Greentree, the filling-station attendant, wiped a greasy hand on his overalls and watched her progress as she turned the car around and headed for the last house down by the creek, where the road dead-ended. Among other things, he was thinking that the car needed a tune-up.

Besides being an auto mechanic, Bert was a CIA agent, as were Hank, Sam, Mrs. Carter, and everybody else in town, except the two newest residents, Julie McLean and Aleksei Rozonov.

The Mustang pulled up in the gravel drive beside the unprepossessing bungalow at the end of the street. To any casual observer she and Aleksei might be visitors who had rented the house for several months. But that was hardly the case, she thought, glancing at the special translucent curtains that covered most of the windows. They gave what appeared to be an unobstructed view of the interior. That was all part of a carefully constructed illusion.

At the top of the porch steps, she took a deep breath before opening the door, bracing herself for the feeling of disorientation she always experienced when she stepped across the threshold. The view from outside was blocked by a wall against which rested a small pine chest. In fact, it was only a small part of the stage set. Inside, the little house was divided into U-shaped compartments, each positioned toward a different window. Facing every compartment were several three-dimensional holographic and movie projectors mounted in the ceiling. As she stood in the hall, Julie pushed a button marked J1 and saw an image of herself walk down the hall and into the "kitchen." No matter how many times she'd seen this happen, it still sent shivers down her spine. It triggered another electronically stored sequence of Aleksei getting up from a couch.

To anyone peering through the special optical filter curtains, it would look as though the two of them were living upstairs. That was precisely the idea. Crossing quickly to the basement door, she hurried downstairs, opened the combination lock on the steel barrier at the bottom, and stepped into the tunnel that connected the house to the real living quarters she and Aleksei were sharing.

When she entered the living room, he looked up, his face telling her that he'd been worried about her absence. "I'm glad you're back. Hramov was spotted in Connecticut last night. He's got to be arriving in town soon."

Aleksei had been on edge all week, just as she had. Waiting in a concrete bunker for the KGB agent to come and try to kill them was almost intolerable. But the next move must be his, and all they could do was sit tight and hope that the CIA's elaborate scenario played itself out as planned.

As she took the groceries to the compact kitchen, she marveled again that this whole crazy place even existed. Just exactly what kind of item in the federal budget had camouflaged its creation? You could stay in Harmony for a week and never guess it hid underground electronics labs that would put Disney's Epcot Center to shame.

Aleksei got up to help her put away the supplies. As he bent to take a can of tomatoes from the bag, he shielded her body from the lens of the close-circuit camera in the corner and brushed his hand possessively against her hip. She pressed her fingers over his and then turned back to the job at hand. Both of them had picked up little tricks that brought a degree of privacy in their fishbowl environment. When Gary Conrad had explained the necessity for twenty-four-hour surveillance, they'd reluctantly agreed. Only the bedroom and bathroom in the small apartment were off limits to the hidden cameras.

A portable cellular phone rang in the living room, and Julie's hand froze in the act of putting some tuna fish cans away. These quarters didn't receive random calls from aluminum-siding salesmen.

Aleksei crossed the room and reached for the receive button.

Bert Greentree was on the line, speaking from his shielded office. "Station one, this is station five reporting."

"Wolfhound here. What have you got for us?"

"He just stopped for gas and inquired about lodging in town. I told him Mrs. Smith sometimes rents a room."

"Thanks." He turned back to Julie.

"You don't have to tell me who's arrived," she said.

HE SPENT TWO DAYS casing the town, getting to know the locals on the pretext that he was working on a travel article for the Paris edition of the *Herald Tribune*. A number of them were willing to talk about the young couple who had rented the small white bungalow at the end of Main Street. "They're snooty, if you ask me," Mrs. Carter said. "Keep to themselves," Bert Greentree explained. "Except to visit Doc Hudson. She takes him there every Tuesday afternoon—regular like."

Slouched in the front seat of his car, with his fisherman's hat pulled down over his nose, Hramov watched the Tuesday ritual with interest. They must have thought they'd picked a good hiding place to be so open, he mused. And it would have been, too, if McLean hadn't left a credit card trail a mile wide from Newport News to Vermont.

It would be as easy as shooting clay pigeons to pick off that bastard Rozonov and his whore Julie McLean right here on the street. But that wouldn't be smart. Better to attach plastic explosives to the foundation of their house and set a timer. That way he could be on his way to Canada to meet the comrade general when the charge went off.

While the CIA had him in custody down at Newport News, he'd occupied his mind with thoughts of what he would do to Aleksei. Somehow, the idea of bombing the defector into oblivion had become an obsession.

For a moment he closed his eyes, as though to block out the unpleasant memories of what had happened during his captivity. At the navy brig there had been hours of intense interrogation, during which he was sure he hadn't told them a thing they could use. The trouble was, when he tried to recall the sessions, he couldn't quite bring them into sharp focus. It must have something to do with Rozonov's banging his head against the concrete warehouse floor. But he'd certainly been thinking clearly enough to make the most of an opportunity to escape when it had presented itself.

They'd been going to transfer him to D.C. But one of the guards had gotten careless. Hramov had taken the man as a hostage and then shot him in the knee with his own gun before disappearing into the city's dock area. From there it had been easy to get back to the room he'd rented. The CIA was hamstrung in their search for him because of the need for secrecy. Apparently the Pentagon wasn't any more anxious to explain Topaz to the American public than the Kremlin was.

"STATION FOUR, this is station seven. Hramov disappeared into the woods a half hour ago. We believe he's on his way to pick up the explosives he hid there."

"Is he heading for station one?"

"We don't have him in sight, but we will as soon as he comes out of the woods."

"We should alert Wolfhound and Bambi to sit tight. I don't want anyone upstairs—or even that reinforced door open—if anything's about to happen."

"Affirmative. But I'm having trouble calling Wolfhound. There's interference on the line."

"Damn! I'll bet the remote controls for the two systems upstairs are malfunctioning like they did last week and producing stray signals on the cellular phone."

"Maybe I should send Sam down to the street toward the creek with a fishing pole. If Hramov's in the vicinity, that should scare him off until we can get the frequency clear again."

"Do that and I'll keep trying to get Wolfhound."

AT THE END OF MAIN STREET, in the bunker, Aleksei pushed the number five button on the automatic dialer to call station five. Instead of a ring-through, all he got was a burst of static from the speaker and a blinking red light on the unit. *Chyort!* He looked at the equipment with disgust. He hadn't much liked this science fiction plan from the beginning, especially since it put Julie's life in danger. His condition for consenting had been that Gary Conrad would keep him fully informed about what was going on. Now the damn equipment wasn't working again.

He turned to Julie. "We had a problem like this with the remote controls on the projectors last week while you were getting groceries."

"Didn't Gary fix it?"

"He thought so. But you can hear for yourself that the communications system isn't working now." He gestured impatiently at the receiver. "I'm going up to do something about it."

There was a sick feeling in the pit of her stomach as he crossed to the cabinet near the five-inch-thick steel door that sealed off their hiding place. She watched as he pulled out a Colt service revolver and checked the ammunition clip.

He weighed the grip uncomfortably. The damn gun had never felt right in his hand. But Borman had balked at the very idea of anyone using a Makarov in a CIA operation. He'd been forced to go along with the change in weapons, since he was out of ammunition clips anyway.

As she watched him tuck the pistol in his waistband, her feeling of apprehension sharpened.

He turned toward a control panel by the door and flipped several switches. "I'd better turn off the system before I leave. It's disorienting walking around up there meeting images of myself."

"Aleksei, stay down here. It's too dangerous if we don't know where Hramov is."

"All the more reason why we have to reestablish communications with our eyes and ears on the outside. You stay at the phone and try getting through to Conrad or Greentree."

Helpless to interfere, she watched in frozen silence as he activated the inside lock and started up the stairs. She knew he'd reached the end of his patience with sitting around letting the CIA make his decisions.

Her hand automatically placed the call again, but she wasn't listening to the static still on the line. Instead she strained to hear any hint of trouble upstairs. Minutes crawled by, but the only thing she heard was the thudding of her own heart.

She was just turning back to the phone when the sound of gunfire made her finger freeze over the dial.

Oh, God! Hramov must be here! He must have come upon Aleksei in surprise. Instinctively her hand reached out and flipped the switch that activated the projection system once again. Then she pressed the buttons labeled A1, A2, and A3. Then, with no other recourse to save him, she fled headlong up the stairs.

AP HARMONY, VERMONT. THREE PERSONS BELIEVED TO BE ASSOCIATED WITH A LEFTIST TERRORIST GROUP PERISHED IN AN EXPLOSION IN THIS SMALL NEW ENGLAND TOWN YESTERDAY. THOUGH FEW DETAILS ARE AVAILABLE, THE FBI HAS INDICATED THAT THE TWO MEN AND ONE WOMAN WERE UNDER INVESTIGATION IN CONNECTION WITH THE MANUFACTURE OF HOMEMADE MUNITIONS. THE BLAST DESTROYED SEVERAL HOUSES AT THE WEST END OF MAIN STREET IN THE LITTLE HAMLET. THE MUNITIONS MAKERS WERE THE ONLY FATALITIES, BUT TWO RESIDENTS FISHING NEARBY WERE TREATED AT AN AREA HOSPITAL FOR INJURIES CAUSED BY FLYING DEBRIS.

ACCORDING TO SERVICE STATION OWNER, BERT GREENTREE, THE BLAST KNOCKED OUT WINDOWS ALL OVER HARMONY. HE ADDED THAT TOWNSPEOPLE WERE SHOCKED TO DISCOVER THAT AN ARSENAL WAS BEING MANUFACTURED AND STORED IN THE QUIET LITTLE TOWN.

THE FALCON'S expression was enigmatic as he finished the short news story on a back page of *The New York Times* and handed the section to his assistant. In a way it was fitting that this whole thing had started with an explosion and had ended with one as well.

Connie scanned the article. "Well, you told me to expect something like this, but it doesn't make it any easier to take."

In a rare show of affection, Gordon reached out and grasped her hand. "Connie, in our profession, we have to be philosophical. I wanted something a lot better for the Raven, too, but it wasn't meant to be."

"I don't like the way we had to work this out. He should have been proclaimed a national hero and been thanked by the President for his tremendous sacrifice."

"Well, at least he has the satisfaction of knowing that the Topaz material got into the right hands. It's already having the stabilizing effect on the balance of world power that he hoped it would."

"We owe him a lot, and Julie McLean too."

Epilogue

His name was Adam Ross. Once he had been a raven. Now he cast his lot with the eagles soaring majestically above the pine-covered mountains. The Black Hills of South Dakota were a perfect refuge for a man with a new name, a new identity, a new profession and a new country, he thought as he looked out over the rugged landscape.

Pushing his chair away from the word processor, he stood up. One thing was certainly true. It hadn't taken long to get used to his new wardrobe of comfortable jeans and bulky sweaters, he thought, stretching his long arms over his head. There was a nip in the air, and snow flurries had already danced past the floor-to-ceiling windows of the redwood and stone house that was perched to take advantage of the mountain view. He was looking forward to seeing the landscape blanketed in white.

The past few months had been difficult, and he knew there were still plenty of problems ahead. But the solitude and natural beauty of this place were having their own healing effect on the wounds of his body and soul. Throwing open the French doors to the deck that cantilevered over the valley, he stepped out and took a deep breath of the pine-scented air.

Nicole Ross, his slender, dark-haired wife, was standing by the railing. Nicole. They'd picked the name together. He loved the sound of it. He loved her. And he owed her so much.

She had saved his life, not just at the warehouse when Hramov had been pointing a gun at his stomach, but also in Harmony, Vermont. When the killer had surprised him working on the electronics equipment and wounded him in the side, she'd flipped the switch that activated the projectors. Suddenly Hramov had been confronted with multiple images of the man he'd come to kill. They'd drawn his fire long enough for the Raven to finish him off.

It had been Gary Conrad's decision to blow up the house and Hramov with it.

"That's what he came here for," the agent had pointed out. "Bogolubov will think you're dead and that Hramov somehow got himself killed in his own trap."

The Raven had seen the wisdom of the decision. The whole point of the Harmony charade had been to satisfy the general's lust for revenge. The amazing thing was that the CIA had been able to direct Hramov's actions with post-hypnotic suggestions before they allowed him to escape. But as Conrad had explained it, "We're not programming him to do something that goes against his training or his character. We're just making sure he does it our way."

Of course, the assassin was supposed to do his job and report back to the general. The gun battle and his death hadn't been foreseen. But they'd made that work for them. And now the Raven no longer existed.

As Adam stepped outside, Nicole turned and held out her hand.

"Well, hello," she said simply. The words were casual, but they conveyed a wealth of emotion. Every time she looked at this man, she realized all over again how deeply she was committed to him. She'd been his wife for only a few months, but already her old life seemed like an eternity away. "What are you thinking?" she asked, seeing the emotions that played across his face.

"How lucky I am to have you."

"I was just standing here marveling at the same thing."

Coming up behind her, he wrapped her in his arms and drew her close against the length of his body as he looked out over the valley.

There were still many nights when he woke and reached for her, needing the reassurance that she was really here with him. If his own change of circumstances had been a necessity, hers had been voluntary. She could have opted out before the charade in Harmony, Vermont, and gone back to her own life. Instead she'd chosen to give up everything familiar to come with him. Every time he thought about it, his heart was pierced with a fierce ache that he'd found a woman like her. He knew it was more than luck. Fate must have intervened in their lives to bring them together.

"How's the writing coming?" she asked softly.

"I finished the chapter," he announced. He was setting down some of his own experiences now, getting more comfortable with English, letting Nicole show him the fine points of the language with her invaluable editing. That project was a form of therapy for both of them. But soon he was going to try his hand at the fictional stories he had wanted to write for so long.

"That's wonderful, but I thought it was going to take you till dinnertime."

A warm smile flickered at the corners of his well-shaped lips. "I believe you mentioned a little incentive for finishing early."

She smiled back, the golden highlights in her eyes glowing possessively as they caressed his face. "Then perhaps you ought to collect your reward."

On the most romantic day of the year, capture the thrill of falling in love all over again—with

Harlequin's

Bachelors

They're three sexy and *very single* men who run very special personal ads to find the women of their fantasies by Valentine's Day. These exciting, passion-filled stories are written by bestselling Harlequin authors.

Your Heart's Desire by Elise Title
Mr. Romance by Pamela Bauer
Sleepless in St. Louis by Tiffany White

Be sure not to miss Harlequin's Valentine Bachelors, available in February wherever Harlequin books are sold.

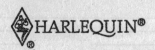

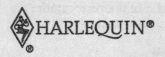 **HARLEQUIN®**

 *Weddings, Inc.*

The proprietors of Weddings, Inc. hope you
have enjoyed visiting Eternity, Massachusetts.
And if you missed any of the exciting Weddings,
Inc. titles, here is your opportunity to complete
your collection:

Harlequin Superromance	#598	*Wedding Invitation* by Marisa Carroll	$3.50 U.S. ☐ $3.99 CAN. ☐
Harlequin Romance	#3319	*Expectations* by Shannon Waverly	$2.99 U.S. ☐ $3.50 CAN. ☐
Harlequin Temptation	#502	*Wedding Song* by Vicki Lewis Thompson	$2.99 U.S. ☐ $3.50 CAN. ☐
Harlequin American Romance	#549	*The Wedding Gamble* by Muriel Jensen	$3.50 U.S. ☐ $3.99 CAN. ☐
Harlequin Presents	#1692	*The Vengeful Groom* by Sara Wood	$2.99 U.S. ☐ $3.50 CAN. ☐
Harlequin Intrigue	#298	*Edge of Eternity* by Jasmine Cresswell	$2.99 U.S. ☐ $3.50 CAN. ☐
Harlequin Historical	#248	*Vows* by Margaret Moore	$3.99 U.S. ☐ $4.50 CAN. ☐

HARLEQUIN BOOKS...
NOT THE SAME OLD STORY

TOTAL AMOUNT	$
POSTAGE & HANDLING	$
($1.00 for one book, 50¢ for each additional)	
APPLICABLE TAXES*	$ _____
TOTAL PAYABLE	$ _____
(check or money order—please do not send cash)	

To order, complete this form and send it, along with a check or money order for the
total above, payable to Harlequin Books, to: **In the U.S.:** 3010 Walden Avenue,
P.O. Box 9047, Buffalo, NY 14269-9047; **In Canada:** P.O. Box 613, Fort Erie, Ontario,
L2A 5X3.

Name: _____

Address: _____ City: _____

State/Prov.: _____ Zip/Postal Code: _____

*New York residents remit applicable sales taxes.
  Canadian residents remit applicable GST and provincial taxes.

WED-F

This holiday, join four hunky heroes under the mistletoe for

Christmas Kisses

Cuddle under a fluffy quilt, with a cup of hot chocolate and these romances sure to warm you up:

#561 HE'S A REBEL (also a Studs title)
Linda Randall Wisdom

#562 THE BABY AND THE BODYGUARD
Jule McBride

#563 THE GIFT-WRAPPED GROOM
M.J. Rodgers

#564 A TIMELESS CHRISTMAS
Pat Chandler

Celebrate the season with all four holiday books sealed with a Christmas kiss—coming to you in December, only from Harlequin American Romance!

HARLEQUIN®

I N T R I G U E®

Harlequin Intrigue
invites you to
celebrate

It's a year of celebration for Harlequin Intrigue, as we commemorate
ten years of bringing you the best in romantic suspense. And to help
celebrate, you can RETURN TO THE SCENE OF THE CRIME with a
limited hardcover collection of four of Harlequin Intrigue's most
popular earlier titles, written by four of your favorite authors:

REBECCA YORK	Shattered Vows (43 Light Street novel)
M.J. RODGERS	For Love or Money
PATRICIA ROSEMOOR	Crimson Holiday
LAURA PENDER	Déjà Vu

This unique collection will not be available in retail stores and is
only available through this exclusive offer.

Mail the certificate below, along with four (4) original proof-of-purchase coupons
from one Harlequin Intrigue Decade of Danger & Desire novel you received in July,
August, September and October 1994, plus $1.75 postage and handling (check or
money order—please do not send cash), payable to Harlequin Books, to:

In the U.S.	In Canada
Decade of Danger and Desire	Decade of Danger and Desire
Harlequin Books	Harlequin Books
P.O. Box 9048	P.O. Box 623
Buffalo, NY 14269-9048	Fort Erie, Ontario L2A 5X3

FREE GIFT CERTIFICATE

Name:_____

Address _____

City:_____ State/Province: _____Zip/Postal: _____

Account # _____ 086 KCG-R

(Please allow 4-6 weeks for delivery. Hurry! Quantities are limited. Offer expires
January 31, 1995)

HARLEQUIN INTRIGUE
DECADE OF DANGER AND DESIRE
ONE PROOF OF PURCHASE

086-KCG-R